PRAISE FOR

GREEN FOREST, RED EARTH, BLUE SEA

"Jim Gulledge's ode to North Carolina takes the reader on a journey through time and place, from the steep hills around Saluda to the fertile flatlands of the Piedmont and the history-haunted realm of the coast. In *Green Forest, Red Earth, Blue Sea*, love, loss, and redemption intertwine across generations. Three lightly tethered tales bring forth a breathing, multidimensional past in believable detail and heartbreaking force. These pages are graced with fortunes won and lost, revenge taken, love gained, and even buried treasure. If this book doesn't stir your love of the Tar Heel state, nothing will."

—Culley Holderfield, Author of *Hemlock Hollow*

"When you marry genuine, compelling characters with a keen sense of time and place, you get *Green Forest, Red Earth, Blue Sea*. Jim Gulledge is a talented and lyrical storyteller, and he has crafted a ripping good story. You'll read it and say, 'Yeah, I know those people.'"

—Robert Inman, Author of *Home Fires Burning* and *The Governor's Lady*

"Jim Gulledge weaves a captivating tapestry of stories in his latest work. Interwoven narratives, brimming with intricate details, bring to life a cast of dynamic characters grappling with the core of human nature: the ever-present tension between light and darkness. Though [the stories are] set against the backdrop of specific historical moments, the poignant joys and sorrows experienced by generations resonate across time. Gulledge crafts characters so intimate you'll find yourself mirrored in their triumphs and struggles. With each turn of the page, the vivid lives of the Bucklands, Elliots, McClures, and their counterparts become intricately woven into the fabric of North Carolina. The narrative sweeps from the deep mountain forests to the salty embrace of the coast, offering a rich celebration of the Tarheel State's natural beauty, customs, and cultures.

"As a native North Carolinian, I found myself transported by Gulledge's evocative descriptions and storylines. He captures the state's essence—its complexities, enduring charm, diverse landscapes, and the remarkable mosaic of people who call it home. This is a must-read for anyone yearning for a powerful story deeply rooted in a richly depicted place."

—Benjamin K. Haywood, PhD, associate director, Faculty Development Center, James B. Duke Library, Furman University

"Jim Gulledge writes with a smooth lyrical beauty about the land he obviously knows and loves. Immersed in those landscapes are unforgettable characters whose stories are woven together just tightly enough to keep you turning the page. *Green Forest, Red Earth, Blue Sea* does more than describe the geographical settings of his linked stories; the title draws the reader through a sometimes magical journey."

—Carter Taylor Seaton, author of *The Other Morgans*

"When good storytelling, deep love for a state, and insight about human nature combine, the result is a captivating, thoughtful, thought-provoking novel that spans generations and regions. Jim Gulledge has crafted a tale that brings places and people to life and traces the history of both, weaving threads that connect stories, lives, and fortunes. With vivid imagery, telling detail, and a heart for humanity, *Green Forest, Red Earth, Blue Sea* offers an immersion into the histories, cultures, songs, and lives that have inhabited North Carolina over time. It all rings true, and 'after all, all that we really ever have in this world is story.' Indeed."

—Laura A. Dean, PhD, professor (retired), College Student Affairs Administration/Student Affairs Leadership, University of Georgia

"Jim Gulledge understands the nuances of the subregions of North Carolina. In *Green Forest, Red Earth, Blue Sea*, his writing reflects what natives of the state have long understood—that the land is a character in all our stories. The people who inhabit Gulledge's world showcase the complexities of our ties to the land and ties to one another. Gulledge writes with the careful voice of a storyteller. His characters are shaped with both a reality and empathy in mind that speak to our own flaws and joys. *Green Forest, Red Earth, Blue Sea* reads as if I'm sitting down with an old friend or family member, swapping tales of times past. The only thing missing is a good plate of barbecue."

—Michael D. Thompson, PhD, assistant director, Monarch Internship Academy for the Humanities, Old Dominion University

Green Forest, Red Earth, Blue Sea
by Jim Gulledge

© Copyright 2024 Jim Gulledge

ISBN 979-8-88824-388-6

All rights reserved. No part of this publication may be reproduced, stored in a retrieval system, or transmitted in any form or by any means—electronic, mechanical, photocopy, recording, or any other—except for brief quotations in printed reviews, without the prior written permission of the author.

This is a work of fiction. All the characters in this book are fictitious, and any resemblance to actual persons, living or dead, is purely coincidental. The names, incidents, dialogue, and opinions expressed are products of the author's imagination and are not to be construed as real.

"A Poor Man's Supper" illustration by Grainger McKoy
"Peachland" and "Wild Horses" illustrations by Josh Cross
Cover art by Suzanne Bradshaw

Published by

3705 Shore Drive
Virginia Beach, VA 23455
800-435-4811
www.koehlerbooks.com

GREEN FOREST, RED EARTH, BLUE SEA

Jim Gulledge

VIRGINIA BEACH
CAPE CHARLES

To my beloved wife, Linda,
and our children, and son-in-law,
who are always in my heart.

And to all our extended families and ancestors,
who are so often forgotten.

Author's Note

THREE REAL COMMUNITIES—Saluda, Peachland, and Beaufort—have inspired me in my attempt to capture the geographic diversity of our beloved state of North Carolina. "Mountains to the sea" as we Carolinians say. As a writer there is a danger in selecting real place settings for a book; however, I believe there is a greater danger in creating imaginary places. Having encountered this trend in recent books and movies, I have simply decided that it does not suit my taste. There are too many wonderful, real places in North Carolina for me to create poor imaginary ones. So, I brace myself to be corrected and scorned for everything that I have gotten wrong about these three beloved communities.

To be clear, I have never lived full time in the settings for my book, but I have enjoyed being in each for periods of time. Much of this book was written in Saluda at the former Snail's Pace retreat center. My ancestors lived in the Peachland area for two hundred years. My wife and I have traveled and vacationed in Beaufort and much of the North Carolina coast. Both sides of my family arrived in the Carolinas in the 1730s and 1740s. I have never lived elsewhere. Those are my credentials. However, I humbly acknowledge that I am not a historian, biologist, geographer, or linguist. I am sure I have gotten many things wrong about these places, and I humbly ask your forgiveness. I am a storyteller doing the best I can.

A few other quick items. Although some of my characters are amalgams of people whom I know, none of them, as far as I know, are thinly veiled members of your family or friends. Finally, I would like to be clear that I am a Christian and have been for fifty years. Some of you may not believe that if you read my book. A number of folks in this story say and do very unchristian things, but we live in a fallen world. All the characters are flawed to some extent. I let them speak and act as they do in order to be honest and pay respect to the truth about human nature. If you like books that dodge issues of race, sexuality, and violence, this story may not be for you. Regardless, I respect your right to not read this novel or to stop reading it at any point that it violates your conscience. Some of my best friends are among your company.

For the brave or foolhardy among you who persist, I hope you will be rewarded with moments of light, healing, and redemption in a world often soul crushing in its darkness, pain, and loss. May you enjoy my love letter to the Old North State.

GREEN FOREST:

A POOR MAN'S SUPPER

Prologue

A RED-TAILED HAWK rose on the currents of the afternoon thermals, gliding round and round the crown of the weather-beaten pine before resting upon an outstretched branch. From his perch, the bird looked out upon the vista that stretched before his keen eyes. Below him, a rustle in the grass turned his attention from the heavens to the earth. A small cottontail emerged from its hiding and nibbled at wildflowers on the edge of the cliff. Before the hawk could muster its instincts to respond, another motion entered the scene just below the rabbit. The head of an eastern diamondback rattlesnake surfaced over the rim of the ravine and flattened out as it wound its way closer to its prey. The rabbit saw nothing and knew nothing until a flash, the sensation of warm fluid oozing into its cranium, then its limbs stiffened and senses darkened. The snake coiled in bliss around the twitching final pulsations of the ball of fur and fluids.

Its revelry, however, was short-lived. In another flash, a convulsion of pain interrupted the snake's pleasures as piercing talons penetrated its flesh and lifted it skyward. Soon, the hawk sat upon his perch once again and tore the eyes from the stilled serpent. Had the bird cared to notice, at that moment a man descended from the peaks above and another wound his way up the rugged escarpment below. The bloodlettings of men were about to play out again beneath the watchful eyes of the bird; but hawks are creatures of the air and take no notice of the affairs of men. Slowly, the raptor lifted and again rode the warm afternoon breeze, oblivious to all hungers but its own.

CHAPTER ONE
Vancie Keller

VANCIE KELLER ROCKED slowly back and forth on the weather-worn porch of the farmhouse. She looked the part of an expensive, French, store-bought doll, and she was as uncomfortable as hell. Mattie had spent all of Friday boiling her clothes in the big washpot in the backyard and most of Saturday pressing them with a hot iron. The result was clothes with creases so sharp that they threatened to draw blood every time Vancie turned. After all of her dancing around, Mattie had finally threatened her life.

"Child, if you twist yourself one more time, it ain't your starched-up dress that is going to hurt you."

Her mother, Lois, had worked her body over in the same fashion in a washtub in the summer kitchen, scrubbing her until she was sure that she would bleed. It was Sunday morning now, and Vancie had been parked on the front porch, hair curled, with instructions to rock just fast enough to fan but not fast enough to sweat. Her only hope of salvation was Big John pulling the wagon around front, loading her sorry self into it, and getting up enough speed for her to at least feel the spring breeze blowing through her hair on the way to another form of torture—church.

Vancie was about the only pretty thing on the Keller farm that morning with the exception of some buttercups blooming by the front steps. Although her family's farm had once been a showplace in the small, mountain community, life had not been kind to the Kellers. Vancie's dad had come back from the war briefly but not in one piece. With part of his left leg gone, and even more of his mind, Marcus Keller never became a real farmer again before his death. God knows he tried. Big John and Mattie tried even harder, but injury and age had left their mark on the Keller place. Even deeper than the gullies in the field were the lines in Lois Keller's face. Though once a woman of exceptional beauty, her husband's death and her family's unrelenting slide toward poverty had wounded her body and soul. All the brightness of her youth had vanished, replaced by a sharp tongue and dark disposition.

Every time Vancie made a false step, her mother's words rained down on her like hail in a summer thunderstorm.

"Go ahead then, you fool child. You are more and more like your daddy every day. Always off in a dream. Well, dreams won't fill your belly, and honor and nobility don't satisfy the bank. You need to get some sense. Look where his noble dreams got him! Life is hard, and it's all about surviving in a tough world. Instead of looking for a man to come along with a buggy load of fancies, you had better be looking for a man to come your way with a pocket full of silver!"

Vancie had heard this speech more times than she had seen lightning bugs in the yard. Fact was, she just didn't care. She hardly ever thought about men and never thought about the considerable beauty that she had inherited from her mother. The only time that Vancie Keller ever saw her own face was on a clear day when she was looking in the creek water for tadpoles. She would rather be wrapped in barbed wire than strapped into a church dress with her cheeks pinched and her body scented with rosewater. As soon as their wagon pulled back into the yard after church and dinner on the grounds, she would drop her dress on her bedroom floor, pull on her britches, and be out the back door to save what was left of the day exploring the woods, creeks, and meadows on the farm.

"Well," said Vancie, going out the back door shouting at her mama, "if I ever find a man, he will have to be standing in the middle of a creek!"

CHAPTER TWO
Josiah Buckland

JOSIAH BUCKLAND'S COARSE, homespun clothes chafed against the sharp angles of his adolescent frame as he strode down the middle of the road into Saluda. He was not alone as he rounded the last curve of the twisting mountain road and came into sight of Main Street. A disheveled and noticeably hungover farmer drove a small band of brown, mud-caked pigs into town in procession about twenty yards in front of him. As he struck the ones bringing up the rear, grunts and squeals joined the growing cacophony that is town on a market day. Josiah felt his insides rear back in revulsion as he was enveloped by the whinnying of horses, the slap of leather reins, shouts of merchants loading and unloading goods, and the squeals of ragamuffin children come to town on their once-a-week pilgrimage.

Sound was not the only thing that assaulted Josiah's forest sensibilities. After a late rain last night, the main boulevard of Saluda had become a cesspool of mud, tobacco juice, pig urine, horse shit, and flies. His deerskin shoes soon reeked with corruption as he labored to suck one and then another up from the fetid muck that passed as a street in Saluda. Let there be no misunderstanding, only necessity and the need to survive had driven Josiah down the mountain. He longed for the silence and solace of massive fir trees, impenetrable rhododendron thickets, and sunlit mountain balds. But, some evil, or a series of them, had come to the high country in recent years.

Loggers had clear cut entire ridges, and other lowlanders had burned off meadows, hoping to coax crops from the rocky, thin soil of the mountaintops. Somehow in their coming, they had brought a plague to the great trees of the Blue Ridge and Smokies. The massive giants that had provided wood for cabins, farm tools, furniture, and forage for black bears and deer were dying off by the tens of thousands. The whole food chain of the high country had been undone for man and beast. Once prosperous settlements and game lands now offered up little to those who clung to their wasting remains for sustenance. Josiah's parents had passed with the passing of the great trees, so he had been driven by hunger and loneliness to the lower altitude of Saluda.

The buildings of the town were aligned in an odd quarter circle arc the length of Main Street. At first sight, it looked like the street had been laid out by a moonshiner rather than a surveyor. However, after staring for a few moments, the logic of the street slowly revealed itself to Josiah. Its timbered storefronts had been built to mimic the serpentine arc of the older road and the newly laid tracks of the rails of the Saluda Grade Railroad.

The rail line to Saluda was a marvel of engineering wizardry that climbed nearly twenty-five hundred feet out of the Piedmont on the steepest grade in the Appalachian Mountains. Dozens of men had died in its making as they routed the railway up the ancient trading path of the Cherokee. Others had perished in its initial runs when train engineers lost their battles with the forces of nature as the behemoth iron horses tried to descend back to the lowlands overloaded with timber and other booty from the high country. Josiah found himself wishing that the townsfolk would all die as a locomotive stalled at the depot released a hiss and then scream of wood-fueled vapor into the already unnerving racket of the town. For a few moments, pandemonium ensued as mountain horses unused to the dawning age of steam and metal reared onto their hindlegs. Pigs scattered, chickens took flight, and wide-eyed children shrieked. It was more than Josiah could take. He fled up a side alley and into the sanctuary of the old livery stable a block removed from the chaos.

Once inside the livery, his sanity returned. The buildings of the façade of Main Street and the angle of the alley somehow absorbed the chaos of man and machine. Josiah breathed in the sweetness of newly mowed hay and the muskiness of placid beasts chewing their cuds in silence. He had never known until coming to town that silence was the essence and necessity of his life. He had always taken it for granted, like the sky, wind, spring water, and the earth itself. Josiah found himself never wishing to leave the livery again.

"Well, if I have to live in this hellhole, maybe I can find some work here. Everybody has to take care of their horse," mused the boy.

Josiah walked through the silent cathedrallike passage of the ancient barn and eventually found a doorway to a lean-to addition out back. He softly rapped on the dilapidated doorway, afraid that it was as likely that some form of vermin would emerge from it as it was that a human might appear. However, after another knock or two, Josiah heard the latch lift and stepped back as the door swung inward on its rusty metal hinges, scraping against the frame. He caught his breath between a gasp and an impulse for laughter at what stood before him.

By the color of his remaining hair, beard, and sideburns, the man in the doorway seemed to be in his late forties to early fifties. However, by his stature he appeared little more than a boy in his early teens. To call him a dwarf would have been a little less than the truth but not by much. At full attention, the man standing on the stoop could be no more than five feet tall. Although he was barrel-chested, other signs of physical weakness prevailed. Small square-lens spectacles perched on the end of his nose, and as he took a step closer, Josiah noticed that his right foot was twisted to the side, producing a pronounced limp.

"Hello, my name is Phineus Coble. I run the livery here in Saluda. What can I do for you, boy?"

Josiah struggled to imagine the man-child before him wrangling horses in and out of the stalls of the livery or feeding or shoeing them, but suddenly he snapped out of his reverie and answered, "Mr. Phineus, I am Josiah Bunyan Buckland, and I need myself a job. Things have gotten hard up in the high country, and I have come to town looking for me some work. Do you have any jobs for me?"

Phineus looked the boy up and down, sizing him up on the outside against a hard day's labor, but then he set his sights upward into Josiah's eyes. Phineus's father had always told him that when doing business with a man, the eyes were the windows of truth. If that was the case, Josiah Buckland's eyes were the windows to heaven itself. In most other ways, the boy was ordinary—tall, angular-framed, and with thick brown hair hanging nearly to his shoulders. Everything about his body was of the earth. In fact, Josiah's body seemed somehow an incarnation of soil, tree, and rock. But not his eyes. When he straightened to full height and his hair fell back from his face, there emerged two of the most startling eyes that Phineus Coble had ever seen. Sometimes when people stand at the right angle at the right time of day, the sky can be partly reflected in the orbs of their eyes. However, Josiah's eyes did not reflect the sky. They seemed to be the sky itself—at times nearly gray and at others dark and sapphire, like the sky in the mountains before the sudden crash of thunder and the fall of rain.

Though Phineus was poor as a church mouse, he suddenly heard himself agreeing to give the boy shelter and meager rations in exchange for six days a week of hard labor. He could not decide if his actions constituted charity or abuse, but his words were spoken into the air before he knew that they had been formed in his head. Josiah responded in pure delight. Tonight, he would not sleep in the rain and would not struggle to sleep over the sound of the rumblings of his empty stomach.

"Thank you, Mr. Phineus. Thank you, sir," the boy muttered over and over as he shook the hand of the tiny man smiling before him.

CHAPTER THREE
The Meeting

JOSIAH WORKED FEVERISHLY at the livery stable, fueled by the deep, abiding gratitude that he felt for Phineus Coble. It was Mr. Phineus who had taken him in when he was hungry and put a meal in his belly and a roof over his head. It was difficult to accept Mr. Phineus's kindness, but Josiah intended to earn his keep with his sweat. Every day, he rose early while the moon still hung in the sky above the sleeping village and long before the roosters, scattered around town, heralded the dawn. He set to work mucking out stalls, scattering oats in the feeding troughs, and hauling bucket after bucket of water from the old communal well at the end of Flat Rock Road.

When the sun finally rose, it flamed with a vengeance. Summer pressed down upon Saluda as the day brightened. The cool night air of the mountain evening dissipated quickly and was replaced by the creeping humidity of July. It would be a long, sweltering day. A hay wagon had been pulled into the barn the night before, and Josiah's work would be to lift the contents, pitchfork by pitchfork, from the bed of the large wagon to the floor of the loft high above. The barn walls, which had sheltered him from the night just hours before, now worked against him as they closed out the few breaths of air that occasionally stirred around the wooden structures on Main

Street. Within a few hours, the dampness of the air clung to his skin and coalesced into droplets which by noon merged into rivulets and streamed down his back, chest, arms, and legs.

Each time Josiah pitched a new forkful of hay into the oppressive air, straw disappeared into the loft, but straw dust and bits of chaff rained downward. They clung to his wet shirt, collected in his hair, invaded his nostrils, and joined the already stinging salt water in his eyes. He peeled his shirt over his head, swiped his arm across his brow, and kept going. There was no point counting the strokes of his arm lifting the hay upward. Day would have slipped away before the last forkful of the dried grass lay safely in the loft. His only duty was to stoop, scoop, pitch, and blink as the debris continued to rain down upon him.

Dinner, when it came from Mr. Phineus, would be simple but ample—a few slices of cheese and a hunk of bread. Water would be drawn in a dipper from one of the buckets carried in for the horses. He felt no anger in the simplicity of the meal; he knew that it was no different than what Phineus Coble would feed himself at noon today. Mr. Phineus lived the life of a pauper. The only luxury that Josiah had ever seen the little man indulge himself was a tin penny whistle, which the boy would sometimes hear him play late in the evening.

Supper would be much the same as dinner, with beans replacing the bread. However, his stomach would not ache from emptiness as it had the many days and nights in the woods when he had worked his way down the mountain trails from the highlands. Unless Mr. Phineus dropped by during the day or a customer delivered or retrieved a horse, the only voices that Josiah would hear would be those of the barn swallows as they darted in and out of the opening at the front of the structure.

Josiah settled into the rhythm of his work and comforted himself with his awareness of his growing strength. He was still a boy, but as the weeks passed, he felt the tightening of the sinews in his arms, legs, back, and chest. Though far from manhood, he smiled at the thought of the recent crackling of his voice and the emergence of small patches of hair under his arms, about his face, and around his cock. Most mornings when he rose, his cock had risen before him in small imitation of its far larger, more intimidating counterparts dangling from the stallions about the barn. At first, these bodily changes had startled him, but now he found them strangely comforting. He'd had to play the part of a man for a long time now. It was nice to finally be growing into the role.

"Hello, boy," said a small, sweet voice from behind him.

Josiah nearly threw his pitchfork into the loft with the hay. Heart pounding, he wheeled around on the balls of his feet and faced a girl standing nearly nose-to-chest behind him.

"What are you trying to do, you little fool, kill me?" Josiah snorted.

The girl lifted her face up to him, and suddenly Josiah found himself lost in the blueness of her eyes. He felt at home again, back in the safety and beauty of the forests in the upper reaches of the mountain summits. The coolness of her breath invaded his space, sweetened the rankness of his own odor, and awakened him from the numbness of work.

As his senses cleared, he became aware of his half-nakedness, ripped his shirt from the fencepost, and pulled the soiled cloth over his damp body. In a panic, he realized that she had awakened more than his sensibilities, so he dropped the tail of the thick, coarse material down rather than tuck it in.

"Are you here to pick up a horse or something?" he stammered.

Her eyes sparkled with delight, and she laughed musically. "Why, you silly boy, do I look like a customer at a livery stable? I was just walking into town to the mercantile and saw you in here trying to bury yourself in a pile of hay with a pitchfork."

Josiah blushed crimson, half in embarrassment and half in rage.

"So, I guess you could do a better job yourself, girl, in your little calico dress," he retorted.

"Well, the only thing that I am sure of is that I couldn't possibly do a worse one," the girl fired back.

Lightning flashed in Josiah's eyes, but even as he felt his heart pounding, he was aware of a great lie. He heard the anger and sarcasm in his voice and felt the pounding in his temples, but inside of himself he knew that he could stand anything that this girl might say to him as long as she continued to speak. The only thing that he could not stand was to never hear her voice again and never fall into her eyes again.

But at that very moment, to his horror, she turned around, tossed her golden hair behind her, and sashayed out of the barn, calling out behind her, "My name is Vancie Keller, and you can tuck your shirt in now."

Josiah stood in the doorway, lost in a wave of rage, shame, and longing. As he looked sadly down the now empty street, a small, sharp voice behind him shocked him back to his senses.

"So, is this why I provide you with room and board, for you to moon around staring off into space after I have given you a job to do?" quipped his employer.

"Oh, I am so sorry, Mr. Phineus. I will get right back to work, sir."

"What's wrong with you today, boy? Lollygagging around isn't like you. Are you feeling sickly?"

Josiah was tempted to simply grab his pitchfork and return to his labors, but to his own surprise he began to pour out his heart to the small, bespectacled man.

"Mr. Phineus, I met a girl. Not just any girl, mind you. I am certain that I met *the* girl, the girl that I will spend the rest of my days with, the girl that will bear my children and love me forever."

Phineus Coble was tempted to mock the excesses of youth, but something in the pain on the boy's face and the vulnerability in his eyes stopped him. Josiah Buckland stood before him, his heart exposed without defense. The wrong word would pierce him like an arrow and poison him with the seed of adult cynicism forever. Also, a wound from Phineus's own youth rose up inside of him, constricting his vocal chords. He knew that a boy could meet a girl and love her forever, and he knew the pain that endured when she did not return the favor. The words that finally came to Phineus were not of his own making.

"What is her name, Josiah?"

"Her name is Vancie Keller, sir."

Two weeks later at dinner, Phineus, with mist in his eyes, approached Josiah at the table, took his right hand, and pressed a small round object into it. Josiah peeled back his fingers and gasped.

"Why, Mr. Phineus. It's gold!"

A small, rose-colored lady's pocket watch, no larger than a dollar, lay in Josiah's calloused hand.

"Where did you get this, sir? No offense, but you are poor. How did you afford something like this, and why are you giving it to me?"

Phineus pulled back the small chair beside him and took a seat, his feet still dangling above the dusty floor. "Josiah, it is too late for me. The feelings that you have for Vancie were there for me too for a girl of my own when I was a boy. However, there are people in this world for whom love will never be more than feelings—small people, crippled people, poor people. I am getting old now. There will never be a girl for me, and there will never be children of my own to whom I can pass my mother's wedding watch. You are as close to a son as I will ever have. I did a reckless thing last week. Look, there is a small clasp on the watch. Press it, and open the back cover."

Josiah followed Phineus's instructions, prying open the slightly dented back of the watch. Newly etched on the inside of the back cover, Josiah found the initials V. K. and J.B.

"Mr. Phineus, it's our initials. You ruined your mother's watch."

"Well, 'ruined' is perhaps a bit harsh. I guess if worse came to worse, the letters could be scratched off, but something in my heart tells me that that will not be necessary. Call it a leap of faith if you wish. A leap of faith in the young and in the mystery of things. You are worth the risk."

Josiah looked at the dwarf of a man before him and realized that there are debts in life that cannot be repaid. Laying his large hand on top of Phineus Coble's diminutive hand, Josiah realized that he now owed such a debt.

Phineus looked him squarely in the eyes and said, "And forget any nonsense about paying me back. Just pick up some nails for me at the hardware tomorrow, and we will call it even."

CHAPTER FOUR
The Stars

JOSIAH PLODDED ALONG the road out of Saluda. Although the livery provided some buffer from the smells and noises of town, at least once a week he simply had to leave. Most people would fear walking out of the comfort and security of community into the terrors of the night, but with each step away from the lights of town into the inky darkness of the country, Josiah felt the tightness in his body and the oppression of his heart lift. For a woodsman on an exposed road without a tree canopy, it wasn't even particularly dark. Josiah's eyes had long ago become accustomed to the soft light of stars, and he found all the light that he needed to lengthen his stride and quicken his pace as he left the clamor of town in the distance.

Soon, all the sounds surrounding him cleared his senses—the murmur of a small stream running along the roadbed, the incessant chirps of crickets, and the plaintive call of the whip-o-will. The air cooled. An occasional cloud blocked out patches of the stars that streamed like diamonds across the heavens. All was now well as Josiah sank into a state of peace, solitude, and healing. Another mile or so down the road, he heard the soft strains of singing and tensed at the prospect of encountering someone on his walk. For a moment, he thought of plunging into the darkness of the forest to avoid human contact.

When he paused to leap, he saw movement to his right in a small meadow. Darting about in the glade, spinning madly like a whirling dervish, a girl's form sharpened into focus. With the light of the stars upon her, she appeared to be dressed in the palest of white. Against her golden hair in the dimness of the night, small meadow flowers stood out in a ringlet around her brow. As she ran and danced, she piped in a clear soprano voice like a nightingale:

"Star light, star bright,
The first star I have seen to-night;
I wish I may, I wish I might,
Have the wish I have wished to-night."

Each time she uttered the lines, she burst into waves of joyful laughter and spun about beneath the glow of the Pleiades. Josiah stopped dead in his tracks, in love with the flower-crowned nymph twirling wildly through the darkness. At that moment, the forest above the field appeared to burst into flame. Josiah shrank back in terror until he realized that the glow was not fire but the full crimson moon rising above the ridge of the hill. Before he knew what he was doing, he dashed from the road, across the small stream, and out into the field. Seeing him in pursuit, the girl fled like a deer before hounds.

Josiah followed as the moon slowly turned orange, then yellow, and finally white, illuminating everything in sight nearly to the brightness of day. However, before he could catch his prey, she leapt from the bright meadow into the darkness of the forest with him just yards behind. Even for a seasoned woodsman, Josiah found the darkness of the forest temporarily disorienting, but his eyes quickly adjusted like those of an owl. He caught a glimpse of her receding dress and took off after her. After chasing her for what seemed like miles, he suddenly cried out in despair, "Stop! Come back."

His voice echoed through the forest, but only silence returned to him. He had lost her. His chest heaved, his legs burned, and his heart ached with emptiness and loss. As he turned to leave in defeat, something happened that he had only seen one other time in his life. Fireflies suddenly illuminated the darkness but not as they do most places. In most places, fireflies pulsate in scattered, twinkling succession. However, in a few magical spots in the mountains, in perfect synchronization, they all spark at the same time. The effect was startling. The woods pulsated from inky blackness to stardust illumination, like a lamp turned nearly to nothing and then again to full flame.

As the fireflies lighted, Josiah saw her no more than twenty feet away. He stepped forward. Darkness fell. Then the fires flared again, and each time they did, Josiah found himself closer to the god-child. In darkness, his hand found hers and pulled her body close. In warm light, her head lifted toward him. In darkness, he kissed her soft, moist lips, and in a flash of light he knew her to be not a goddess but the girl that he had met at the livery a few weeks before. As their lips parted, Josiah reached to the depths of his trouser pocket, retrieved the cold, golden circle of the watch, and pressed it into the small hand of the puzzled girl. Vancie smiled faintly, tightened her hand around it, pulled away, and bolted into the night. Her form grew ever smaller and dimmer as she retreated.

CHAPTER FIVE
Jagger Hill

JAGGER HILL STEPPED lightly down from the passenger compartment of the train. A cloud of steam enveloped him as the engine belched its last breaths after the long struggle up the mountainside. Once the vapors cleared, Jagger got his first glimpse of the village of Saluda in its workaday squalor. His attraction to Saluda was not to what it was but rather what it might become with his help. He had spent months poring over maps of the Southeast, looking for a small town poised for the opportunity of explosive growth and great wealth. Saluda was the winner.

Although it was little more than a pig path now, the coming of the railroad would make the village the first point of arrival for goods being exchanged between the high country and low country. Jagger knew opportunity when he saw it, and Saluda held prospects for great opportunity. Unlike so many other men, he did not place all his faith for success in his intellect and unbridled drive. Jagger held his ace in the hole in the leather bag dangling in his left hand. He had possessed his wealth for nearly twenty years, so long in fact that a few good turns had swelled his initial fortune. However, the years had also clouded Jagger's memories of its origins. He had affected the role of a gentleman for so long now and spun such stories about the blueness of his blood that even he had begun to believe them. The real story of the source of Jagger's wealth lay deeply hidden within the dark, sheltered recesses of his own mind and heart. Hidden from all he met. Hidden after all these years even from himself.

Jagger had forgotten many things. He had forgotten the hardscrabble life of his boyhood, working on a rock-strewn farm, chopping cotton by day, and being beaten by his foul-mouthed immigrant father by night. He had forgotten the idealistic young man who had gladly marched off to defend the honor of Dixie in exchange for escaping the rot of his childhood.

Most of all, Jagger had forgotten Robert Laurens. He had met Robert early in the war and was immediately drawn to him. The Laurens had the life that Jagger had longed for as his stomach twisted with hunger in the fields. Colonial blue bloods, the Laurens had built upon their privilege and nobility by erecting one of the finest plantation houses in the low country. That did them little good as the tide of the war turned unrelentingly against the South. The grand palace, populated now by women, Robert's own sickly, pasty-faced child, and a few remaining Negroes, stood trembling on the brink of extinction.

Terrors about the fate of his family and several near misses on the battlefield had caused Robert to lose faith, and in a moment of weakness he had poured out his sorrows.

"Jagger, you are my best friend. Promise me. Please, promise me. If we fail, if I die and you live, promise me that you will go back to Penland. I have a secret there. A way for my family and for you to survive after the war. There are crypts behind the main house in the woods. Crypts of all the Laurens who ever lived at Penland. In my grandfather Henry's crypt, there is gold. Lots of gold. Enough for all of you to survive and start a new life. I didn't even tell Lucy. Promise me if anything happens that you will save them."

Jagger did make a promise that night. Thirteen days later, Robert Laurens died midmorning from a rifle ball to the head. In the confusion of battle, it escaped the notice of all survivors that the ball had entered the back of Robert's head and had exited between his eyes.

Jagger kept his promise after the war and went to Penland. However, the few malnourished, diseased occupants who remained were never aware of his visit. He came in the night and only paid his respects to Robert Lauren's grandfather. If he ever justified anything that he did, his justification was that nobility had failed and proven itself unworthy. The victor of war is the survivor, and to the survivor goes the spoils. Jagger Hill was a survivor.

He strode with confidence down the wooden walkways of Saluda, a town which he knew in his heart he would soon own. Tipping his hat to the younger of the ladies passing by, he surveyed the town, taking inventory of each building, wagon, and person and sorting what he might keep from what he would not. Suddenly, Jagger grasped for a porch post, struggling to keep his equilibrium as a dirty, brown-haired street urchin careened into him at full speed.

Regaining his footing, Jagger grabbed the youth by the nape and spat invectives at him as he took the boy's hair in his other hand and jerked his head backward. Jagger stared down into the lad's eyes with shock and revulsion. Two grayish-blue orbs pierced him like spears. Jagger felt like he would fall into their depths and be consumed. He jolted back in horror at the sensation of being small and falling into an infinite expanse of space.

The boy looking up at the man experienced a terror of his own. Every instinct honed for survival in the forests brought Josiah to full alertness. Josiah looked into Jagger's face and had the disturbing sensation that it did not look like the real face of the man. The man's real face lurked somewhere deep behind the outer mask of the man. Josiah shivered, jerked himself free from Jagger's grasp, and lunged backward. Babbling, he said, "I am sorry. I was just on my way to the hardware to get some nails for my boss. Please forgive me for being careless."

Then the boy bolted down the boardwalk. Jagger quickly composed himself, adjusted his clothes, and promptly buried any memory of the encounter with the youth as deeply as possible in his psyche. He had no desire or capacity to retain any experience with a young hoodlum that had somehow made him feel like less of a man.

CHAPTER SIX
The Falls

VANCIE CAREFULLY FORCED her way through the thickets of rhododendron and laurel along the banks of Colt Creek. Occasionally, the ground cover became so dense that she had no other choice than to take to the waters of the stream, gingerly jumping from rock to rock as she slowly worked her way closer to the falls. At times, the excruciating pace of her progress discouraged her, but she found herself cheered by the almost imperceptible increase in the volume of the now not so distant falls. The walls of the holler closed in on both sides of the creek. Had it not been nearly noon, she would have already been shrouded in darkness.

The sun only penetrated the depths of the gorge from late morning to early afternoon, but for now, the bright, golden rays warmed her shoulders to offset the iciness of the chilled water splashing over her bare feet. Like the brown trout hiding in the murky swirl of the waters, she continued her struggle up the stream. Vancie heard few sounds other than her own breath and heartbeat, the cascading waters of the stream, and the occasional piping and warbling of the forest birds. As far as her senses could reveal at this moment, she was the only human being upon Earth. This sensation continued unbroken until she made her way around the last bend before her first view of Pearson's Falls. Vancie became aware of the sudden rush of her own breath as it came into full view.

The sun rested at the top of the cataract, illuminating the water in a whiteness that stood out in blinding contrast to the emerald hues of the surrounding woodlands. As magnificent as this view was, that was not what had taken away the young girl's breath. At the foot of the three-tiered wall of water stood Josiah Buckland, the teenaged boy she had encountered at the livery and with whom she had cavorted under the stars. However, he was transformed. He had stripped off his clothes on the bank of the pool of the falls and now stood with his lean, muscled shoulders and taut buttocks facing her. He rinsed his shoulder-length blond hair in the foam of the last tier of the falls, rotating his young body as the sun poured down through the white waters upon him. He stepped from the water fully exposing his angular face, strong chest, long loins, and the dark encircling web around his fully matured manhood. Vancie should have been embarrassed and had been trained to know shame, but at that moment she felt only the thrill of being in the presence of Josiah Buckland without any of the artificial barriers that separate man from woman. She knew that it was a sin, but for a moment she felt that she stood before some long ago and long since forgotten god of the forest and waters.

Paralyzed momentarily by surprise, Josiah stood statuelike before regaining his senses and wading out across the pool to reclaim his clothes. Vancie knew that she should retreat but instead found herself crossing the sandbar to him, ripe with well-intended, insincere apologies for her invasion of his privacy and dignity. Her advance caused Josiah to freeze again before her. Despite his embarrassment, he simply stopped and turned to her. Vancie watched with rapt, mesmerized attention as the last glistening drops of water slipped across the surfaces of his body and dripped down the tips of his fingers. She braced herself to laugh, cry, or scream, but no sound came. In sheer amazement of her own actions, her spirit rose forth from her body and watched her fingers wander to the straps of her cotton dress. Slowly, they twisted until the clasps opened, dropping her flower-patterned dress around her feet.

In some strange gesture of equilibrium within her irrational mind, she revealed herself to Josiah Buckland. The just ripening curvature of her hips and small milky breasts stood exposed to the widening glare of his gray eyes. Her small belly stretched down to the auburn triangle of her own emerging identity as woman rather than girl. For several moments, they stood silently in a strange state of comfort before each other, no more self-conscious than the mares and stallions sharing quarters back at the livery. Josiah abandoned all pretense of retrieving his clothes as he stepped forward in heightened excitement to sense Vancie more fully. She felt her nipples tighten into small, taut knots as he sniffed the sweetness of her hair and ran the edge of his fingernail across her neck from ear to shoulder. Josiah stepped back momentarily as he felt his stiffening phallus rise to close the small distance between them. At that moment, Vancie felt the exhilaration of the dew at his tip finding the moisture of her own body that had not come from the stream but from some place of mystery within her. Desire overcame her, and she fell with him into the mossy bank of the stream.

Cascades of dripping water seeped from the banks of the small grotto and slipped over moss, leaf, and rock in rhythmic profusion around them as their young bodies joined. The first human sound of the afternoon emerged from Vancie as a muffled cry erupted from her lips. However, the sensation of pain was followed by wave after wave of mounting warmth as Josiah pressed himself within her and began thrusting in an ever-increasing, instinctive fury. The young lovers' frantic bodies pressed more deeply into the mossy bank, and their fingernails pressed more desperately into the flesh of each other's shoulders until Josiah erupted within her. She felt herself transported in spasms of heat and muscular release. The young lovers lay panting together with lips separated, but their shoulders, nipples, hips, and genitals remained locked in a moisture-dampened, slowly loosening union. Josiah muttered, "You are like a dream from another world."

Those words from his lips ran through Vancie like a lightning strike. As the last bit of Josiah slipped from her, he stood once again exposed to Vancie's full gaze. She stared in shock and despair. The orbs that moments ago had seemed egglike were now small and tight against his frame, and his cock, ropelike before, dangled nearly flush to the bottom of his torso. His once-shining blond hair hung ordinary, damp, and brown upon his shoulders. Whatever spell had bewitched her had faded like morning mist on a summer's day. The god-man, mighty and awe-inspiring, now revealed himself as a tall, lean, awkward teen, scampering self-consciously around the beach gathering his clothes and pressing them to his bare body. "Why, you are only a boy," Vancie blurted.

Instantly, she realized the wound her words caused and wished to reach out and regather them to her mouth. The damage was immediate and deep. Josiah froze, blushed crimson, and desperately pulled at his tangled trousers until he had covered what remained of his badly mangled manhood. Vancie fled in embarrassment and shame.

CHAPTER SEVEN
Retreat

STUMBLING BACK DOWN Colt Creek and running the entire way to the Keller farm, Vancie tried to distance herself from the memory of lying with Josiah Buckland. What devil had possessed her to give herself away to a boy in the middle of the woods? What if Mama Lois found out? She would disown her and turn her out onto the road. Vancie stopped long enough to take a short bath in the creek on her mother's farm. She needed to wash the last vestiges of Josiah Buckland from her body and her mind before entering the house and falling under the piercing gazes of Mattie and her mother.

She had barely stepped onto the back porch when the first assault of words struck her like lightning from the kitchen.

"Where have you been, girl? I thought I done told you to be out there weeding that garden before the briars and the brambles be the only thing we got left to eat. What you been up to with yourself?" Mattie spat, training her milky eyes on Vancie.

"I've just been down to the branch and lost track of the time," Vancie mumbled.

"I expect that there be more to the story than that," Mattie fired back, "but I don't have no more of my time to waste today on a trifling girl. Get yourself to the dining room and set the table so I can get you and your mama some dinner before it get dark."

In disgust, Mattie turned back to the stove and her duties. Vancie bounded up the hall stairs to her bedroom, past her mother out on the front porch shelling beans, and slipped into her room, closing the door tightly behind her.

Thank God Mattie is half-blind, thought Vancie as she took off her mud-stained clothing and hid it under the bed to be slipped into a boiling pot later in the week.

Her nakedness made her self-conscious, so she quickly put on clean clothes and went downstairs to set the table and try to slide back into the ordinary routines of life on the Keller farm.

For a while, Vancie thought that she had gotten away with her ruse. She immersed herself in her chores and carefully avoided any contact with town, especially the livery. However, several weeks after her encounter on Colt Creek, she awoke one morning overwhelmed by surges of intense nausea. She barely had time to grab a chamber pot by her bed before she heaved the previous night's supper and successive waves of greenish-yellow phlegm. She broke out in a cold sweat fearing that her gags had awakened her mother, but when her bedroom door squeaked open, things became worse than she had feared. Mattie stood with arms akimbo and feet planted firmly in the doorframe.

"Well, looks like baby girl may have lost more than the track of time in the woods," sighed Mattie sourly.

Within the hour, Mattie had delivered the bad news to the mistress of the house. Lois Keller sat in her porch rocker, teeth clenched, madder than a red wasp.

"Damn fool child, the spitting image of her weak-willed father. Well, Marcus Keller may not have done his duty in protecting this family from the sins of this world, but, by God, Lois Keller will not make the same mistake."

She was not about to let some stray mongrel destroy what was left of her family and farm. It had been hard enough for her to hold on to what remained of her life with no man and a child. Her daughter would not relive the struggles and hardships of her own life. The best Lois could tell, the baby couldn't be any bigger than a tadpole at this point. If she acted quickly, there was still time.

CHAPTER EIGHT
The Barter

BEING WORKED OVER for church was the norm for Vancie, but this Saturday and Sunday morning had been particularly trying. Mattie had boiled her in the tin tub like a batch of crawdads on Saturday, scraping over her skin with a hard-bristled brush and a cake of lye soap. By Sunday morning, a new dress had appeared from nowhere, and for the first time in her life her mother had pinched her cheeks until she thought they would bleed before applying a light coat of reddish powder to them. A small silver cross had been hung around her neck, and she was hauled out the door, loaded like grain into the buckboard, and driven to church in Episcopalian silence. She and her mother had taken their pew in the old Green River Church for one of its last services before being vacated in the fall for the new church rising on the hill above the transforming town. Who knew that the arrival of one stranger in the area could create such a ruckus.

Mr. Hill sat just two rows in front of them in his Sunday finest. Within days of his arrival in Saluda, he had bought the failing mercantile. In rapid succession, other buildings downtown had taken on new ownership and new vitality. The small town buzzed with carpenters, masons, and painters as the community underwent a period of renewal and excitement unlike any other in its history. Mr. Hill's wealth had become legend, and his reputation in Saluda soared as small portions of his largesse trickled out to the hardscrabble folks scattered throughout the hills surrounding town. First the railroad, and now this. Of all the changes, perhaps the most stunning was the new Green River Church whose spire rose above the ridgeline of Saluda.

Vancie had grown used to her mother's clenched jaw in recent days, but she was puzzled by her mother's detached presence in church. After a while, she made an imaginary line from her mother's steely stare to the object of its attention, and it seemed to lead to Mr. Hill. Her curiosity at the end of the service only rose as she watched her mother beat a hasty path to the man and engage him in a very long, hushed conversation in a corner. Halfway through their chat, Vancie felt a cold chill as though being watched from her abandoned pew in a now nearly empty church. Turning her head to see when her mother might be ready to go, she met the methodical stare of Jagger Hill as he eyed her up and down. Vancie felt like a horse at auction, having her teeth bared and hooves inspected. There was more whispering between her mother and Mr. Hill, but this time it ended in formal smiles and polite handshakes.

Without a word, her mother retrieved her and escorted her to their buckboard. It would be nearly a week before her mother finally told her that she had been bartered away to Jagger Hill for the price of the remaining debt on the Keller farm and the promise of a privileged life for her as the first lady of Saluda. Days later, Vancie was wrapped in white silk and a veil, delivered red-eyed to a private service at the unfinished church on the hill, and married to Jagger Hill. Later that night, he raped her for the first of countless times. Each time, she survived by holding tight to her memory of the tenderness of Josiah Buckland. Numbing herself to all other things, she retreated into the solitude and darkness of her own private hell, which she would not share with another living soul.

Vancie never blamed her mother. How could she have known? Though reluctant, in the end Vancie knew that she had agreed to the marriage. Life with Jagger had hung before her, tinged with darkness perhaps, but solid, safe, and substantial. A life with Josiah at that time had appeared ethereal and uncertain, all heart and no head. How could anyone have ever known who judged by outward appearances? Jagger Hill had not been watched long enough to see what kind of fruit fell from his tree. The Almighty in heaven might see the human heart, but the rest of us dumb beasts are subject to the mistakes of judgments made with the eyes.

Although Vancie wanted to die, she knew that she would live. The knowledge struck her when she looked into the eyes of her sweet baby boy and saw staring back the blue of her own eyes and the gray flecks of the eyes of Josiah Buckland. She knew she would live because Jagger had finally tired of her and sought his satisfaction from Delilah Hart and others in a bed above one of his many businesses in town. She was a mother now and would live if for no other reason than for the well-being of her child.

CHAPTER NINE
Delilah Hart

Delilah Hart lay sprawled out on her big mahogany bed clothed in a pair of pink bloomers and nothing more. Her silk sheets had been pushed down to her footboard. Two girls in their early twenties sat on each side of her bed, alternately fanning themselves and then their madam with paper church fans. It was that unbearable time of afternoon in the summer when every breath of air stilled and the cicadas droned. Even though all the hallway doors were flung open, there was no breeze to catch. A big clock on the mantel ticked each sultry minute as her girls fished small chips of ice from a metal bowl and ran them across Delilah's glistening forehead. She allowed the resulting moisture to creep in small rivulets across her cheeks, down her neck, and around her ample breasts.

"Thank God for ice stored during long mountain winters and for the connections in town to have portions of it delivered on deadly summer afternoons."

Delilah was out of uniform. Although her profession required few clothes in the late evening, what really made her feel naked was the complete absence of any makeup. The heat and humidity of the morning and afternoon had robbed her of every dab of rouge, powder, eye treatment, and perfume. Though still a good-looking woman in her natural state, she would not be caught dead without the full application of every weapon in her arsenal, each of which was spread out on her dressing table across the room. It just wasn't professional, and she knew that she would have to pull herself together during the next few hours.

She was hoping and praying for rain. Most summer afternoons in the mountains, clouds would gather, the air would still and thicken, and the sky would weep cooling rain for an hour or more. On those days, it was a whole lot easier to rise from bed, apply her face, pull on layers of clothing, and sashay down the stairs to meet her gentlemen callers in her full glory. On the days it did not rain, every bit of the same preparation had to be executed, but she carried out the process in abject misery. She lay still, waiting to hear which type of day this would be. Within moments, her answer came. The brilliant light outside of her windows dimmed, birds became silent, and the first distant rumbles of thunder reached her ears. Her breasts rose as she heaved a great sigh of relief. Soon, the cooling rain poured off the eaves of the roof, past her window, and spattered into the dirt below.

With a wave of her hand and a slight smile of appreciation, she dismissed the girls, who exited with the chilled bowl and closed the door gently behind them. Delilah sat up in bed, her breasts filling and sagging only slightly as she swung her feet downward, fishing for her slippers. Finding them, she rose. She retrieved her sheer dressing gown and pulled it onto her bare shoulders.

The room had not yet completely cooled, so she did not bother to button the front of her gown as she proceeded to a small table without a mirror. She sat lightly, picked up a one-bristled brush, and began to dab the veins of leaves onto the small white porcelain plate in front of her. Every working woman needs a pastime, and Delilah's was tole painting. Although usually the distraction of dried-up Southern spinsters, she found the silence and fine detail of the craft soothing. Several years ago, a traveling botanist had dropped in for the evening and in gratitude had left his sketchbook as part of his payments for services rendered. For a long time afterward, Delilah had paged through the journal and marveled at the amazing variety and beauty of the flora. One day, she became brave, purchased a few white plates, paint, and brushes from the mercantile and set to work.

Delilah's first attempts were crude, but her skill improved. Now, she found herself able to duplicate the art of the botanist. It felt good to take pride in her efforts. Today, a small display of trillium took shape before her. Suddenly becoming aware of time, she changed locations to the mirrored table on the other side of the room.

This was her work table. Dozens of cosmetics were spread out before her. Expertly, she selected small jars and began the transformation for the day's work hours. By the time the social hour began at eight, she would have become the fantasy of every farm boy, merchant, peddler, and lumberjack cued up for the evening to spend time with her and her girls. This being a weeknight, she had to look especially good because she would probably be spending most of her evening with Jagger Hill. Ever since he had settled in, he had become a frequent customer.

At first, Delilah had fixed Jagger up with some of the younger women. However, word had come back to her quickly that Jagger took his greatest satisfaction in inflicting pain. If he had been some two-bit farmer, she would have thrown him down the stairs herself. However, his wealth and growing power created a shield of immunity for his cruelty. Although there was no pleasure in the job, Delilah decided to take the bastard on herself rather than run the risk of him hurting one of her girls. He fucked like a lineman driving railroad spikes, but Delilah knew her limits. She kept a small revolver in the drawer by her bed and knew how to use it if necessary.

Dabbing a last layer of powder across her cheeks and bosom, she rose from her dressing table, cinched up her breasts, and stepped into her gown. She pulled it up around her. She rarely felt remorse about her work. Her profession had begun early for her and had saved her from starvation. However, last week she had caught sight of Jagger's wife as her buggy rolled down the rutted main street of Saluda. Such sorrow marked the young woman's face. Deliliah knew that most of that came from Jagger. For the first time, she thought about the women of the men in her life. The thought had left her dead inside, so she had quickly retreated back upstairs to her sanctuary. As for tonight, there was no time for such thoughts. Her visitors awaited.

CHAPTER TEN
The Ferryman

JOSIAH BUCKLAND MAY have arrived in Saluda at noontime, but he had left in the dead of night. Mr. Phineus had come to him after dinner with the news of Vancie's impending marriage to Jagger Hill. Josiah thought of begging her to reconsider, but what incantation could he have spoken to undo the bewitchment of betrayal that had fallen upon her. Truth be known, his own anger and pride had not contributed to a spirit of reconciliation. He hated to turn his back on all the kindness that Mr. Phineus had extended to him, but after the delivery of the news he said a tearful goodbye to his boss, threw his few worldly goods into a sack, tossed it over his shoulder, and eased out of the back door of the livery.

Quickly, Josiah had slipped out of town and made long strides for hours, putting as much distance between himself and the source of his pain as he possibly could. Although it violated all his survival instincts, he found himself on the first of a series of roads and trails that would take him back to the high country. He had no idea what he would do when he got there. His parents were long since gone. He had no siblings, and his extended family had never emigrated from the highlands of Scotland. Once again, he was completely on his own. As morning neared, Josiah was stranded on the banks of the upper stretches of the Green River. He could go no farther without the help of the ferryman. Searching the riverbanks for the scoundrel, he saw the old man's raft bobbing in the early mists of the morning a few dozen feet away. To provide a little extra protection from unexpected strangers and wild animals, the old man had anchored the raft a little ways out in the channel.

At first, the raft appeared to be abandoned, but as Josiah peered into the obscurity of the near dawn, the mist stirred and a figure rose up slowly from the craft. Josiah found himself involuntarily taking a step backward as the apparition came into sharper focus. Rising before him was the broad-shouldered figure of a silver-bearded old man more than six feet tall. The frightful thing about him was that he was armed not with a pistol or rifle but with some type of spear. He stood astride the ferry still shrouded in semidarkness, lower legs wreathed in mists. In his right hand, the ferryman was holding a small, crudely made two-pronged triton tipped with a frog.

"Why, hello, boy. Come to join me for some grub?" the old haint shouted.

Josiah snapped back to his senses and realized that the ferryman had been on his knees, gigging the last of his breakfast under the shroud of the late night before the sun chased his prey away. The ferryman used his muscled arms to draw the rope from the water and haul the craft back to the shoreline. As the raft closed the short distance, Josiah got a better look at his breakfast host. A floppy, old broad-brimmed hat lay lightly on the top of the old man's bespectacled, lined face. Tobacco stained one corner of his chin and streaks trailed down into the tangle of his beard. Faded overalls draped the rest of his slightly stooped frame. Josiah had seen the man before.

"Ain't much of a talker I see," said the old man as he lurched from the raft onto the riverbank. "Catfish got your tongue?" he quipped, chuckling softly at his own wit as he whipped a straight-bladed knife from a creel at his waist.

Once again, Josiah instinctively took a step backward. "Why, no. Nothing has got my tongue," he retorted. "I just need me a way across the river."

The old man made his way to a small fire ring on the riverbank, struck a small piece of flint against the metal of his knife blade, and ignited the preset tinder piled up in the middle. A small blaze rose up, and the ferryman added twigs and then sticks in a methodical fashion. Once the blaze was secure, he dropped the creel next to a flat rock, fished out the first of its contents, and expertly sliced the heads from the squirming frogs and cleaved off their stilled back legs. Silently, he returned to the raft, retrieved a cast-iron pan, tossed a bit of fatback into it, and dropped the frog legs into the soon sizzling skillet. The aroma of frog flesh, salt, and fat filled the morning air.

"Never answered my question, boy. Want some grub? And by the way, ain't I seen you before?" the old man grumbled as he stirred the contents of the pan.

"Well, yes, I would like something to eat, and you saw me a while back when I crossed the river in the other direction when I was headed down from the hills."

Josiah remembered his first crossing painfully. To pay the ferryman, he'd had to part with a silver belt buckle that had belonged to his father. He did not suspect that the spirit of charity had fallen upon him since then, so he anticipated that he'd have to pay a painful price to get back to the other side. The ferryman leaned in a little closer toward him, peering through muddied spectacles.

"Well, a lot of people pass this way, but I do seem to recollect seeing you afore," grunted his cook as he squirted tobacco juice to one side of the fire.

You ought to remember me, you old thief, thought Josiah.

It was not that he denied anyone a living, but the belt buckle had been worth a considerable amount more than he would have paid if he'd had silver coin. Nothing had come back to him in the exchange. At least this time he had a few coins, pressed into his hand by Mr. Phineus as he left, and he was getting breakfast out of the deal to even up his last trip on the ferry.

When breakfast was golden brown, the old man sat the pan on the ground between the two of them and let Josiah gingerly retrieve his portion from the scalding grease. Though some townsfolk might have turned up their noses at the contents, meat of any kind was a rare treat for the boy. Josiah blew on each limb until it cooled, pulled the meat from the bones with his teeth, chewed with gusto, and sucked the bones until the last drop of grease was gone. Releasing a sigh of contentment, he balanced back on his haunches.

The ferryman broke the silence, announcing, "Now, that will be one quarter dollar for your passage and another quarter dollar for your grub."

Josiah launched to his full height and spat, "What! That is robbery. You never told me that you were charging me anything for my breakfast. I ought to go back to town and bring the sheriff down on you, you old reprobate."

Menacingly, the ferryman replied, "Settle down there, sonny boy. I just asked you if you wanted any of my grub. You could have said no. Now, you don't have to cross this river, but you owe me for that food. By God, you will be paying me."

The crook reached over to the rock, retrieved his knife, and wiped frog guts and blood into the dew of the morning grass. Josiah was madder than hell after being jilted and now robbed, but he was no fool. Somehow, the old devil had calculated exactly how much money was in his pocket. It would cost him everything but his life to settle accounts with the ferryman and continue his journey. The last thread of his dignity was going to be left on this side of the river, but Josiah would just have to silently accept this butt kicking. His only comfort was that nothing would ever bring him back this way again. The boy fished into the deepest recesses of his pocket, extracted the two silver coins, and dropped them into the eagerly extended wrinkled hand. The ferryman smiled back in return, exposing the gaps left by several missing teeth.

Without further ado, the two of them kicked dirt onto the remaining embers of the breakfast fire, stepped lightly onto the ferry, pulled up the rope to draw them to the other side, and began Josiah's silent retreat from everything that he had found and loved during the past year. The ferryman looked down upon the boy stoically. Years ago, he had lost count of how many country simpletons he had shaken down. The problem for him now was that the thrill was gone, and all that remained was the mind-numbing drudgery of crossing and recrossing the river.

CHAPTER ELEVEN
The Wood Carver

LIKE AN EXECUTIONER, Josiah stood in the yard of his homestead, an ax clenched in his hands raised to its zenith above him. Time and time again the blade fell with violence, cleaving hunks of the chestnut tree trunk. The wrath of the noonday sun beat down upon his head and bare torso. He lost himself in sorrow, pain, fury, and sweat as the ax rose and fell in rhythmic cadence. Although he had left her behind in Saluda months before, the specter of Vancie Keller occupied every waking moment of his days and haunted the darkest recesses of his nights. Josiah remained deeply wounded by her rejection, but he had been driven to a state of near madness by Phineus Coble's news of her marriage to Jagger Hill. Every long-considered strategy of reconciliation had fallen like flaming bridges across insurmountable chasms. Faint hope in an instant became fatal despair. He had lost her. Josiah Buckland, young and foolish, had lost the light of his life to the darkest and most corrupt soul that he had ever encountered.

He paused, sweat dripping from every part of his body, and shuddered at the memory of his encounter with Jagger Hill on the sidewalk of downtown Saluda. The hair on his nape rose in spite of the sweat as the name and vision of Hill congealed in his brain. Josiah then did the only thing that he had found to be effective in relieving the tyranny of his thoughts: He moved.

Hitching a chain to one end of the remaining six feet of the log, he dragged it across the dust, weeds, and chicken shit of his yard into the shed beside the barn. He had thought about killing Jagger Hill, but Mr. Phineus had finally made him accept that Vancie was bound to him by the iron manacles of the law. After several tortured hours, Josiah gathered his few possessions and retreated to the only other home he had ever known. It would never be where he wished to be, but he would simply have to make the best of the choices, other than murder, that remained available to him.

Since his return to his father's old homestead in the high country, the shed had become his sanctuary from the pain of the outside world. Dark and musky from old hay, the outbuilding provided relief from the noonday sun, yet the cracks in the roof and sideboards still emitted enough light for his craft. Josiah had become a woodcarver. Farming had never been a profitable enterprise in the thin, rocky soil of the highlands. With the felling of many of the great trees from disease, he had been gifted the raw material to churn out a steady stream of chairs, sideboards, bedframes, and wagon wheels. His new profession lent itself well to the daily practical needs of the thrifty, no-nonsense Scotsmen who populated the mountaintops of the Blue Ridge. As Josiah heaved the roughed-out log upright in his workspace, he knew that it would never support the weary bodies of his neighbors at night, house their tableware, or rock their children.

Josiah sensed that a lovely young woman lay imprisoned within this wood. For weeks, she had called to him in his dreams, begging to be set free from captivity. Now, like a knight of old, he had come to her rescue. He picked up a small hatchet from his worktable and proceeded to hack away at the chestnut bark. With each blow, he exposed part of her smooth skin beneath the coarse shell of her imprisonment.

For hours upon hours, day after day, Josiah hacked, gouged, sawed, chipped, and polished until the beauty of her face emerged, the tresses of her hair cascaded over smoothed shoulders, and the elegant arms of her freed body wrapped themselves in front of her around a great mystery. Driven beyond reason, he left a great bulge on the front of the emerging figure where it should not have been. Days ago, the bulk of her breasts, hips, back, and limbs had been winnowed down to their scale in the real world. However, a great mass had remained in her midsection. Josiah stepped back in wonder as he puzzled over the crude, formless mass that marred the emerging essence of Vancie Keller. He could not understand why his vision of the beautiful figure blurred in her midsection. Perhaps fatigue had gotten the best of him at the end of a long workday. In exasperation and defeat, he slowly placed his tools on his workbench and retreated from the shed for his evening meal.

CHAPTER TWELVE
Mama Lois

Mama Lois sat bolt upright in her cast-iron bed at the end of a dark hallway in her old farmhouse. The golden strands of her hair had turned to the bluish-gray of gunmetal and were now wrapped tightly about her head like a diadem. Her grandson, James, had occasionally seen her tresses unfurled when Mama Lois pulled loose all the pins and clips that held it in place and unleashed it to its full length down to her knees. She would sit in a small rocker on the back porch, taking sections of it in her silver comb and working rainwater from the barrel down the strands until she eventually squeezed it from the tips into a basin at her feet.

In those days, when her tongue remained sharp and her temper quick, the boy thought of the stories that he had been told of Medusa and her strands of snakes. When James was young, the old woman seemed to hate the boy, more for simply breathing than anything that he had actually done wrong. But in recent years, as her mind dimmed, her heart softened and her face brightened any time that he entered the room. It brightened more than when Mattie brought in her meals, more even than when her own daughter, Vancie, appeared.

James found her affection to be even more mysterious than her hatred had been. Whatever grudge the old woman had held had burned away like the sultry dampness of an August morning after a night of rain. Mama Lois had simply lived long enough to forget precisely who and what it was that she was supposed to hate. She was lucky that James was a boy and not a man. A puppy can be whipped and will come back time and again, believing that a stroke rather than a swat is just around the corner. A dog will strike back.

"Hey, Mama Lois!" James chattered as he emerged from the darkness of the hallway into the full morning light of the old woman's bedroom. He leapt up on the bed, rattling her breakfast tray as he snuggled in beside her.

"Well, good morning to you, you rascal," the old woman squealed as she pushed her tray down to the foot of the bed.

A rooster crowed down in the yard beneath her window.

"Now, boy, what is it that the rooster says?"

"Why, Mama Lois, the rooster says, 'Doctor Gaston! Doctor Gaston,'" responded the boy with pride.

Mama Lois cackled and hugged the boy close. This was their great secret. James had discovered that Mama Lois could talk to all the barnyard animals and understand their every reply. She had explained that the rooster was a particularly good friend of hers. Any time he saw that old sawbones, Dr. Gaston, heading up the road in his buggy, the bird would scream out the doctor's name to give Mama Lois time to lock the parlor door and buy herself a day or two of reprieve from his endless probing, sticking, and fussing.

Their days were spent in endless hours of barnyard tales, gliding on the front porch swing and singing silly songs that Mama Lois had been taught as a child in Ireland. Mattie did all the cooking, and Big John kept up the garden. Mama Lois was free all day long to lighten James's heart and cure him of the endless melancholy of life with his mother and father back at Orchard Cove. Wednesdays at Mama Lois's were days to breathe deeply and freely, to be silly, loud, and juvenile, all things that were banned at his father's house.

"Sing that song to me again, Mama Lois, the one about the dog, the cat, and the fiddle."

She did, and James, bouncing, leapt over the old woman's legs each time the cow jumped over the moon.

"Tell me that you will never leave me, Mama Lois. Tell me that you will always love me."

The old woman pulled him tightly to her side and replied, "He will never leave nor forsake thee."

Her tone and most of her words comforted James. He puzzled over her use of "He" for a while but finally wrote it off to the dimming of her mind. She made many small mistakes these days.

"He will never leave nor forsake thee," the old woman chanted once again before lapsing into her morning nap.

CHAPTER THIRTEEN
Of Pear Trees and Plott Hounds

MANY PEOPLE THOUGHT James to be an unusual looking child. He had clearly inherited the golden hair of his mother and her prominent cheekbones, but the combination of her features and his odd bluish-gray eyes set him apart from all the other boys at his school. The fact that his father owned more than half of Saluda did not help either. He had pumped a fortune into the town, but that had not gone far to tamp down its citizens' jealousies. Though strong, James often found himself an outsider and suffered when he heard the whispered taunts of "ghost boy" or "wolf child." Rejection by his peers drove him to entertain himself on his own. So, when he could escape his father's watchful eye, James wandered the forests and creeks of Jagger Hill's considerable land holdings, following streams, turning over rocks, and tracking game.

Once in the woods, he felt safe from his peers and his father. Though his father had hundreds of acres of land, his only joy in nature seemed to come from owning a large piece of it. Often, James was deeply disturbed by his father's orientation to the earth. Last spring, the normally bountiful pear tree on the front lawn at Orchard Cove blossomed, but by fall it had borne no fruit. One beautiful fall morning, James bounded down the steps of the manor house and froze in his tracks. Jagger Hill stood like a lumberjack in the front yard of his newly occupied barony, with the sleeves of his dress shirt rolled up, ax in hand. The white steps and yellow-sided levels of the mansion soared before Jagger like an ostentatious wedding cake. With horror, James realized that the object of Jagger's wrath was about to be his favorite tree.

"But, Father, pear trees don't bear fruit every fall. Sometimes, they just store up for a big harvest the next year!" pleaded James.

If Jagger Hill heard the boy, he paid no mind. The ax rose and fell, slicing into the trunk and into the boy's heart. The boughs of the tree and their golden leaves quivered with each blow. Before he knew what he was doing, James had crossed the yard and wrapped his eight-year-old arms around Jagger's legs.

"Please, Father, just give it another—"

But before he could finish his sentence, James felt the right side of his head explode as the back side of his father's hand struck him with stunning force. James rolled across the lawn, felt the light of day darken, and was momentarily deafened by the ringing in his ears. When his hearing returned, he heard his father spewing invectives.

"No damned tree is going to suck nutrients and water from my land and give nothing back in return, not for the long haul or even the short one. 'The tree that does not bear fruit is cut down and cast into the fire.'"

It was the first and only time that James ever heard his father utter a word of Scripture. The blows to the root of the tree resumed as James lay stunned on the ground. He jumped up when he heard the crack of the trunk as the ancient tree toppled backward and shook the ground. By late in the day, the help had crosscut-sawed the tree to kindling. Old lumber from the barn, dead brush, and lamp oil were added to the wreckage, and by dark, Jagger's prophetic words rang true as the sweet smell of burning pear wood rose into the starry night sky.

As devastated as James had been by the destruction of his favorite tree, he had no notion of what other brutal lessons of nature his father would drive home in the coming year. By the next summer, the pear tree had been largely forgotten except upon the rare occasion that James stumbled in the remaining indentation in the lawn when he played there. Last fall had brought an unusual act of kindness shortly after the destruction of the tree. Jagger had bought a handsome tall hound and a matching bitch from the estate of a timber baron on the other side of Sassafras Mountain. The baron had been experimenting with a new type of hound that would be fearless in ferreting out the last of the black bears that ruled the high country. Mr. Plott had nearly mastered the new breed, and upon hearing of a hound more fearless than a bear, Jagger was consumed with lust to own one of the first breeding pairs. Late in the spring, the male had his way when the bitch came into heat, and by fall eight puppies whimpered in the run by the barn.

Joy overwhelmed James as he passed the pen with the writhing puppies each day. He could smell the aroma of new puppy as he walked by the enclosure, but he knew better than to think that he would ever touch them. His father had owned dogs in the past, and he owned them as he owned everything in his dominion—exclusively. At one point, two of Jagger's dogs had dropped their litters the same week. A few months later, thirteen pups yapped behind the fence, well beyond the reach of James's eager little hands.

This time, his father shocked him by announcing that James was to pick and name one of the young male hounds. Jagger hoped that ownership of such a masculine beast might make a real boy out of his doe-eyed son. The boy spent too much time with his weak-willed mother, and if there was ever to be anything hanging between the boy's legs it was going to require intervention on Jagger's part. Upon hearing his father's offer of a pup, James could not control his delight and danced around his father like a pup himself, proclaiming, "His name is Sport. His name is Sport. That's my pup's name!"

Jagger looked down with mild disdain and left the boy to his embarrassing exuberance.

In the coming months, James and Sport were as inseparable as Jagger would allow, but James had been given strict instructions by his father "not to ruin the animal." This meant, at least in Jagger's presence, that he was to show the dog no signs of physical affection. James was to follow a strict regimen of controlled feeding, teaching of voice commands, and the gradual introduction of game scents to awaken its primal instincts. When the help killed rabbits and other fare for the family table, James was allowed to take the pelts to expose the pup to their hides and the scent of blood.

James would have done anything to have a dog of his own, so he followed his father's instructions with great precision. However, when he knew that his father was safely away in town, James would occasionally steal a hug from his new best friend. After much preparation that summer, the day came for Sport to get his first official hunting trial with James and Jagger Hill. By then, Sport could track the carcass of a rabbit that James had dragged throughout the grounds of Orchard Cove and hidden in the brush for a reward when found. Today, the pup would have his first go at live rabbits.

Jagger descended the steps of the house with his gun over his shoulder. Within an hour, Sport had jumped a rabbit in the brush along an old fence line, and the hunt was on. James thrilled as Sport made his first shrill attempts at baying as he pursued the rabbit. Instinct and older dogs would teach the pup to slowly circle the rabbit back to where it had been jumped. Jagger ran for interception, rapidly outpacing James's shorter legs.

James struggled behind, wading through the swampy areas of the lower pasture and painfully fighting his way through patches of excruciating cane briars. Still a considerable distance behind, his heart pounded with pride when he heard the echoing report of Jagger's gun. Tearing his pants as he ripped his way loose from the briars, James crested the hill and gazed down the slope with horror. Jagger stood at the bottom of the hill with a slight wisp of smoke rising from his gun. Sport lay at the foot of a large oak tree in a pool of his own blood. Running up to his father, James opened his mouth to scream, but no sound came. His father broke down his gun, ejecting the shells.

"Damn fool dog chased a squirrel up a tree rather than follow the trail of the rabbit. You can never fix that in a dog."

CHAPTER FOURTEEN
Big John

BIG JOHN STOOD deep in the growing darkness of a pit of his own making. The last thing Miss Lois had told him that she needed was a new root cellar. Now she lay dying in the house in the last hours of her life. The old cellar had been slowly crumbling for years, so Big John spent the last few days digging in the earth to keep himself out from underfoot as womenfolk tended to Miss Lois's needs. As he worked, he could occasionally hear the keening of Miss Vancie as the hour neared.

Yesterday, as he cut the walls of the cellar with his spade, he could hear his daddy's voice say, "Now, John, you make all of them walls in that ditch straight. Don't you go messing up. One of these here days, somebody will dig up this here ditch and say, 'That man that dug this ditch, he dug it up for the Lord. It sure is purty.'"

It had been a long time since he had heard his daddy's voice in his head. He tried not to think of such things. His daddy had died young in years but old in body and mind. He was worked to death on a cotton plantation near the coast. Big John tried to remember as little from those days as possible. He hated taking his clothes off at night and seeing what he could of the ridges that marked his back, torso, and chest. A whip had engraved them when he was a boy. There would be more of them, but as soon as the war ended, he had taken off with Aunt Mattie for the hills. His mama and daddy were both dead by then.

He and Aunt Mattie ran for the mountains because they were the farthest thing they knew from the coast. There weren't many Black people in the mountains. Many of the White people blamed them for the war, but the Kellers had taken him and Aunt Mattie in. They probably had worked about as hard on the Keller farm as they had on the plantation, but the Kellers worked shoulder to shoulder with them. Mr. Marcus had done his best, but he was busted up bad from the war. Miss Lois had a sharp tongue, but she had worked from sunup to sundown as long as Big John had known her.

Big John did not care. He was free. Though he did not own the earth he dug in, he was not owned by the man and woman who did. He loved the earth, its smell in the spring and its touch as he busted coal-black clots of it in his enormous hands. Unlike most men, he did not shy away from plowing fields, digging ditches, planting trees, or burying the dead.

The winter earth was hard as he cut out the new cellar walls, and Big John knew that he would be digging in the frozen earth again within days, this time no deeper than six feet. It would be his last favor to the old woman for taking him and Aunt Mattie in. He tried not to think what would become of the two of them when Miss Lois passed. Miss Vancie was a good woman too, but she had gone and married the devil. He had seen his kind many times before when he was a boy. Every time Mr. Jagger's shadow fell on him, Big John made a cross in the yard from sticks to undo the hex. Just thinking about him gave Big John the chilly bumps, so picking up his spade he cut a little deeper into the cold dark earth and found a rhythm of work that drove all thoughts from his head.

CHAPTER FIFTEEN
The Ice Storm

SLEET PELTED THE brim of James's hat like pellets of steel. If Big John had not dug Mama Lois's grave yesterday, the funeral would have been postponed. A front had blown into the mountains during the night, bringing with it an icy mist and an imminent threat of snow. Snow might indeed come, but for now icy projectiles continued to fall in sheets as the small band of humans huddled like cattle beneath the fir tree at the back of Mama Lois's house.

James watched his own breath materialize and then dissipate inches from his face. Despite his heavy coat and broad-brimmed hat, the cold sneaked into the seams where one piece of his wool clothing met another. The boy pressed himself close to his mother and felt the warmth of her gloved hand as he reached up and took her small, strong hand into his own. Her grip reminded him of Mama Lois.

Even in the last days of her life, as cancer ate away at her insides, Mama Lois's grip retained the tensile strength of a fencing foil. James used to wince and attempt to pull his hand away when she would take it into her own. He could never reconcile her small frame, especially in old age, to the crushing power of her clutch. Perhaps it came from year upon year of picking cotton in the flatlands during her own childhood and youth. Perhaps it just came to those who lived long, worked hard, and suffered unbearable sorrows. There are things of the earth that break the body, mind, and spirit of the half-hearted. To remain in the shadowlands of this world, the strong-willed have to hold on tightly to life, lest they be snatched away without warning. James tightened his grip on his mother's hand as the preacher droned on.

Mama Lois had been what the people of the hills refer to as a hard-shelled Baptist. No card playing, no drinking, no dancing, nor musical instruments even in church. On a few occasions, James had attended church with Mama Lois late in her ninety years of life. Though a religious woman in a severe sort of a way, she said that her absences from church in her latter years would be forgiven because an old woman has lost all the padding on her rump to sit respectfully and endure hours of hellfire and damnation preaching.

"The Maker understands such things and makes concessions to the bony-assed late in life."

When she was in church, she sat straight-backed, her shawl wrapped tightly around her shoulders and her iron-gray spectacles pressed to her face. Mama Lois was a stern woman, but James had seen her on the periphery of a barn dance with a smile stealing across her lips and her foot lightly tapping the ground. Even a lifetime of hardships and eons of churchgoing in the mountains could not completely extinguish the flame lighted in her family in more pagan corners of Ireland.

To dampen that flame, Mama Lois never missed the foot washing services on Sunday nights. If there was indeed any sacrament in life to counter the fires of hell, it was foot washing. There was a rawness in peeling off socks and stockings, baring calloused, smelly feet, and walking forward barefooted and rooted to the ground. The ritual stripped away all pretense of being anything more than the dust of the earth.

"Ashes to ashes and dust to dust," droned the preacher as he scooped a handful of frozen black clods of earth and scattered it over the cover of the exposed pine box six feet below.

The boy felt a brutal sense of loss. His greatest loss was his grandmother, but Mama Lois's house had also been his sanctuary from his father and his tyrannical oppression at Orchard Cove. Now, there was nowhere to hide.

James lifted his grayish-blue eyes from the hole, tears streaming across his frozen face, and looked up at his mother, Mattie, and Big John. Tears streamed down their faces too, and James imagined them simply becoming salt-tinged additions to the sleet as it continued its assault upon all things warm and living.

The only dry eyes he saw were the dark orbs of Jagger Hill as he stared out blankly across the mist-shrouded ridges. His mother's husband and his own father, Jagger, stood apart from all the other mourners, touching and being touched by no one. His feet shuffled impatiently in the frozen slush beneath them, and James sensed his father's readiness to bolt for the carriage upon the utterance of the last "amen." Without warning, James realized that his father had shifted his gaze and was now staring back at him with a venomous countenance and furrowed brow. Jagger Hill, in the leadlike grayness of the day, had been caught off guard once again by his son's haunting, transcendent gaze.

Where in hell did he get those eyes? His bitch of a mother has blue eyes, and my own are nearly black. Why does that boy look like a damned wolf staring back at me? And where have I seen those eyes before?

Jagger racked his brain, searching back through the years. James smiled faintly at his father, but his smile was not returned.

CHAPTER SIXTEEN
Encounter

It had been a hard year for James. The death of his dog and the devastating loss of Mama Lois had left the boy hollow inside. Finally, a morning dawned without his father in the house or the prospect of his return for the entire day. Jagger had gone to Asheville on business and would not return until late that night. James had been banned from the house to "give his mother time to rest."

After wandering aimlessly about the yard for a while, James wildly ran several miles down the road from Orchard Cove and finally plunged into the forest. Escaping the heat of the day and the oppression of home, the cool of the forest enveloped James and slowly stilled his racing heart. For over an hour, the boy moved from tree to tree in the pathless woods, dodging the occasional laurel thicket and briar patch. After great effort, he came to what appeared to be the faintest and most crude of trails. He was not even sure that it was a trail, but by midmorning the path took on greater definition, leading him deeper into the heart of the great forest.

By noon, his efforts had brought him to a small rippling stream, cascading noisily over rocks. He amused himself by turning over stones, looking for salamanders and crayfish beneath them, but the attractions of the stream paled in comparison to the allure of the thunderous noise coming from more deeply in the woods. James found the roar irresistible as he forced himself through the thickets lining the creek, edging nearer and nearer to the source of the fury. Within minutes, he emerged from the thickets of the forest into a small opening at the foot of a magnificent waterfall. The white foam of the cataract bounded from boulder to boulder as it leapt from the heights, descended the wall of the gorge, and plummeted into the boiling cauldron at its base. The cool mist billowing from the cauldron soothed his fatigue.

As clouds thinned overhead, the curtain of the fall morphed from gray to dazzling white. James's knees slowly buckled, and he fell to the rock beneath him. Kneeling, he was enveloped in light, mist, and sound as leaves rustled gently around him. He lost any sense or capacity for words. Everything became feeling. Later, when some ability to think and speak returned, the word that would finally come to him was "oneness." In Orchard Cove, everything was separate. There was house, mother, father, help, animals, and tree. Here, everything blurred. Here, everything was one and alive—sky, water, light, rock, and tree. The words separating these things seemed ridiculous. All things were one, and life pulsed in everything, even those things like rocks that James had believed always to be dead. Nothing was more or less alive than another. Nothing was more or less alive than himself. He now heard his own heart beat in rhythm with wind, water, and tree. At first, everything just seemed to pulse with energy and life, but soon James had the odd sensation of another joining him.

His eyes told him that he was alone in the forest, but his heart was at war with his eyes. There was Other, and it wasn't the birds in the trees or the trout in the stream. They were on his side. Whatever had joined James at the falls had joined them too. The sensation was so foreign that he had no words for it. Later, he would realize that this feeling might be what others called peace. James had known no peace in his life, but he knew the comfort of a quilt at night in the winter. Whatever came to him came in that way. It settled over and around him, but in the end it was not something settling over him but rather someone.

In his bliss, James knew three things: If this presence continued to grow, he would die from joy, this experience could not last, and finally, he would spend the rest of his life seeking this sensation again. Too soon, he felt it slipping away. He wanted to cry out in despair and longing, but he knew that would do no good. Whatever had come to him did not answer to him. Within moments, things were separate again. James was ravenously hungry, strangely sad, and frightened as he became aware of lengthening shadows. Rising from the rock, he turned away from the waterfall and marched silently toward his house. Fortunately, he found a more clearly marked trail for his return, and his trip home was uneventful. At one point, he saw what appeared to be an old, dilapidated building in the distance, but the sun was too low in the sky for any more exploring today.

CHAPTER SEVENTEEN
The Church

THE CARRIAGE SLOWLY crested the ridge as it struggled for traction on the newly graded road. Jagger's heart swelled with immeasurable pride as the white spire of the newest of his creations soared into the cobalt sky before him. This was a structure worthy of praise and a fitting focal point for gleaming Main Street. Every town worth its salt possessed a church that dwarfed all other structures and reminded everyone, every day, of what it was to come before magnificence. All the dots scurrying back and forth in Saluda, perhaps soon to be called Hillsdale, needed to be kept in perpetual remembrance of what it was to be small and insignificant.

For a few moments, Jagger was lost in the revelry of his own joys and had forgotten his travel companion, who was tucked into the far corner of the seat beside him. Vancie sat in silence, staring blankly ahead with her empty azure eyes. The boy had been dropped off with Mattie at the Keller farm; she was minding his fever, which had sprung up the day before. Mattie and her nephew kept up the place until Jagger could make arrangements to sell it.

Whatever this day meant to Jagger, to Vancie it was just another episode in an endless struggle to keep alive her withering soul. She walked in lands of shadow, oblivious to the town below, the gleaming white church before her, and the finery that enveloped her. Jagger had spared no expense for this day. The most luxuriant fabric in Charleston had been shaped to her hourglass figure. It tightened around her tiny waist and lifted her fully mature breasts to the observation, desire, and envy of every man and woman in the crowded sanctuary. They would all be sanctified in the best of their own clothes, but however polished on the outside, the coarseness of their insides would still harbor lust for her husband's wealth and the riches that nature had bestowed upon her.

According to the Gospel of St. John, no one had to tell Jesus what dwelled in the hearts of humans, and no one had to tell Vancie either. Her private musings were suddenly violated by the sharp crack of the buggy whip against the straining, damp flanks of their horses and the sharper crack of Jagger's tongue as he broke what remained of the quiet of a sad Sabbath morning.

"Sit up straight, damn you! And slap a smile onto your stupefied face. I didn't spend a damned fortune in Charleston on clothes, hats, and jewelry to have you behave like some cowering yard dog this morning. You are Mrs. Jagger Hill. Sit your ass up straight, and act like it. We are about to pull up to the front of the church."

The carriage rested in a circular drive before the doors of the gleaming edifice. Throngs of people from the town below crowded the drive and entrance foyer of the church. Heads turned and eyes widened as the occupants dismounted.

"Why, Mr. and Mrs. Hill, good morning to you. It's a fine building indeed, sir. Yet another major step forward for our small town. Why, you are looking magnificent this morning, Mrs. Hill. Never prettier I would say," said someone in the crowd. Suddenly, the crowd's chatter was muted as the rector strode out onto the church steps and proclaimed to all the faithful:

> *"Lift up your heads, O ye gates; and be ye lift up, ye everlasting doors; and the King of glory shall come in.*
>
> *Who is the King of glory? It is the Lord strong and mighty, even the Lord mighty in battle.*

Lift up your heads, O ye gates, and be ye lift up, ye everlasting doors; and the King of glory shall come in.

Who is the King of glory? Even the Lord of hosts, he is the King of glory.

Glory be to the Father, and to the Son: and to the Holy Ghost;

As it was in the beginning, is now, and ever shall be: world without end. Amen."

Adoring hands from all sides reached out to touch the Hills as they mounted the steps to the foyer. The hush of the elect already inside brought the new arrivals to silence within the coolness of the brilliant sanctuary. Light streamed in profusion through a miasma of colored glass as the sun finally broke through the morning mists of the mountains. Sonorous tones poured forth from the organ, which Jagger had purchased on a whim while in New York last spring.

After everyone took their seats, the liturgy began, and the first congregants of Green River Holy Episcopal Church poured forth their prayers, praises, and petitions of consecration of a new church and a new day. Nothing of the newness of her surroundings penetrated Vancie's mind or heart. There was no new day, only another day and then another. But she was jolted to awareness when it was time for her to move. Kneeling benches were dropped, mounted, and raised again in preparation for the Eucharist. A gleaming silver plate, pitcher, and chalice rose into her consciousness as Jagger subtly tightened his grasp on her elbow and raised her now animated body to his will. The priest intoned:

"Be ye not unequally yoked together with unbelievers: for what fellowship hath righteousness with unrighteousness? And what communion hath light with darkness? And what concord hath Christ with Belial? Or what part hath he that believeth with

an infidel? And what agreement hath the temple of God with idols? For ye are the temple of the living God; as God hath said, I will dwell in them, and walk in them; and I will be their God, and they shall be my people."

Vancie advanced down the aisle before Jagger like a puppet on a string until she found herself before the newly hired parish priest. His pale appendage extended bread to her cupped hands, dipped the morsel into the cup, and lifted it mechanically to her mouth. She felt a small part of her brain come to life, though it wasn't due to the overwhelming presence of the Magnum Mysterium. The faint aroma of the bread had breathed life back into Vancie with long-forgotten memories of the goodness of the kitchen and of flour, lard, and milk kneaded into the sustenance of life itself. Memories of her mother, her old wooden breadboard, and the burst of heat from her stove assaulted her mind, heart, and spirit. Vancie set her jaw and stifled simultaneous desires to cry and collapse beneath the weakening frame of her body.

At just the right moment, the sting of tannic wine burst forth from the dampened morsel in her mouth and cleared her senses like smelling salts. She knew little of God and far less of church, but she returned to her pew awake as she had not been in a long time. Sight, sound, and smell poured into the vacuum of her soul and nearly swept her away with its force. All her senses were heightened. Color from the windows, robes, and worship implements dazzled her. Music permeated her very being, and the smells of candles and flowers soothed her. The pronunciation of the benediction interrupted Vancie's rejuvenation.

"The peace of God, which passeth all understanding, keep your hearts and minds in the knowledge and love of God, and of his Son Jesus Christ our Lord: And the Blessing of God Almighty,

the Father, the Son, and the Holy Ghost, be among you, and remain with you always. Amen."

In her heightened state, Vancie turned to Jagger to see him discreetly spit the small purple-stained mass into his white handkerchief and effortlessly return it to his breast pocket.

CHAPTER EIGHTEEN
Rosemary O'Shay

IN THE WEEKS following her last communion, Vancie's spirit remained strong, but terror crept into her heart as she watched her body slowly waste away. It began with dark circles under her eyes that refused to fade regardless of rest. She felt her body slowing incrementally each day as her waistline shrank, her hair thinned, and her gums bled. Before long, she found herself bedridden from exhaustion. Although Jagger shunned her in disgust, he allowed Rosemary, one of the kitchen staff, to bring her meals and make weekly trips to the apothecary and retrieve the medicines prescribed by Dr. Gaston. The ancient healer faithfully arrived at her bedside each week, mumbled a new diagnosis, and assured her of a better response to the next elixir.

She was no fool and paid him no mind. Vancie Keller knew dying when she saw it. She had recently seen it in the face of her own mother. Her fear was not for herself. Dying was her only route of escape from Jagger Hill. Her terror was for James. With Mama Lois gone, James would be left with Jagger and no buffer between the boy and the man who believed himself to be his father. Even when assuming James his son, Jagger was unspeakably cruel to him. What would become of the boy without her to throw herself between them? Jagger would never allow James to flee to Mattie, and her age made that an impossibility anyway. Mattie would invoke enough of Jagger's wrath when he discovered that Vancie had willed her parents' farm to her and Big John.

Somehow, she had to get the boy back to his own father, but Vancie had no idea where Josiah fled when he left town in the dark of night. Even if she knew where to find him, she was too weak to reach Josiah with the boy. Vancie knew that she would have to have an ally, but Jagger had so controlled her life since their marriage that her circle of friends was nonexistent. The only person she saw on a regular basis was Rosemary. Jagger had returned from a business trip to Boston with Rosemary O'Shay in tow. The poor girl had barely arrived from Ireland in full flight from famine when Jagger had scooped her up to add to his unnecessarily large house staff. Jagger collected human beings the way many people collected livestock or furniture.

He was particularly attracted to Rosemary because of her mastery of all things baked. Even in his bed at the hotel, he had been overcome by the aroma of bread, scones, pastries, and pies rising up the stairway from the kitchen. Before hard times had descended upon her in the old country, she had immersed herself in the mysteries of wheat, rye, and barley. When the blight arrived, Rosemary had risked her life crossing an ocean in search of prosperity only to be snatched up like a housefly in a spiderweb. Sharing confidence with poor Rosemary would be foolhardy and a risk that could cost Vancie and James their lives. However, she was going to have to trust somebody with her secret, and her options were limited.

Early the next day, Vancie reached out her arm and pulled James to her bedside when he entered to give her a morning kiss.

"James, my darling, Mommy has a gift this morning for you, but it is our secret and you must never share this gift with anyone other than one person."

Vancie pressed the golden watch into the boy's small, open hand. His eyes widened as he fingered the timepiece.

"In the near future, a special friend of Mommy's is going to come to you. He will be tall, with brown hair and gray eyes. When you are introduced to this man, show him your special watch. Then tell him that you know about the secret place in the back of the watch. You can trust this man. He is our friend. Show no one the watch other than him. Do as he says, and go with him if he asks."

James looked puzzled but could tell from the distress on his mother's face that now was not the time for questions. He allowed her head to fall back on her pillow and waited until her breathing became deeper and regular before he slipped out in silence from the room.

Later that morning, Rosemary brought Vancie's breakfast tray and methodically dropped her medicine into her tea. Rosemary's eyes widened to saucers as Vancie poured out her tale to the poor house servant.

"Your story is safe with me, Mistress Hill. Don't be to worrying. Just drink up your tea now, and get yourself some rest. I will find him. I will find him for you."

Vancie fell back into a stupor and slept the remainder of the morning. Rosemary took her tray back to the kitchen, put her dishes in the sink, pulled a stool to the cabinet, and put the dropper bottle in the far back corner of a high shelf above all the medicines prescribed by Dr. Gaston. The dropper bottle now contained only spring water.

"I am not a bad woman," Rosemary mused. "I would do the mistress no harm, but the mistress is weak like the stars, not strong like the sun and the moon."

Her beauty had drawn Master Hill to her, but she knew that Jagger Hill was no admirer of beauty. Beauty was a fleeting fancy. Master Hill loved strength, and Rosemary knew that she was a strong woman. She had drawn her strength from the rocky earth that nursed the once plentiful grains of Ireland. Earth gives strength to the worthy. She alone in this house was a child of earth and worthy of a man like Jagger Hill. She alone was worthy of the life he could offer.

CHAPTER NINETEEN
The Body

Vancie's body lay silent, dwarfed by the sturdy walls of the chestnut box and silver ornamentation that now encased her. She was finally contained and utterly subject to Jagger Hill's every desire or whim.

"Now, now, pretty one, rest your weary body and mind. I will take care of everything from now on," whispered Jagger. But he lied. He would certainly take care of everything, but she really was no longer that pretty. Her high, fine cheekbones, her ample bosom, and the redness of her lips remained thanks to the skill of the undertaker. Even so, Jagger missed the grace of her movement as she swept about the house performing his will and the soft subservience of her hushed voice in response to his commands. What he did not miss were her eyes. Well, the cowed look of them, perhaps. But not the white-hot flash that on the rarest of occasions revealed the rage and contempt she bore for him. As a final farewell to that spark of freedom that had remained in her eyes, Jagger reached into his vest pockets, removed two heavy gold coins, and pressed them firmly into her sockets. Stepping back, he found her to be beautiful once again.

Tomorrow, the stream of the bereaved would arrive. On Wednesday, the funeral would take place at his church with a late afternoon burial in the churchyard.

"In final victory, I will turn a skeleton key in the lock of the new Hill family crypt, grieve for the appointed number of days, and then set about the business of installing a new mistress of Orchard Cove," Jagger droned methodically.

Suddenly, something orange flashed in the darkness outside of the drawing room window. Jagger strode to the massive door of the house, threw it back against the wall, drew his pistol, and stepped onto the broad porch. In his wildest imaginings, he could not have anticipated what peered up from the center of the drive beneath him. That damned old Black housekeeper from the Keller place stood trespassing in the darkness, flanked by other torch-bearing darkies four or five deep on either side. He had no reason to recognize any of her other shiftless conspirators, but the one immediately to her right seemed like it might be that old Black preacher Andy from that ramshackle church in the woods.

"What do you want, washer woman, and what are you doing trespassing on my damned property in the middle of the night?"

For a moment, only silence and the darkness of the evening answered him. Mattie Fort stood before him, arms akimbo, eyes closed, and softly humming as her weight shifted methodically from one foot to another. Without warning, she froze, her yellow eyes blazed to life, and a piercing cry escaped her lips that made the hair on the back of Jagger's neck rise.

Pointing her crooked finger up from the small circle of light to the darkness above, Mattie keened, "Devil Man, you old Devil Man, the land I stand on it ain't your land. The land which I stand on be the earth. The earth it done been here before you, before me, even before the mountains and the hills were here. And the Lord of the earth and of the heaven he done sent me to you tonight. It don't be the ground that be damned by Him. You be damned by Him, and he done sent me to this house tonight to take that girl lying in there back to her mama in the ground, back to the earth of her farm, and back to other folk that you don't know nothing about. Get out of our way, Devil Man, and leave us to our work."

The absurdity of her challenge evoked Jagger to break into gales of laughter. But as his chest swelled and muscles tightened, an image paralyzed him in midrespiration. The piercing, yellow menace of the old woman's eyes as she drew a few steps closer to the bottom of the stairs filled Jagger with dread.

She transformed before him into some primordial emblem of authority, power, and danger. The form of the washer woman faded and was replaced by a shapeless specter of the forest that stalks and disembowels its prey in a silent frenzy of tooth and claw. For the first time perhaps in his life, Jagger's self-confidence cracked. Without warning, a deep hesitation seeped into that crack as the old woman's companions hummed and chanted some dark, sonorous incantations of solidarity as they advanced toward the steps of his home. The reality that he did not just face some old Black bitch but rather a phalanx of flaming might congealed in his consciousness.

His hand slipped slowly to the trigger of his gun, which hung tightly in his hand, but his merchant mind quickly calculated the bullets in the chamber and the foes before him. Even if he took some of them down, one torch was enough to reduce him and all that he had labored for to smoldering ruins. What if in a reckless frenzy they decided to use Orchard Cove, a strongbox of paper and coin, as a pyre for Vancie's worthless corpse? He treasured his pride. He jealously nurtured and protected it from all challengers, but at what price tonight? Would he sacrifice everything for a lifeless, White trash farm girl whose only worth was that she used to be the wife of Jagger Hill? Hell no. She would not take from him in death what he would not have conceded to her in life.

Slowly, almost imperceptibly, he lowered the pistol and stepped silently to the side. The old woman, eyes still blazing, slowly mounted the stairs with a massive Negro attached to each of her arms, supplanting any weakness in her aged body. She was an unreckonable force as her flaming spirit fused to their frames and strode up the steps and set about her work. Jagger had not even shaken himself from his stupor before the three emerged from the house with their prize. One of the men came out first, carrying the small, limp contents of the coffin wrapped in a worn, crazy quilt. The other man guided the old woman with one hand and with the other lifted a torch. Her eyes no longer blazed but had returned to their milky blankness.

Jagger thought at first that she would pass in silence, but at the last moment she pulled herself free and announced like a prophetess with great authority, "We ain't done yet, Devil Man. We got her, but we done torn your house near up looking for that child. You done spirited him away somewhere tonight, and if we knowed for certain it wasn't to some hidden place in this hellhole, we would be dropping this torch before we leave this place. Our business with you be half-done tonight. As God above is my witness, that child don't belong to you, and he won't always be with you. You just keep yourself worrying about us, but we is the least of your worries. Devil Man, you got a worry that you don't know nothing about."

In silence, she descended the stairs, mounted the creaking seat of the buckboard beside Big John, and rocked back and forth on her perch as the mules ferried the passengers into the darkness. Jagger watched the flickers of their orange torchlight until the wagon rounded the bend at the far end of the drive.

Quietly, he walked back in the house and closed the door. He straightened furniture disarrayed by the intruders. Rounding the doorway of the drawing room, he slowed his pace until he stood resolutely before the coffin, now empty except for two neglected gold pieces. Deftly, he returned them to his vest pocket. With his left hand, he reached up and pulled down the cover of the velvet-lined casket.

Speaking out loud in the empty room, Jagger pronounced, "My luck that they thought I knew where the boy is. He will pay when I do find him, but there will be time for that. More important details to attend to first. There will be no viewing of the body tomorrow.

Word will be sent in the morning that I have been overwhelmed with unbearable grief. The casket will be sealed and will lie in state in my church tomorrow. People in town will think me all the more admirable for loving with a love which wounds. Otherwise, plans will proceed on schedule. As soon as I get clear title to that farm, I will take care of that crazy old bitch."

With no further fanfare, he retired for the evening.

CHAPTER TWENTY
The Peddler

THE SPLINTERED SEAT bounced up and down beneath the skinny ass of Emile DuPont as the peddler's goods swayed on the eaves of his covered cart. He had long ago left the smooth dirt roads of what passed for civilization in these parts, and now he climbed the badly rutted paths of the high country. Huge hemlocks pressed in upon him, deepening the gloom that permeated the woods and his soul. One more farmstead and he could happily turn his traveling mercantile around for the brighter valley floor far below him. Emile attempted to spit from his parched mouth as he lashed the backside of his mule.

"Get up then, damn you," intoned the Frenchman. "And damn you too *liberté*, *fraternité*, and *égalité*," he shouted into the oppressive air of the dense forest.

Emile had fought in the wars of the Old World and as a mercenary in the wars of the new. Completely disillusioned, he had simply ridden away from the battlefield, bartered his military artifacts for dry goods, and headed for the hills. If there was freedom to be found, it was in the solitude of the mountains not in the company of humanity.

Occasionally, Emile would pull into town and quickly resupply his cart with food staples, lamp oil, tinware, and tools. With the treasures and necessities of life in tow, he headed upward to the remote hollers of the mountains to peddle his wares at a substantial profit. This fueled his freedom on the open road. On this particular trip, he had made a potentially disastrous mistake. Leaving town, he encountered a farmer with a freshly fermented barrel of muscadine wine. Though a Frenchman would rather drink mud from a work boot than drink this purple swill, Emile had wrongly assumed that these hill people also thought of the pressings of the grape as a necessity of life. He had underestimated their ignorance. Every time he had tried to unload some of the brew, he was showered with the scorn of Bible thumpers as they spewed invectives at him for his pagan ways. Now, the barrel weighed down his wagon and darkened his mood as its contents splashed back and forth in the oaken keg.

"I should just pull to the side of a bridge and feed this piss to unsuspecting fish below," fumed Emile. "I should let it run down the pilings like pee down the leg of an old man who cannot hold his water."

He resisted the temptation and held out faint hope that his next customer might be a fool. The wagon jolted to a halt. Cursing with a soup of French and ill-conceived English, the peddler dismounted the wagon seat, waded into the mud, put his shoulder to the wheel, and pushed. The cart rocked forward but then back again. Emile had a tantrum, jumped to the side of the conveyance, and lashed the poor mule with all his strength. Baring its huge teeth and shrieking, the animal lurched forward, freeing the cart. Sweating, Emile mounted the wagon seat and continued his assault on the mountain.

Within the hour, the peddler's eyes were blessed with the curls of white smoke rising from the last outposts of his journey. He would not have put this much effort into the climb if the man in the cabin ahead had not been his best customer. Though young, he was a hermit who apparently prized his freedom and solitude even more than the peddler.

"*Bonjour*, my young friend!" shouted the Frenchman.

"Hello," called back Josiah. "Just in time for dinner."

Emile winced at Josiah's invitation. He knew what passed for a meal at this cabin. He craved some venison with fresh herbs, but that was a fool's desire. As he dismounted the wagon, his nose crushed the last of his hopes. His nostrils flared as they met the unmistakable stench of bear meat festering in its own fetid fat. Emile took an involuntary step backward as he cleared his senses with a whiff of a lavender-saturated handkerchief, kept in his pocket for just such occasions.

"Oh, too much the pity. I have just eaten," piped Emile. "Just time for a little business and talk before my return to the valley."

Though a man of few words, Josiah tried to hold up his end of the conversation as he handed the merchant his list and his money. Emile opened the flap at the back of the wagon and added the items to an old wooden packing crate. When finished, he handed the crate down to the young man. However, before crawling from the wagon, he took a tin mug and drew off a cup of the wine. Passing the still frothy drink down to his unsuspecting customer, Emile bounded from the cart. When he straightened back to his full height, the mug was passed back to him.

"Sorry, Emile, no offense, but it just isn't time for this. Maybe some other time. So, how has business been?"

Once again, the Frenchman was tempted to pour out the wine, but bad wine is still wine. Holding his nose, he gulped down the whole mug. He spat the remaining purple-tinged saliva from his mouth but smiled involuntarily as he pondered the aftertaste.

"Maybe it is not so bad after all," he hummed. "Oh, business is good, so good it's been hard to get all of my food supplies. Big gathering up at the Orchard Cove with the death of Monsieur Hill's wife. Wiped out most of the flour and sugar in town."

As Emile turned to conduct his final business with Josiah, the young man's appearance shocked him. Josiah was silent and ashen-faced. Without uttering another word, he retreated to his cabin and slammed the door behind him.

"Damned rude hillbilly," fumed Emile. He drew another pint of wine, dropped the flap of his cart, and shook the reins of his mule for the descent to the valley. Within hours and after several stops for refills, Emile found himself lonely and morose. The freedom of the open road was overrated. Though he satiated his desires with pleasure and escape, sometimes the aloneness was crushing. Distant rhythms of music revived his spirits. Peering from the side of his cart through the tangle of trees, he caught sight of a ramshackle building on a hill deep in the forest.

CHAPTER TWENTY-ONE
The Road

JOSIAH'S PULSE QUICKENED on his way down the hill, but he remained strong until the stark, gray framework of Vancie's old farmhouse shattered his soundness of mind. At that moment, everything trembled and fell. Like the banks of a muddy Southern river at flood stage, huge pieces of Josiah cracked, liquefied, and slid into the tumult of the flood. Collapsing from within, he felt his knees buckle and he fell into the earth of the last furlong to her house.

A cry pierced the air, more animal than human, as his scarecrowlike form hit the greasy clay of the road embankment. Pain seared through Josiah's heart like the blade of a knife taken from the flame and pressed to the raw flesh of a gaping wound. Time ceased to exist as he writhed first in a gaping inaudible cry and then in convulsions of flesh. In a kaleidoscope of images, every memory of Vancie was unleashed like a primordial flood as he rolled about on the damp ground. Memories of her haunting blue eyes and the redness of her lips hit him again and again.

Never in all his years in exile had Josiah wished to die, but spinning through the blackness of these moments, he wanted to die. To die to pain. To die to memory, longing, and loss. Josiah begged with all his soul to the white afternoon clouds and blue sky that he might fall into forgetfulness of everything that it was to be mortal. In his delirium, he had lost all perspective of his surroundings and convulsed with a start when a voice said, "We put her around back, boy. We laid her out beneath that old hemlock to the back of the place."

The furrowed face of Mattie, the Keller's washer woman, loomed above Josiah and blocked the mocking brightness of the afternoon sun. From the wash sink in the kitchen, the old relic of a Black woman had seen the thin form of the mountain man lurch into view at the top of the hill. Mattie still knew him. She had never believed he had chosen to abandon Vancie. Many times in the swelter and glistening sheen of worship in her old wreck of a church, she had heard Brother Andrew say, "Faith is being sure of what we hope for and certain of what we do not see. This is what the ancients were praised for…"

Mattie was an ancient. Her brown eyes had long since milked over, but an imperishable flame lived within them, by which she saw things unseen by younger eyes.

"Git up, boy. Git your raggedy self up off of that ground, and go see to her. That poor gal done waited all her life away in this here world and part of her life in the other waiting to see you. Go show yourself to her."

Josiah rose up from the ground by a force not his own. Bone coming to bone and flesh to flesh, he crossed the last hundred yards around the corner of the house to the shaded space beneath the towering hemlock. Spirit failed flesh once again, and he fell through time. Hot tears scalded his cheeks, dripped salt into his mouth, and showered the earth. Only one word formed and passed over and over from his lips into the shaded air beneath the tree: "Vancie."

His gnarled, blistered hand reached out and wiped the dried grass from the name carved in granite beneath his palm: "Vancie."

"I said git yourself up. She had a boy."

Why did Mattie seem intent on twisting the knife in Josiah's heart by reminding him of the child that Vancie had with Jagger Hill?

"Why should I care about the boy? He has a father."

"You're the boy's father," Mattie spat back at him.

Josiah froze.

"You're the boy's father, and unless I be wrong, your boy is in a whole lot of trouble." Mattie lifted her milky eyes toward an ever-darkening sun. "He's headed to the old church in the woods, but you need to head to the waterfall."

CHAPTER TWENTY-TWO
The Whipping

MORE THAN ANY other time, James dreaded dinner at Orchard Cove. Sometimes, he could get away with eating breakfast or lunch with the help at a kitchen table, but never at dinner. Even though he and Jagger were now the only ones who dined at Orchard Cove, he was required to wash and dress for dinner. He sat at one end of the long mahogany dining table and Jagger at the other. Full components of china serving dishes, crystal goblets, and sterling silver flatware closed some of the space between the two of them. Most evenings, they sat in candle-lit silence as James listened to Jagger crunch the bones and suck the marrow from quail, chicken, duck, goose, cow, or occasionally deer. Vegetables, bread, fruit, and desserts were mandatory parts of every dinner, but they were an afterthought to Jagger. Most dinners were spent in silence, but James was not to be so lucky this evening.

Coolly, Jagger pulled a leg from the roasted chicken on the platter in front of him. "Where were you this afternoon, boy?"

James felt every fiber of his body tighten. Could his father possibly know that he had in a moment of madness violated the edict to stay out of the woods?

"I just walked downtown to buy some candy," James lied.

Silently, Jagger rose from the table.

"Then could you begin to tell me why Mr. Taylor, my land surveyor, told me that he saw you out on Tryon Road?"

James felt his body grow numb and cold. "Well—"

"Shut your damned mouth," growled Jagger. He closed a little more of the distance between them. "You and I both know what is out on Tryon Road, and it's not a candy store."

Immediately, James understood that his mother no longer stood between the two of them to absorb Jagger's abuse. Jagger pounced like a puma. Imported china and crystal shattered in fragments around him, and silverware clattered as Jagger ripped his son from his chair and pinned him stomach down to its arm. Before he could utter a cry, Jagger jerked twice on the back of his trousers, popping buttons, peeling down underwear, and exposing his bare buttocks.

James had no time to form thoughts of shame. Modesty is the least of your problems when you are in the grips of a madman. Jagger ripped his belt free from his own pants, and the narrow leather strap struck like a diamondback rattler across James's exposed backside. Time after time, it tore flesh and released small channels of blood. James cried out the first time, but after that the mind-numbing pain produced only a gaping hole in his face, like a fish from which air but no sound emerged. It was a good thing that Jagger had him pinned by his neck to the chair because James felt his flailing legs tense, weaken, and then dangle loosely from the sidearm. There was no more pain. His brain ceased to process any sensation as Jagger's arm rose and fell blow after blow. Not only did his strap fall, but words spewed from his mouth.

"How dare you defy me, you little piece of shit. Don't think that being my seed will save you. You have always been like her—fair-haired, weak, and a prissy dreamer. If I didn't think that I could beat her out of you, I would kill you right here."

Not out of mercy, but from sheer exhaustion Jagger stopped. Now, the only sound came from the dining room door, which slowly creaked closed as the help retreated to the kitchen. No one would save him. Jagger tossed James's limp body to the floor and allowed his blood to stain an expensive Persian rug. James lay paralyzed with pants and underpants around his knees. Jagger retreated to his sleeping quarters in silence.

For hours, James lay on the floor unable to move. Jagger had every reason to assume victory, but in those hours James came to a stark realization: His father was right. His soul bubbled with the essence of his mother. He felt her in every fiber of his being. However, as hard as he tried, he could not find a single shred of Jagger Hill within him. How can a boy be only his mother and none of his father? As hard as James sought, he only found his mother and some mysterious, unnamable other. That other was not Jagger Hill. As he lay on the floor, one other insane realization came to him: As soon as he could get up and walk, he was going back to that church because his mother was calling him there. If he bled out crawling on his belly to that building, then that is where he would die. He might have to use Jagger Hill's last name in public, but from this night forward, he would be James Keller.

CHAPTER TWENTY-THREE
Church Too

JAMES LIMPED SLOWLY and painfully up the trail into the woods. He could feel rivulets of blood trickling down the backsides of his legs each time he established a new foothold and tensed his thigh muscles to step upward. His backside felt like it had been swiped by the claws of a puma, and the steeper the trail became, the fainter he grew.

"I know that I have only been here once before, but it didn't seem to take this long," he moaned.

Just when James thought he would have to lie down on the trail and die, he heard the obscure but certain sound of music as he caught sight of the top of the church shanty on the ridge.

It wasn't a sound like the sonorous bellows of the organ at Green River or the lighter sound of a piano; this music was compiled entirely from the human voice. James had never heard such music. He wasn't even sure that it was beautiful; but as he drew closer, it became clear to him that the music was pure and raw. He lumbered through the dirt-swept yard of the dilapidated building, unaware of how many people might be harbored inside. Whether a dozen or a thousand, people are hard to count when they are one. Whoever was inside of this church sang as one. Their words rose and fell, soared and crashed like the waves of the wild Atlantic. They came though the walls, through the newspaper-stuffed holes of broken windows, and rattled the doors hanging precariously on fragile rusty hinges. Suddenly, what had seemed like only sound changed to meaning as the words took root in James's brain:

> "I am a poor wayfaring stranger a travellin' through this world of woe,
> And there's no sickness, toil, or danger in that bright world to which I go,
> I'm going there to meet my Savior,
> I'm going there, no more to roam.
> I'm just a poor wayfaring stranger on the road to that bright world to which I go."

Slowly, James mounted the steps, took the door by its handle, and stepped inside. He stepped from hearing a song into a song. Fifty or so people sat not straight-backed in pews but in a circle. Right arms and left arms rose and fell in tomahawk fashion with the cadence of the music. Voices barked, croaked, shouted, and keened in a maelstrom of power, unity, and praise:

> "Come ye sinners, poor and needy,
> Weak and wounded, sick and sore,
> Jesus ready stands to save you, full of pity, love and power
> He is able, He is able, He is willing
> Doubt no more."

The room spun about James as an usher pulled him into the center of the circle beside the resolute song leader, whose right arm rose high above her head and then fell in perfect rhythm like an ax. James gasped as he recognized the first face in the room. Mattie stood like a lighthouse in the midst of crashing waves, her eyes beaming down upon the boy with a tenderness and compassion greater than James had known in a long time. Around him words rose, swirled, and fell:

> "There is a fountain filled with blood flowing from Emmanuel's veins
>
> Its blood can make the foulest clean,
>
> Its blood availed for me,
>
> Its blood availed for me-e-e, It's blood availed for me.
>
> Its blood can make the foulest clean, it's blood availed for me."

James no longer knew or cared if his own blood still flowed down the back of his legs. He no longer cared about Jagger Hill or Orchard Cove. As he swooned in a sea of sound and solace, he knew that Jagger Hill had never been a real father to him and that Orchard Cove was a house and not a home. Other faces emerged from the crowd: the great head of Big John; the red-nosed visage of the peddler, Emile DuPont; Phineus Coble, the odd little crippled man who had kept the livery; Delilah Hart, the pretty lady who lived in the boarding house downtown; and the pale, stricken face of his father's kitchen girl, Rosemary. These people never darkened the door of Green River and probably would have been thrown out in the yard if they had tried. The music swelled louder and the room spun, and several people split off from the back rows, went to a side room, and returned to the center with basins of water and towels.

One by one, people stopped their singing long enough to go from the circle, remove their paper-patched brogans caked with mud, and expose their calloused, arthritic, smelly feet to the coolness of spring water and the softness of the touch of bent-kneed apostles intent on washing away the soil and toil of the earth. James was lifted up, placed in a straight-backed chair, and unshod. An ancient, bespectacled man looked up at him from bathing his feet as the music reached a crescendo:

"This is my father's world
And to my listening ear
All nature sings,
And round me rings,
The music of the spheres.
This is my father's world
And let me ne'er forget
For though the wrong seems oft so strong,
He is the ruler yet."

Never had James known such love, healing, tenderness, and release. Tears streamed down his face—for the first time in his young life, tears of joy rather than sorrow. Rosemary pressed through the crowd pushing a salt-tinged piece of the best bread he had ever tasted to his lips. Emile followed her with a wooden cup, pouring a bracing brew of muscadine wine into his mouth.

He intoned in a broken French accent, "These are the body and the blood, broken and shed for you."

Through the stinging astringent grape in his mouth and the blur of salt water in his eyes, James noticed that the church had a balcony. Two people were sitting in it side by side. His eyes cleared and with a piercing cry, he shouted, "Mother! Mama Lois!"

The child collapsed into darkness and music.

James fell through oblivion, swirling in images of the clapboard church, the vortex of song, and ghosts from the past. When he finally opened his eyes, he was out in the yard propped up on a quilt. He became aware of several things simultaneously. Much to his embarrassment, he knew that someone had doctored his backside. Streaks across his buttocks pulsed in soothing heat from some country poultice. Tree branches and inquisitive onlookers smiled down at him from above. But he became most aware that he was famished. James did not ever recall being so hungry, and the aroma of freshly baked cornbread and other mysterious food scents in the air almost made him cry. One of the faces staring down at him was Mattie's.

"Hungry?" she asked.

"Starving," James replied.

"Well, we got a cure for that."

Other scents in the air were mysterious because they were beneath his father's standards of anything that a White person would ever eat at Orchard Cove. He was introduced to the staples of most poor Black and White people in the South. Pots and pans bubbled to the brim with pinto beans, collard greens, and buttery cornbread. Instead of the usual fatback, at great sacrifice one of the poor farmers offered a young shoat for the feast. The small pig had been cooked in a pit all night over hickory and oak and washed over with vinegar and chopped red peppers from neighboring gardens. Since there wasn't nearly enough meat to serve fifty hungry farmers, tradesmen, and their kin, the precious meat had been picked clean from every bone on the pig, head and all. It was then submerged in chunks in the boiling cauldrons to flavor the collards and beans with the essence of glistening, smoky, hot-spiced pork.

The only other meat on the table was a grotesque platter of frog legs, but sides of mountain onions, pickles, and chowchow filled out the table along with blackberry, blueberry, and damson cobblers. Huge crocks on each end of the table were filled to the brim with cold spring water and new apple cider chilled in the creek. On a table by itself off to the side, a wooden keg marked "Grown Ups Only" was getting a lot of use.

"Child, this is just an old, poor man's supper. You ought to come on back and see us come fall when we has a real dinner on the grounds," rumbled Big John.

James didn't care what Big John called the spread. He didn't even care that he didn't know the name of half the food he was putting in his mouth. He just ate with wild abandon, waited upon by kind strangers who hugged his neck and filled his plate. Even Miss Delilah, who used to work in town, came over, drew James's cheek to her ample breasts, and told him what a fine man he would be someday. With great surprise, James noticed that when she returned to her table it was to a seat beside a beaming Mr. Coble. They seemed like an odd, but happy, pair.

As he ate, glistening hog drippings coated his tongue with their goodness. Sweet, melted butter slid with coarse salty cornbread down his gullet. Tart, vinegar-coated greens, pungent spring onions, and sour blackberry juice joined in quick succession. Soon, the salt did its work, and James slaked his thirst with jar after jar of spring water and cider. Within the hour, he collapsed back on the quilt in a stupor of pleasure and misery. The misery had been brought on by his hedonism and the first fragmentary memories of his vision in the balcony.

Mattie saw the pain cloud his face.

"Lamb, you saw what you saw. Won't no ghosts or no haints. Sometimes, the curtain gets thin between this world and the other one. They ain't forgot you. He's never going to leave or forsake you. You can count on that."

Nothing in Jagger Hill's house had prepared James to count on that, but he found Mattie's words strangely comforting. He stretched out on the quilt and slept; but for the first time in a long while, he slept in peace.

CHAPTER TWENTY-FOUR
Fire-Breathing Dragon

RAGE BURNED WITHIN Josiah's chest as he took long strides down Flat Rock Road toward town. He had no time or inclination to reflect on his first entrance to Saluda that had been a thousand years ago, and he was now consumed by his obsession of settling an old score. For years now, all his anger had been channeled into the hard labor of his exile in the high hills. He knew that Jagger Hill had not literally killed Vancie, but perhaps he had done worse. From what little information he had, he knew that Jagger slowly tortured her through his actions and inactions, squeezing the will to live out of her until her spirit lifted from her body in despair. He thought about finding Jagger in his home and burning it to the ground, but even in his rage his moral core pulled him back from the abyss. He could not risk hurting others in his attempt to extract vengeance on Jagger, and he could not sacrifice the time in senseless acts of rage. It was a long way to Pearson's Falls, and he was unsure how much time he had and what kind of trouble James might be in. Though Mattie saw more than most, even she did not see all things.

Different routes to the falls flashed through Josiah's fevered mind, but none provided any particular advantage over another. He feared arriving at the falls in a state of exhaustion, but he feared even more arriving too late. As the morning waned, the miles ticked by until

Josiah looked up and saw a larger and more chaotic Saluda. Gone were the ramshackle storefronts and mud-rutted streets of the town. Josiah jostled his way through the noisy, crowded main street, astounded by gleaming buildings plastered with banners that trumpeted the obscene name of Jagger Hill.

The noonday train sat parked at the station for the firemens' and engineers' lunch break. The iron behemoth crouched close to the tracks, menacingly spewing steam from each side of its massive head. Josiah stopped, surrounded by streams of strangers passing to and fro in manic procession. Steam not only billowed toward him, but he also felt a fire rising within him. If only he had an ax capable of putting even the smallest dent in Jagger's train, he would break his own arms in the effort. The long rifle hanging from his right hand would obviously do the iron-clad engine no harm. Sadly, there would be no slaying of this dragon by any weapon at his disposal.

Suddenly, an idea congealed in Josiah's mind, and a slight smile spread across his face. Maybe the mountains themselves offered a weapon. He slipped past the distracted pedestrians, swung between the engine and fuel car, and mounted the side of the train. As he had hoped, the small crew had all departed for the hotel for lunch. With no treasure on board, they had felt no need for a security detail to remain with the train. Josiah stared in great confusion at the dials and gauges before him. Had the train been headed upcountry, Josiah wouldn't have been able to move the beast, but the train pointed downward toward Tryon. He only needed one control, and he soon found it.

With one strong jerk, Josiah released the brake on Jagger's train, a vital source of his riches. The passenger train had already passed through that morning headed to Asheville, and there would be no obstructions on the tracks. The hulk of iron slowly pulled away from the platform. In only minutes, it slipped through the edges of town with several wide-eyed citizens following in futile pursuit. Even over the course of a few hundred yards, the train was already gaining momentum. The wind whistled through Josiah's dampened hair as he threw shovel after shovel of coal into the flame-filled belly of the great serpent slithering its way around bend after bend.

It would soon arrive at the intersection of the train tracks with the old Cherokee trading footpath. If his leap from the train did not kill him, his plan would place him far closer to the falls in a more rested state. For now, he reveled in the sweat and passion of feeding the beast. Flames leapt from the door of the boiler, and steam enveloped Josiah as the train plunged down the hillside toward the edge of the escarpment. With a last jerk on the overhanging cord, the monster issued a bloodcurdling scream.

Josiah lunged from the side of the train and tumbled end over end. His rifle flew into the surrounding brush. A roar and a final explosion came as the full coil of the train jumped the tracks at the escarpment's edge and plummeted into the abyss of the flatlands. Beyond the range of Josiah's vision, the train fragmented, like a meteor, into thousands of chunks of molten metal, raining down the cliffs of the mountainside and igniting small brushfires. The terrain was too steep for human habitation, but reptiles retreated to their holes, woodland creatures to their burrows, and birds to the safety of the heavens. Josiah lay stunned for a few moments, his vengeance partially satiated. Slowly he rose, searched out his gun, reclaimed it, and set out limping for the falls.

CHAPTER TWENTY-FIVE
Rendezvous

AFTER THE CHURCH supper ended, James picked his stepping stones carefully and made his way up the mossy bed of Colt Creek. The falls had been calling him since his first visit, and he knew this place also held some special meaning for his mother. It challenged his imagination to picture her ducking rhododendron branches and crawling over downed logs. The louder the falls became, the more her spirit stirred within him. Ever since seeing her in the balcony of the church, he had racked his brain for other places where, as Mattie had said, "the curtain might be thin." This might well be a snipe hunt, but just the sensation of being in the forest made James feel close to his mother and satisfied in his hatred for his father by defying him once again.

He knew that Jagger would be searching for him. James was on the run, living off the kindness of church folk at the poor man's supper. Jagger nearly killed him the last time he saw him, and no way was he going to tempt fate again by returning to Orchard Cove. James had burned all his bridges behind him. He was just trying to lose Jagger on the trail long enough to double back to town at night and hop a train down to the Piedmont or up to higher mountains. Anywhere would be better and safer than Saluda. However, before he left he wanted to see his mother one more time. Although vivid, the memory of her on the balcony had faded a bit already. Just one more time and he wouldn't have to take Mattie's word for it; he would know that his experience was real.

Gnats and mosquitoes tormented him as he proceeded up the creek, sweating and swatting at biting things seen and unseen. When he could no longer stand it, he finally caught his first glimpse of the falls. In the midday sun, the waters glistened with radiance as they tumbled over the top of the ridge. James forgot his miseries and steeled his courage for a steep climb up the rocky, precarious stairs leading to the top of the falls.

Jagger Hill had never known such a state of rage. Slapping laurel branches right and left, he charged like a bull down the old trail to the top of Pearson's Falls. Hardly anybody even remembered that this trail existed, and Jagger was counting on James coming to the falls by way of the creek bed. When that kitchen bitch, Rosemary, had finally betrayed Vancie's oldest and best-kept secret, Jagger thought that he might burst into flames.

Jagger could not believe that he had contaminated his table with the bastard son of a White trash farm girl and a hillbilly. He had forgiven the farm girl because of her beauty as breeding stock, but to think that she had already been poked by that boy before he had his way with her enraged him. His only relief was that he had lived in shame for twelve years thinking that he had sired a pasty-faced, gray-eyed weakling. At least he had escaped the greater shame that would have come if his "heir" had ever reached manhood and inherited his hard-won fortune. There was still time. Not for the kitchen bitch, Rosemary, though. Imagine her thinking that he would make the same mistake all over again in return for her loose lips.

"Hell, no," he had boomed at her. "I don't care what you think I owe you. I never asked anything of you, bitch."

The next mistress of Orchard Cove would come with papers from New York or Boston. His days of lying with mixed-breed dogs were over. Even though the outing of James's secret had saved

Jagger greater future embarrassment, he was not willing to take any chances with the boy. He had not worked for the last twelve years to become the laughing stock of Saluda. He could ship Rosemary out of town on the next train. Hell, with his investments in the railroad he could even make a little money on her ticket. She had already provided a double yield. Not only had she told Vancie's secret, but she had been hanging out at the ramshackle church in the woods. James had told her about his attraction to Pearson's Falls. He might not be there, but it was a start. Jagger would track him to hell if he had to. Rosemary was easily enough shed, but James was personal and would require a personal solution.

Jagger reached down and tapped the butcher knife he had retrieved from the kitchen. On the way to the kitchen, he had passed his gun case with some of the finest rifles and handguns in the state. They would not do. He knew who the boy was, but the boy still thought that he was his father. He wanted to be close and see the look of betrayal in the bastard's eyes when he twisted the blade.

Suddenly, Jagger teetered on his heels as he reached the end of the trail and stared down into the cascading waters of Colt Creek. He backed away from the edge and stooped down behind a large rock in a clump of hemlock trees. Huffing and puffing, he waited and hoped that this entire afternoon had not been a wild goose chase. After about an hour, he was rewarded for his efforts. James's head bobbed as he rose and stooped beneath rhododendron branches, making his way slowly up to the base of the falls. Within moments, his slight frame and blond head disappeared, and Jagger realized that James had started the ascent of the rock stairs beside the falls.

CHAPTER TWENTY-SIX
Pursuit

JOSIAH PANTED AS he crashed through one obstacle and then another, working his way up Colt Creek. Mattie's words still rang in his ears: "He is your boy. She named him James after your father."

He would never completely understand what made Vancie turn from him to Jagger Hill. He never knew the man. However, he had encountered him on the old plank sidewalk many years ago, and despite the man's finery, Josiah had felt the hair rise on the back of his neck. Years ago, his father had taught him that a man should trust his instincts. You don't have to understand them, just trust them. If Mattie was right, James would never be completely safe until he got him out of Saluda and away from Jagger Hill.

He knew though that he couldn't put all of this off on Jagger. Even though he and Vancie had been attracted to each other at the falls and had even come to love each other, Josiah could not escape the sickening feeling that the two of them had sped up a clock that day that might have been far kinder to all involved if they had just waited. He and Vancie had loved each other, but so many of their decisions had been motivated by fear rather than trust. But, there are no real ifs in life. They chose, and the only life they would ever know together in this world was the short, tragic one that they had lived. But maybe it was not too late for a life with James. Josiah had no idea how he would convince him that a complete stranger was actually his father. First, he had to find the boy.

After the lead from Mattie, he had picked up James's trail hours ago, but it was hard to follow. The boy tread softly in the woods and had already proven his tenacity to the seasoned woodsman. Josiah was not so lucky. He was leaving a great deal more evidence of his passing as he clipped branch after branch with his long deer rifle. The rifle made following the trail more difficult, but he learned his lesson long ago about going into the woods unprepared. Josiah had vague memories of the distance to the falls; but as he questioned himself, he was encouraged by the sound of falling water and his first glimpse of his destination. He stopped, frozen in joy and terror. He had just seen his first view of his son halfway up the fall stairs, but he also glimpsed Jagger Hill emerging from a hemlock thicket at the top of the ridge.

Jagger could hear James's footfalls. Hiding took no real effort; he simply stepped behind the largest of the hemlocks. James puffed and panted his way over the last fallen log onto level ground on the western side of the stream. Although the breeze was refreshing and the view dizzying, James had not climbed to the top of Pearson's Falls for sightseeing. During the climb, he had held his breath in anticipation of catching even a fleeting glimpse of his mother. His hope waned with each stair he climbed, and it completely collapsed when he pulled himself over the last obstacle at the top of the falls. He looked around in silence and then broke down in tears. Wave after wave of pent-up sorrow racked his small body.

"Well, you are the girl that I always believed you to be," Jagger said as he stepped from behind the tree.

James froze. He had not laid eyes on Jagger since the man had nearly beaten him to death. Freezing was a big mistake. Before James could move, Jagger had closed the small distance, grabbed James by the hair with his right hand, and wrapped his left arm under James's armpit and across his small torso. The attack had forced him to the edge of the falls, facing downward into the ravine. The only thing that separated the two of them from falling to their death was the small ledge in front of them. James's heart beat like a drum as Jagger released the hold on his hair, whipped the butcher knife from his belt, and held it against James's throat.

Jagger pressed his hot, foul breath against James's ear and whispered, "Well, Father Abraham might not have had the guts to sacrifice his own son, but I am no cowering woman like him. You are bad seed, and it's time that your father cut his losses and started all over again. I came all the way up here today to slit your throat and remind you just what a piece of worthless trash that you really are. No one to save you here."

James could not breathe with the knife up against his throat and knew that he was doomed, but glancing to his left, he saw what he had come to Pearson's Falls to see. His mother stood on the top step of the falls. He knew that he would soon die and join her, but the sight of her stirred some last streak of resistance within his soul. With his free arm, he reached for his belt, retrieved his own straight-bladed knife, and plunged it into Jagger's thigh. Jagger howled like a wounded beast and dropped his own knife in pain. He flung James down onto the ledge. As his knife skittered over the falls, Jagger yelled with rage and pulled his right foot back to kick James into the ravine. He never brought the leg forward.

James just heard a loud crack in the ravine below and felt a spatter across his upturned face. Jagger teetered for a moment with blood running down his face from a dark, gaping hole between his eyes. Then he crumpled forward, catapulted into the violent cataracts of Pearson's Falls nearly sweeping James over the edge with him. James dug his hands into the clefts of the rock and felt Jagger tumble over him. He slowly backed away from the edge. By the time he was able to stand, another grown man loomed over his small, petrified body.

Mustering the courage to look up, he stammered, "Who are you?"

Josiah looked down into the boy's upturned eyes and caught his breath. Vancie's eyes peered back at him—not just her blue eyes but the flecks of his own gray eyes scattered about the orbs.

"Son, I don't know how to tell you this. There is no reason that you would or should believe a complete stranger after all that you have been through, but I am your father."

James stared up blankly into the haunting eyes that looked down upon him. He should have laughed at the lunacy of what the stranger said to him, but his mother had told him to trust a man like the one above him.

"What is your name?" James asked.

"I am Josiah Buckland."

James reached into his damp right pocket. He pulled out a small gold pocket watch, and Josiah gasped.

"My mother told me when she gave this watch to me that it held a secret."

With his index finger, he tripped a small latch on the dented edge of the watch and the back panel sprang open to reveal the initials *V.K. and J.B.*

Epilogue

All the goodbyes had been said, and James and Josiah now stood by a canoe on the Green River. Within moments, James would leave all that had been bright, fair, dark, and evil about Saluda.

He was eager to be going home with his father. Under other circumstances, it would break his heart to leave behind the place so closely connected to his mother, Mama Lois, Mattie, and his new church family in the woods. But as he watched Josiah step into the back of the canoe, he made his peace with leaving. James lightly followed him and pushed with the paddle at his father's command to launch the vessel into the flow of the stream.

As they paddled, James watched otters play along the banks, ducks fly past overhead, and innumerable turtles slip off of logs into the ever-flowing stream of life. The sun beat down upon them on the rare occasion that they floated out from the huge arboreal canopy overhead. In the warmth and silence of the afternoon, James grew drowsy and slowly leaned back against his father's chest and legs. To the young boy, Josiah smelled like the forest itself. Scents of mud, deer hide, trees, and river water soothed him as he slumbered in the cradle of his father.

He, his father, and the river became one as the boat yielded itself to the energy of dancing waters. He felt Josiah bend slightly and kiss his matted hair. Instinctively, James fingered the smooth, cool case of the watch within his pocket and invited the spirit of his mother to join them. After many hours, the canoe reached the last furlongs they would travel on the Green River as it slowly widened to more open waters.

A cry punctured their peace from a promontory. Perched as erect as a cornstalk in the garden in summer, Mattie sat in the buckboard with Big John on the landing. If her sounds were words, James never heard them. But he saw her with cane raised in a last salute as he and Josiah glided beyond the river into open waters. Although James saw only Mattie and Big John, he heard a sharp intake of air from his father. Years afterward, Josiah would tell him that he had seen the blond-haired love of his youth in the buckboard beside Mattie and that his heart had opened as he took in the last of her that he was to have in this world.

The sun set as they entered the dazzling vast expanse of a lake, and James caught a flash on the top of the cliffs to his right. A great osprey dove from the clifftop, plummeting downward before them. Within seconds, the bird hit the surface of the water and showered them with spray. In a clumsy, methodical fashion, it emerged from the water with a large silver fish thrashing in its talons. Straining above the weight of its catch, the bird rose, and the red rays of the sun caught the wet flesh of the fish and set it ablaze with sparks of fire and gold.

RED EARTH:

PEACHLAND

Prologue

THE FEAR OF frost hung like the sword of Damocles over the orchard. A few weeks earlier, it would not have mattered. If the cold had come then, the fruit would have been no more than small, hard nodules pressed tightly to each tree branch. A few days later, only the smallest points of white would have peeked from the swollen casings of the blossoms. However, spring is treacherous in the Carolinas and comes in fits and starts. First, a burst of stinging cold and then a lull of sickening warmth rolls in as nature whiplashes all living things between the grinding stones of the seasons. This was "just spring," the time between seasons that promised life in one hand and threatened death with the fist of the other. All plants, beasts, and humankind now stood naked and exposed to the vagaries of nature.

It appeared that it was too late for the peaches. All the pink and white blossoms of the orchard now waved back and forth in glorious profusion against the warm background of a dazzling blue sky. When nightfall came, the heavens would exert no effort in holding the accumulated heat of the day close to the mantle of the Earth. The temperature would plummet; and in the early morning hours, death would come. Slowly, the cells of each blossom would crystallize, freeze, swell, and rupture. Small, wet, pink masses like tissue paper would be left dripping from every branch of the trees. There would be no peaches this year. No syrup dribbling down children's chins in late July. No pies for covered dish suppers at the churches this fall. No jars of golden fruit lining the cellar shelves to stave off hunger in winter. No cash to satisfy the hungrier creditors at the bank.

All the mowing, spraying, sweating, pruning, and praying had amounted to no more than human fury. Within hours, death would come to the orchard, and potentially to its stewards, in the grinding poverty of the coming year. For now, the only harbinger of the cataclysm was a lone, gray mourning dove whose plaintive call echoed through the branches of forty acres of the damned.

FAMILY

CHAPTER ONE
Fire

As night fell and the temperature inched toward the killing zone, dark shapes appeared and began to methodically weave their way through the trees of the orchard. Slowly, they found their positions equidistant from each other around the perimeter of the grove. Bending in the night, the phantoms tidied up the edges of rounded piles of the dry, brittle bones of peach trees long since dead. For five years now, every branch pruned in the spring, blown down by summer thunderstorms, victimized by disease, or broken by ice had been added to the mounds around the orchard for just such a night as this. Nature had contributed to their mass by adding layer upon layer of briars, poison oak, poke weed, and blackberries as the seasons passed in succession. The brush piles had already served the farmers well, yielding many a rabbit during hunting outings in the fall and winter, but now came their greatest hour. Each of the forty mounds stood more than eight feet tall and rose up like silent sentinels around the orchard.

The humans now invoked the slumbering spirits of the dryads and called for their aid. The first of the flesh genuflected before one of their ten piles of brush, anointed the rattling branches with kerosene dashed from a rusty metal can and leapt backward after tossing a match forward. The effect was immediate. A small ball of fire erupted at the base of the pyre like a meteor strike in the night. Red, yellow, and orange lapped around the cone, slowly circling the brush, creeping upward as it banished the night and cold. Slowly, the face of a man was illuminated. The dirt-smudged, lined visage of Paul Elliott, already glistening with a fine sheen of sweat, flamed out like a jack-o'-lantern in the night.

Though only thirty years old, Paul's high-cheekboned face carried the memories of the Great War and the realities of daily survival on a failing, red-clay farm in the Piedmont. The Spanish flu had wreaked its havoc on his family shortly before his return from France, so the boy soldier had simply had to transition from one attempt at survival to another as he returned to a stalwart mother and a heavily mortgaged farm. Fighting the Germans had quickly been replaced by an unending battle with poverty, nature, and the land itself. Checking the security of the flame of his first fire, Paul grabbed his shovel and fuel can and dashed like Prometheus to the next waiting mound of brush.

On another side of the orchard, the process repeated itself—darkness, spark, flame, and then light. This time the feminine form of Paul's wife, Pearline, emerged like an avenging angel. Brushing back the perspiration-moistened tresses of her auburn hair with her forearm, Pearline's green eyes glowed with a frightful beauty and resolve as she fought frost with fire. Each of her movements displayed grace, strength, and confidence as she expertly cast fire from her hands and moved on from one mound to another, steadfastly defending her front in the war. At her feet scrambled her arms-bearer, a slender, solemn ten-year-old son named John Rudolph Elliott. The boy faithfully carried their kerosene can with both hands, struggling to keep his balance as they worked their way down the edges of their side of the orchard. There was no time for words, but the boy sputtered grunts as he huffed and puffed at his mother's heels.

On the third side of the grove, darkness and cold held fast. A muscular figure stood silently in the night, watching the distant flames intensify on two sides of the orchard. The orange glow did nothing to assuage the sting of his freezing toes in his battered brogans below him. He shifted silently from foot to foot, trying to coax circulation back into his frozen toes. Even if he had had company, there would have been no words on his part. There had been none now for ten years. The war had taken millions of souls and the influenza millions more, but for Rory Faulkner, the war to end all wars had robbed him of his memory and voice.

Rory's last memory of youth was of throwing his body on top of Paul Elliott as a mortar shell exploded beside them. Shrapnel stole his past as a piece of metal cracked his skull, but his voice appeared to have been ripped from him by the sheer trauma of sending a farm boy into more hell than he could bear. When he and Paul arrived at the field hospital, Paul discovered that Rory Faulkner did not really exist. Apparently, the boy had been some underaged recruit who had lied and forged his way into the military in a starry-eyed, misguided search for glory and honor. The damned little fool had gotten his just reward, lying fixed-eyed, mangled, and mute in his hospital bed; but he also had saved Paul Elliott's life.

Paul was not sure how much honor there had been to the war; but there was still a shred of it left in him, so he had taken the boy under his wing. He brought him home in misguided mercy to fight nature with his fledgling family. Pearline had welcomed Rory as her husband's savior, but his mother, Jule, had spat out the black juices of her snuff in disgust when she heard that Paul had brought an idiot, stray-dog boy with him into his upcoming marriage and onto her farm. Though only half a man, Rory watched for the signal. When it came, he too made fire, illuminating his straw-colored hair, blue-gray eyes, and mute soul.

Jule Elliott stood watch on the last side of the orchard. Though she believed that all their efforts were a fool's errand, she stood her ground. The dark angles of her Choctaw face were set like flint against the darkness. When the signal finally came, she lit her pitch-covered stick, uttered a primal cry, and touched it to the oily fuel doused upon the dead, tangled branches. Flames leapt like the hounds of hell up the sides of the brush pile, licking at the stars and the feeble crescent moon. Jule's gray hair whipped about her face as the mounting fire created a vortex of wind and flames. From above, an owl looked down upon earth, wind, fire and five solitary figures as it searched the edges of the orchard for vermin fleeing the mounting holocaust.

JULE
"Little Bear"

CHAPTER TWO
The Journey

A FEW MONTHS later, Jule Elliott slipped off during the night for her secret journey. As Paul, Pearline, John Rudolph, and the idiot had slept, Jule had crept silently to the barn and mounted Hennie, one of her two now startled mules. Although the mules were mainly used for plowing, it was not unprecedented for them to be ridden. What was unprecedented in these parts was for an old Indian woman to ride a mule bareback and better than a man down the sides of county roads in the middle of the day. Such behavior would attract far more attention than Jule desired. If she rode steadily, she would reach her destination by sunrise and return the following evening before every sheriff in the state had been notified of her abduction and every creek dragged for her body. Let them all think what they may, even an old woman needs a bit of peace and quiet once in a while. Within moments of leaving the farm, she began to find her peace. It was a moonless night, and she rode beneath a star-spangled sky.

As Hennie found her rhythm, Jule began to remember bits and pieces of the stories of the creation from her Choctaw childhood. Soon the heavens came to life, and creatures, heroes, heroines, and villains animated the stage above her, battling for supremacy of the nighttime sky. Almost without awareness, she began to hum and then softly to sing long-forgotten songs of her people, their travels and travails. At times. she could hear the murmur of Dison's Creek and then Little River providing music for her words. Thus, Jule Elliott passed the night, occasionally taking to the woods for a few moments to allow the rare car or truck to speed by completely unaware of a ghost from another time about her business in the darkness.

In the wee hours of the morning, just as the birds began to stir and the crickets and frogs began to still themselves, Jule arrived at her destination. In a long-abandoned cotton field, a great mound of earth rose before her. The land around it had been farmed for years, but the hard-scratch farmers had neither the time nor resources to remove the mound. They simply saw it as an obstacle, like a creek, swamp, or pond that cut into their productivity and deducted from their bottom line come harvest time. The dullards never seemed to question why the pan-flat landscape of the Piedmont was so violently interrupted by such a great upheaval of the earth. The Whites did not wonder nor did they ponder deepness or mystery. They only gouged the earth for what they could take from it. They did not guess. They did not know, but Jule knew. This was the work of the relatives of her people.

Jule slid effortlessly off Hennie's back and began her slow, methodical ascent of one side of the mound. Tree sprouts and the occasional rock helped her with her footing as she proceeded up the steep incline. For an old woman, she was still remarkably agile and strong, so within minutes she arrived on the top of the mound in time to be bathed in the first golden rays of the October sun. For a moment, she stood blinded but reborn. The light of the dawning day soon brought warmth and drove the evening chill from her bones. Holding her hand over her copper-furrowed brow, she looked out across the top of a sea of surrounding trees with sporadic indentations where fields lay. In the quiet of the autumn morning, she could hear meadowlarks and the murmuring of a nearby creek, which would have watered the ancient fields of corn and provided the means for purification in this holy place.

The mound now stretched before Jule empty, but once a thatched temple would have risen there and these people, just like her people of the West, would not have dwelled here year-round but would have come after the harvest to purge their bodies with violent herbal drinks, scrape their skin with rocks and shells until blood flowed, and dip their bodies in the deep places of the stream. She knew no name of these related peoples for this place, but to the Whites it was called Town Creek. Though the mound was not of her people, she was far too old to go again in this life to her own peoples' mounds in the West. She would go there again only on her last walk from this world. She came through the night to this place to purify herself of the life of the Whites, even her own child and grandchild, and to remember, perhaps for the last time, her people and their beginnings here atop the earth.

CHAPTER THREE
"Mother"

JULE DID NOT know the name of the first people of Town Creek, but she knew the name of her own mound: *Nanih Waiya*, "Mother." Among her people there were two stories of her birth, one short and one longer.

In the short version of "Mother," Nanih Waiya was there in the beginning. Nanih Waiya was always there. From "Mother," the Creator fashioned his first people. He molded them from her. The Creator called these first people Choctaw. After they were shaped, they crawled through a long, dark tunnel. From it, they emerged and saw first day.

In the longer story, her people began in the far West beyond the Great River. In the beginning, there were two brothers, Chata and Chicksah. Their first lands had not been carefully tended. The forests were felled, the earth was not restored, and the waters were made unclean. Creator, Nanapesa, was angry with his people but had mercy upon them. To Chata and Chicksah, he gave the magical pole and sent them forth with their people in search of a new land to treat more kindly. Each night, when the first people made camp, the pole was planted in the earth and when the people awakened the next morning, they would break camp, pack their belongings, secure their children, and travel in whatever direction the magical pole had come to lean in the night.

After traveling for a great number of days, the people awakened and the pole stood upright. They had found center. In this place, they buried the bones of their ancestors, which had accompanied them on their great journey in sacks of buffalo hide. Upon these bones, Nanih Waiya, "Mother," rose. Mother was center. Soon, the peoples discovered that even this good, new land could not support them all, so Chicksah took half of the peoples to the North, and they became the Chickasaw. Chata kept the other half with Mother and they became her people, the Choctaw.

Jule closed her eyes and pretended that she stood upon Nanih Waiya. She began to twirl around in the morning sun as she had as a child, and the hem of her skirt flared out revealing alternating patterns of diamonds, circles, and crosses stitched around its circumference. When she had sewn this skirt, she adorned the bottom of it with the ancient symbols of her people, suggesting the snake, sun, and crossed stickball clubs of the Choctaw. For a few moments before becoming tired and winded, she was a girl again. She was "Little Bear." Her people were divided into clans: Wind, Bear, Deer, Wolf, Panther, Holly Leaf, Bird, Raccoon, and Crayfish. Her clan was Bear, and because of her fierceness and strength as an infant, her parents had named her "Little Bear."

Later, at the reservation, Jule's White name had been assigned to her. Not even something beautiful like Jewel but instead Jule. What is Jule? It has no meaning. And then they had made her last name to be Oklahombi. She bristled at it because it looked and sounded too much like Oklahoma, that hell of grass, wind, and fire that her people had been exiled to in her mother's childhood. Although all her childhood had been spent corralled with the remnant of her people in that terrible place, in their stories and in her young heart she always knew that her real home was far away and a place of deep forests and quiet rivers. That is why she had left her drunken father and broken-spirited brothers after her mother died and traveled back to Nanih Waiya. She had not had a magical pole, but she knew to travel toward the rising sun. So week after week, that is what she had done until she came at last to Mother.

CHAPTER FOUR
Homecoming

WHEN JULE CAUGHT her first glimpse of Nanih Waiya, her heart broke and tears rolled down her cheeks. In the stories of the Choctaw in the hell of grass and fire, Mother stood proudly in the forest of her people, crowned by their temple. Now, she lay mortally wounded and crownless, her forests slashed and burned and the resulting devastation littered with the shacks of hardscrabble White farmers and their families. Jule stood at the edge of the great wound in the shadows of a clump of remaining trees.

In the distance, Whites slapped their mule's behinds with long leather straps and cursed their children when they got underfoot during the work of the day. Ragged clothing flapped about in the breezes on wooden fences. An occasional dog barked a warning to any potential visitors who dared to transgress the hard new boundaries of ownership of her peoples' Choctaw land. The work of the Whites was complete. For decades, they had stolen her peoples' world by war and even more so by treaty. The final and greatest blow had come in the Treaty of Dancing Rabbit Creek. After that, the great stealing ended, and her people were marched westward.

Now, the thieves crawled about the corpse of Nanih Waiya like scavenging insects. Jule would not even be able to come to Mother in the darkness. The hounds would attack her or give away her presence to their masters. Her greeting and farewell to Nanih Waiya would be one and the same, a few furtive glances stolen from the darkness of the trees before moving on to she knew not where. Certainly, not back to the West. A thousand miles of walking, hiding, foraging, and stealing lay behind her. She knew nothing of what lay east, north, or south of Mother, but she knew that it was all now the White man's world. Eventually, they would catch her. When they did, they would kill her, enslave her, send her back West, or plant their seed in her.

For months, she had been brave. She had been Little Bear. Now, she felt small, young, alone, and afraid. Jule decided to try to sleep until dark and then begin tomorrow to search the backwoods and swamps in the vain hope of finding some remnant of her people who had escaped the all-seeing eyes of the Whites and their long grasp. She lay down beneath a clump of fruitless, wild muscadine vines and listened as her stomach growled in protest at its digestion of the last bits of a rabbit she had eaten yesterday evening. Intense hunger and overwhelming fatigue battled for a while until exhaustion won and Jule knew nothing but the heat of the afternoon and the darkness of her own closed eyes and broken spirit.

She awoke with a start, suddenly aware of a large White man looming over her. Before she could even roll to her knees, he had her arm in the iron grip of one of his hands. Without speaking, he tossed her up onto the saddle of his horse, mounted behind her, and broke for the road, one hand on the reins and his other pressed into her abdomen. Reaching the road as darkness fell, he cantered steadily away from Mother and the last vestiges of Jule's people. Her cries and protests drifted unanswered into the mist of the evening as the horse quickened its pace. Each time she cried out, the rider pressed her a little more tightly against him—enough to calm her, but never enough to create pain.

None of the things that Jule would have expected from a White man ever came. He did not gag her, slap her, or curse her. He simply rode undeterred through the darkness. After what seemed like hours, he slowed his pace, wrapped his reins around his saddle horn, and slipped his free hand into his saddlebag. Within seconds, Jule smelled the familiar aroma of deer jerky. Her captor loosened his grip enough for her to free a hand, grab the morsel and greedily gobble it down. Next came a quick sip of water from his canteen and then nothing but the rhythm of the horse until the coming of dawn.

CHAPTER FIVE
East

As the first rays of light penetrated the tree canopy along the road, the rider veered into the forest somewhere in Mississippi. As easily as he had hoisted Jule up onto the horse, he swung her down upon the ground and then dismounted the weary animal.

"Rest now," he murmured. He stroked the beast's wet muzzle, then turned his attention to the girl. "If they catch you, they will fuck you and kill you," he barked. "That's what they did to my grandmaw when my maw was a girl. They caught her alone one day, fucked her, and then killed her. She won't no Choctaw. She was Catawba. Don't matter. She was an Injun. That's what White men do in their spare time. They fuck and kill Injuns. That's probably what I would do too if I didn't have some Injun in me."

He continued, "I'm Jubal Elliott. Your people are gone to Oklahoma and the corners of swamps that you will never find. I'm taking you to North Carolina. You will be dead here in a week. These goddamned people hate Choctaw. We'll have to figure out what to do with you onest I git home. Take that blanket off the horse and make you a pallet in the bushes with the chiggers. They will eat you alive, but they won't kill you. Too dangerous to travel by day till we git you farther from here."

Then after a flood of words, they suddenly stopped. Jubal pulled some corn pone out of his saddlebags, gave her one, wolfed down the other, and curled up in the pine needles on his side with his hat pulled low over his face.

"What if I run away while you sleep?" Jule muttered.

"Then you will git fucked and killed," Jubal said and within minutes was snoring loudly.

Jule was tired, but she stood for a few minutes studying her captor before spreading out the horse blanket. Curled up in a ball in mud-caked road clothes without having shaved in days, it was hard to size the man up. He had long legs, big hands, and broad shoulders. What she could see of his hair and beard was dark and shiny. His cheekbones were high like those of her own people, but before he had nodded off she noticed that his eyes were green. If he had wanted to put his seed in her or kill her, he had already had his chance. She reckoned that she was as safe with him as she was going to be with anyone and safer than being on her own. The biggest problem was just being so near a White man. They stunk, and this one was no exception. Weariness finally overtook her. Jule spread out the horse blanket downwind from Blue Eyes and was asleep within minutes.

Their pattern continued like this for weeks, sleeping by day and riding by night. Occasionally, Jubal would have to leave her alone for a while and slip into a town for supplies. The great, green forests and red-clay fields of Alabama, and Georgia slowly slipped by. For a while, passing through the hills of the Upstate of South Carolina, she thought she saw a blue wall of mountains to the west. Mountains were only a tale to her, so she was never sure. Though the landscape changed slightly, the basic elements remained the same: red dirt, pine, and hardwood forests. Incessant humidity and ill-kept cotton fields in search of their former glory enveloped them. To break the monotony, at times she had searched for the signs of the clans of her people. Somewhere along the way, she had seen or heard Wind, Deer, Wolf,

Holly Leaf, Bird, Raccoon, and Crawfish. Bear she had seen only as a skin stretched out upon the door of a barn to dry. Panther now seemed only a ghost of the past.

Traveling at night, it was almost as through the land was unpopulated. The rare signs of humankind were the occasional lantern in a window or the bark or bay of the occupants' dogs. Other than the dogs, the only sounds were owls, frogs, crickets, and the wind. A few nights later, they crossed into North Carolina and a few nights after that they rode up the long entrance road into the center of the Elliotts' own cotton farm. A small frame house with low lights stood before them. When Jubal knocked softly, an aged Red woman slowly opened the door. She beamed at the sight of her long-departed prodigal son; but when she finally recognized the form and face of Jule behind him, Ola Elliott stared at her with such a mixture of recognition, shock, and pain that before Jule realized it, she had taken a slight step backward. In the eyes of Ola Elliott, her long-dead mother had just stepped out of the night and the past onto the steps of her farmhouse porch.

PEARLINE

CHAPTER SIX
The Walk

SOMETHING CAME ALIVE inside of Pearline Campbell in the springtime. The crisp, cold nights and sunny, cool days of March awakened her and invoked the spirits of the clans of her ancestors from the Scottish Highlands. During much of the year, she felt displaced in the flat, red-earthed world of the Carolina Piedmont.

As a child, when her grandmother sang her ballads of the Highlands, she had often felt that she would have fared better if her people had landed along the ridgelines of the Appalachians as had so many of the Scots and Scotch Irish; but her people came to America through Philadelphia, settled in Pennsylvania, slowly migrated down the Great Wagon Road through Virginia, and finally took root in the red clay of central North Carolina. This land was foreign to a people from jagged mountain crags and deep, frigid lochs; but the land of the Piedmont was readily available after the end of the Cherokee Indian Wars and, better yet for the frugal Scots, it was cheap. So, this is where Pearline Campbell found herself—at home in the cold of winter and brightness of spring and somewhat deadened in the clammy humidity and oppressive heat of summer and early fall.

Early on this spring morning, she had awakened with a start, snuggled underneath the weight of her nighttime quilt. She felt energized from her first moments of consciousness and eager for a quick breakfast and then a long morning walk in the fog of the creek bottom before the sun eventually burned away the magic. She rose quickly, dressed in her everyday clothes, grabbed a small slice of ham and a cold biscuit from their supper last night, and was out the door. From upstairs, she could hear the first stirrings of her parents from their own night's sleep as they readied for a long day of hard work. Pearline would be back before they finished their breakfast but had left no note as to her whereabouts. Her parents were long accustomed to her early morning rambles and, other than thinking her peculiar, had no objections as long as she stayed on Campbell land and far away from Mabry property. The Mabrys were known to have MacDonald blood among their kin, and several generations of life on a new continent had not resolved several hundred years of strife between the Campbells and the MacDonalds.

Free from the confines of the house, Pearline took in a deep breath of the fog-rich morning air. She then sighed in satisfaction and opened herself to the arrival of full light, descending across the pasture to the trail along the creek. After a few minutes of walking, she found her senses opening to the first warbles of songbirds and the last, haunting hoots of the night raptors. It was the reversal of the gloaming. In the gloaming in the evening, sunlight transitions to starlight. But in the early hours of morning, starlight fades and the sun begins to flex its muscle. Even in the fog, Pearline felt the process beginning and she sang softly:

> *"For the beauty of the earth,*
> *For the beauty of the skies,*
> *For the love which from our birth*
> *Over and around us lies,*
> *Lord of all, to thee we raise*
> *This our hymn of grateful praise.*

For the beauty of each hour
Of the day and of the night,
Hill and vale, and tree and flow'r,
Sun and moon, and stars of light.
Lord of all, to thee we raise
This our hymn of grateful praise."

She walked along the creek, absorbing the sounds of the muddied waters tumbling over small stones. The pitch blackness of the opposite bank of the stream slowly came into focus, revealing the outlines of tree saplings, brush, and wild grape vines. At this point on the creek, the waters were wild and a bit fierce for the flat terrain of the Piedmont. Pearline reveled in being lost in the sound. It reminded her of songs of wilder waters far away:

"The water is wide, I cannot get over
Neither have I wings to fly
Give me a boat that can carry two
And both shall row, my love and I
A ship there is and she sails the sea
She's loaded deep as deep can be
But not so deep as the love I'm in
I know not if I sink or swim
When cockle shells turn silver bells
Then will my love come back to me
When roses bloom in winter's gloom
Then will my love return to me."

As Pearline remembered the last line of the tune, she became aware of an unusual configuration in the silhouettes across the creek. The haphazard shapes of nature settled into the distinct outline of a man. She was startled, afraid she had stumbled across a stranger or, worse yet to her parents, a Mabry. However, as the fog thinned and light asserted itself a bit more, she recognized the face of Paul Elliott.

CHAPTER SEVEN
The Bridge

Not a Mabry. Not a MacDonald. Even her grandmother would approve. The Elliotts had been border dwellers in Scotland and celebrated for their expertise in stealing English livestock. Once as a child, Pearline had asked her grandmother when their Elliott neighbors had come to America and if they also had come on a big boat.

Her grandmother had responded, "Well, lass, I don't know exactly when the Elliotts came here or the size of the boat; but the only thing I do know for certain is that if they came by boat, then they stole the boat."

Paul Elliott seemed much less the scoundrel than his ancestors as he stared back across the creek at her early on this spring morning.

Though Pearline knew that part of Paul's family came from Scotland like her own, she had heard the stories about his mother being an Indian from out West. In fact, she had even heard the stories about his grandmother being an Indian from a local tribe. Looking at him this morning, it appeared that the stories were true. Strong angular frame, dark shiny hair, chiseled features. Tall like his father, but dark like his mother. Among a lot of White people, there would be revulsion at the reminders of the early people, but whatever should have taught Pearline Campbell to be repelled by the sight of Paul

Elliott was not working on this morning. In fact, ever since she had first seen him at school as a child, she had always been strangely drawn to him. Today was no exception.

Within minutes, she found the two of them walking south along opposite sides of Fishing Creek in perfect accord. At first, they walked in silence, intensely conscious of each other but exchanging no words. The light and woodland sounds of the morning increased in beauty and volume, and for a while the sounds of nature were enough. But soon, Pearline feared that they would walk the entire length of the creek in silence. From experience, she was painfully aware that Paul Elliott was a man of few words. Once, she had caught a ride into town to pick up groceries at the Redfern Store with Paul and his mother, and the boy had not said a word going or coming. If the silence was to be broken, it was hers to break.

"Paul, I think this is one of the prettiest mornings that God has ever made," ventured Pearline.

After a pause, Paul shot back, "Looks kind of like yesterday morning."

The words fell flat in the warming morning air.

"Don't you think it's beautiful?" probed Pearline.

"I think folks decide what they think is beautiful. To me, machines are beautiful. I like to work the thresher, run my grandaddy's cotton gin, and hope to have my own tractor someday. People think up machines to do their work, and when they work right, it is a beautiful thing," uttered Paul in a surprising cascade of words.

"But don't you take pleasure in the beauty God placed around you?" Pearline pressed.

"I don't know about God, but I take pride in a hard day's work, well-tilled fields, a full barn by wintertime, and a life well lived. If there is a God, I think he just expects us to figure things out for ourselves," Paul said.

Although Pearline found his words hollow, the sound of his voice in the moist air took her breath away.

"I think He wants us to know Him and enjoy Him forever," Pearline said with equal conviction.

The two walkers had not noticed the gradual narrowing of the creek as they continued on their way. By the time they made their last pronouncements, they found themselves no more than ten or twelve feet apart. Pearline also saw that a tree had fallen across the creek and now provided a footbridge connecting the short distance that separated them. Before she could even think, Paul had leapt up on the tree trunk and stepped to the middle of it. Pearline stood frozen in her tracks. Somehow, she knew that if she joined him there that her life would never be the same. Her mind spun. He was handsome. She had always been attracted to him. By all evidence he was moral, hard-working, and kind, traits not to be taken for granted among men. Her hesitation was that there was something missing in Paul that was present in the women in his life.

There was a mystical force from the Highlands in her and also perhaps present in Paul's mother and grandmother on hilltops among their own kind. That force that drew your gaze upward from the earth to mountains and the heavens beyond. That force that spoke of the beginning of all things and the intimacy of union and communion with it and others.

Paul stood proud, and Pearline knew it would always be a struggle for him to reach out to another or accept help from stranger or friend. He would help, but he would not be helped. He stood unaware of greater things, independent and earthbound; but before she knew what she had done, she found herself on the log inching her way out to his confident arms. When he took her hands, she gazed into his brown eyes, the color of the creek water below her, and yielded to who and what he was. Paul bent his head downward and kissed her warmly, firmly, and passionately. Afterward, as they stood on the bridge embracing, she heard him mutter, "And I think you are beautiful too."

PAUL

CHAPTER EIGHT
Passage

WHEN WAR HAD finally come, it had come quickly. On the day of his arrival in France, Paul Elliott experienced the first of many of his encounters with the ironies of war. After being marched and shoved down the gangplank of his troop-transport vessel shoulder to shoulder with the other human livestock being vomited from the bowels of the ship, he came to a jarring halt at the end of the incline. There, he paused at a processing station. As papers were checked and rechecked, he watched with wry amusement as an underling carefully recorded on a small Red Cross card that Paul Elliott has made safe passage across the cold, gray Atlantic to the hallowed shores of Europe.

Within weeks, the officially stamped document would arrive in the postbox of the Elliott farm planted on a red dirt road outside of Peachland, North Carolina, USA, and announce to his mother, father, and new girlfriend that the one they loved was safe and sound in France. The irony was that by the point they read the happy news, he could already be lying dead in a trench somewhere on the front. Somehow, that seemed much like the crossing of the Atlantic, both horrifying and mildly humorous.

Paul had underestimated the shock of war from its very beginning after being driven by wagon down Lawyer's Road to the local enlistment office in Wadesboro. Up until that day, he had chosen the occasions upon which he would be naked and the company that he would be keeping under those circumstances. Within minutes after arriving at the enlistment office, he stood in his shorts with his clothes bundled in his arms in a long line with other country boys. Minutes later, he lost the clothes and the shorts. Seconds later, he lost his dignity as a surly Army assistant had him spread his legs and cough as he inspected his privates for God knew what. Red-cheeked, he stumbled on through the assembly line being prodded, probed, and pricked in rapid succession with one device after another. When his neatly pressed uniforms were handed to him at the end of the line, he felt strangely proud but oddly violated.

The shocks at the enlistment station were just the beginning of the convulsions in Paul Elliott's life during the coming weeks. For his entire existence, he had rarely left Anson County for any reason other than the occasional hunting or fishing trip into the Uwharrie Mountains. Now, the worried face of his father, the stoic face of his mother, and the ashen, tear-stained face of Pearline became memories as he chugged ever northward toward New York City across an increasingly unfamiliar landscape. As a boy from a rural, Southern farming community, Paul struggled on the densely packed troop train filled with an ever-increasing diversity of humanity as more men were packed into the compartments at numerous short stops along the route.

By the time the locomotive approached New York, Paul was surrounded by a profusion of dialects, profanity, and general noise that made sleep all but impossible. He attempted to talk with his neighbors en route but often had to pretend that he heard their responses to his questions due to the cacophony. Paul only thought his senses were overwhelmed. By the end of the second day of his travels, his train and dozens of others pulled into the cathedral vaulted dome of Grand Central Station and disgorged their contents at the entryway to New York City.

Emerging from the station and falling into line with his comrades-in-arms, Paul was struck senseless by the noises of the city but marveled at the towering skyscrapers. Suddenly, he felt himself Gulliver cast ashore among a landscape of giants. When his senses began to clear, he noticed that there were a lot of pretty girls in New York City. Most of them were sporting the new bobbed haircut, which made some of them look too much like boys. However, others' eyes sparkled beneath their curled bangs, and their feed sack dresses swished about curvy hips. Long strings of twisted beads bounced on ample breasts, and a good day's trapping of fur encircled some milky necklines.

Paul's revelry was short-lived. A drunken G.I. spun through the doors of a bar, plummeted across the sidewalk, and knocked Paul out of formation onto his ass in the street. Before he even had his first hint of a thought, he was on his feet and had sucker punched his drunken assailant. Boyhood days of defending himself from calls of "half-breed" had given him a hair trigger. Blood spattered across Paul's hand, the drunk's mouth, and a few innocent bystanders. Strong arms scooped under Paul's own, lifting him off his feet. Others gathered up his wounded comrade, and the two of them were marched around a corner and up a series of steep steps, then thrown into a downtown makeshift jail cell outfitted for soldiers for just such special occasions. An hour or so later, Paul got his first good look at his sparring partner as he rolled over and turned his swollen, blood-encrusted jaw toward him.

"Well, hell. Red Jordan," said Paul slowly in surprise. He chuckled.

CHAPTER NINE
Letters

July 23, 1918
My dearest Pearline,

Honey, you must have been worried sick not hearing from me for the most of two weeks. The Army has rules, and I got to be careful not to give away too much about our orders or what we might be up to here in France. If I do, Uncle Sam will cut holes in this letter, black out my words or even throw it away. So I'm going to stick to the basics. You ain't going to believe who I ran into in New York City, and I do mean ran into. Well, to make a long story short, it was Red Jordan from back home! What are the chances that a country boy from Anson County can run into another one from the same place in New York City? I hadn't seen Red since he dropped out of school and joined the Army near two years ago. They had sent him to Georgia of all places for his training while we was seeing if we were going to be getting into Europe's war. Once we met up in New York, we was able to pull some strings and got to bunk up on the way over the ocean. Sweetheart, a man needs a friend on a trip like that.

There were 14,000 of us crammed together on a big troop transport ship called the Leviathan. I puked my guts out most of the way here. For days, there were waves bigger than the windmill back home on the farm. The scarier thing though was that we had Spanish flu onboard the ship. There was one whole floor of the boat where they took down doors and turned them into make-do hospital tables. Several times I heard whistles on deck for burial at sea. With flu spreading, the captain wouldn't even keep the bodies on board to send back home. It's the kind of thing that you just can't think about. When I wasn't sick or scared, Red had me laughing my tail off telling stories, playing setback with an old deck of cards and some new buddies and smooching on pictures of Hollywood girls that he brought along to keep him busy in the fighting. Now speaking of fighting, I feel a lot better about that because meeting up with Red has lifted my spirits. The Army is so disorganized that I'm really thinking that they won't get us away from a place called Brest where we first landed and to the front until the shooting is over. You keep up your spirits cause I will be back home kissing on you before you know it.

Your war boy,
Paul

P.S. Of course Red thought that the name of the town where we landed was funny.

August 18, 1918
My darling,

Well, it took a while for the Army to get their act together, but we are finally on the move. Red actually got changed to my battalion, so we have been bouncing together on the back of an old truck down some of the worst roads you've ever seen. Not only is my rump sore, but my stomach aches from the food and my heart hurts knowing that with the coming of spring and the men off to war that you have been having to help my mama and daddy as well as your own with the planting. No girl of mine as soft and pretty as you are ought to be out in a red clay field having the sun toughening up her soft skin. Please keep on a big hat and long sleeves when you can because I want you to still be as white and soft when I get home as you are in my dreams in this sad excuse for a country. It's those dreams of touching you and lying with you some day that is keeping me going. Every time I think about you and your red hair and green eyes, it makes me hate the Germans all the worse.

There is going to be some hell to pay when the Army finally gets me and Red to the front. Our officers don't tell us nothing, but I heard a lieutenant say something the other day about us going to the Argonne Forest. I don't know much about France or what town's battles are near, but it doesn't sound like a bad idea to be out in a forest. I'm hoping that me and Red drew long straws. As soon as they get us there, I will write to you and give you the lay of the land. Give my love to mama and daddy and tell them not to worry about me. I have always been luckier than I deserve, and I don't intend for this war to mess with my charmed life. After all, who could be luckier than the farm boy that gets to be sweet on you.

Handsome as ever,
Paul

September 30, 1918
Dear Daddy,

Please hide this letter and don't tell Pearline that you heard anything from me. Things has gotten worse than I can tell her. They finally got me and Red up to near the fighting. Turns out that Argonne Forest is not a good place. It's along the front that cuts through a big part of France and it's got about a million Germans on one side and about as many more Doughboys and Frenchies on the other. I haven't slept in days. Big guns rain hell fire down on us day and night. I have seen more rats, cooties, and cockroaches than we did when we tore down that old rotten barn and outhouse a couple of years ago. Stories have been spreading about hundreds of airplanes that drop bombs, gas that eats your guts out, and machine guns that true to God cut men in half. I would never tell you these things cause I know that they will worry you sick, but Daddy, for the first time I think that there might be some chance that I might not be coming home.

You and Mama took good care of me as a boy, and I slept at night knowing that I was being kept safe by the two of you. You was strong and Mama with the Injun in her was just plain scary sometime, but the Army has put your boy somewhere where a mama and daddy just might not be enough. I think I may be truly scared for the first time in my whole life. Last night, I dreamed that I never got to marry Pearline and have our own children. It was more of a nightmare because she ended up marrying that devil Dred Mabry. Daddy, that just can't happen. I got to keep her safe. I am embarrassed to ask because I ain't religious, and I know that you ain't neither, but could you sneak down to the church after dark and say a prayer for me. I know that that is a desperate thing for a boy to ask his daddy to do for him, but I am a desperate man.

Your boy,
Paul

P.S. Will write with better news soon.

October 8, 1918
Daddy,

I am still living, but Red Jordan is dead. An artillery shell took his head off three days ago in front of my very eyes. Another one nearly got me, but some crazy boy came out of nowhere and threw himself on top of me. He is hurt real bad, Daddy. A hunk of hot metal went through the top of his head. The boy ain't said a word since it all happened. I got some wounds of my own, but nothing that will kill me. As awful a letter as this is here in the middle of hell, if you ever got down to the church it just might have worked. They are saying that I might get moved back toward the coast to a place called Auteuil and possibly even sent home. Somebody found out that Mama is Choctaw and that I know some of her language. I can't say no more, but something is up. This part might get taken out of my letter. I am happy about coming home but surprised that I didn't hear from you after my last letter. Will write soon, but hope I get a letter from you first.

Heading toward home,
Paul

P.S. If this boy lives, I got to do something for him. He saved my skin. Strange thing is nobody seems to be able to figure out who he is. Tag says Rory Faulkner, but nobody seems to know him. Might be bringing him home as my souvenir from my good times in France!

November 1, 1918

Dearest Paul,

There is no easy way to tell you this. I am so glad that you have dodged most of the heavy battle in France because I have to break your heart. Darling, your daddy died a month ago this Thursday. The Spanish flu got him and so many others here at home, especially children. Your mama hasn't said a word or cried a tear since it happened. We buried him under a big oak by the pond. She stayed down there all one night singing and chanting things I can't begin to know. She suffers in her own way. Life is harder, but the women here are strong. You will have a home to come back to. I have asked that your commanding officer deliver this news to you. I know that you aren't too high on chaplains and such, but I pray for you every night and all day long. Please come back to us soon. We love and need you so badly.

Your eternal love,
Pearline

December 10, 1918

Dearest, darling Pearline,
I am coming home.

Paul

Two months later, Paul returned to the States. After walking up the long drive to his house, he stood surveying the ruins of what was now his and his mama's farm. As hard as Jule and Pearline had tried on their own, two strong women couldn't do the work of two strong women and two strong men. Nature was winning. Briars and brambles cascaded over fences. Poke weed and cedar sprouts were taking back the fields, and erosion was bleeding the red clay into the creek. Paul just thought the war was over. With a long sigh, he said, "Come on, Rory. We got a hell of a lot of work to do."

His mute companion at his side followed him like a bird dog up the last few feet of the drive and into the omniscient stare of his mother. She stood with crossed arms on the front porch.

CHAPTER TEN
The Wedding

TWO YEARS AND a war later, the not-as-young lovers returned to the footbridge, Paul accompanied by his border-dwelling Methodist family and Pearline by her Scottish-Presbyterian clan. Both groups were equally confused and angry about gathering for a wedding in the woods rather than a church. As much as the couple withered under their families' ire about not having a proper church wedding, the choice had freed them from choosing which church they might be married in and thus which family would prevail and which would lose in the contest. With both families scowling at their respective child and their Protestant rivals, Paul and Pearline became man and wife.

Paul came over the bridge first, his hair slicked back, and his bony, muscular frame draped with a suit coat, string tie, and cotton dress britches. His brother-in-arms, Rory, came with him, and his bird dog, Bonnie, slipped in quietly after the two. After a short pause, a fiddle warmed up softly to "Be Thou My Vision," and as the hymn started, both families in a moment of rare solidarity began to sing heartily:

"Be Thou my Vision, O Lord of my heart
Naught be all else to me, save that Thou art
Thou my best Thought, by day or by night
Waking or sleeping, Thy presence my light

Be Thou my Wisdom, and Thou my true Word
I ever with Thee and Thou with me, Lord
Thou my great Father, I Thy true son
Thou in me dwelling, and I with Thee one

Riches I heed not, nor man's empty praise
Thou mine Inheritance, now and always
Thou and Thou only, first in my heart
High King of Heaven, my Treasure Thou art

High King of Heaven, my victory won
May I reach Heaven's joys, O bright Heav'n's Sun
Heart of my own heart, whate'er befall
Still be my Vision, O Ruler of all."

As the song softly resolved, the vision of Paul's heart walked across the bridge. Pearline, bedecked in ivory lace and crowned with a ringlet of wild flowers from the meadow, approached. With every step, Paul's heart rate and respiration increased. The vision took his breath away—alabaster skin, red lips, and auburn hair blowing gently about her small, tanned shoulders. Within moments, Pearline reached him, placed her soft hand within his brown, calloused one, and promised her eternal love to him. Then she accepted her ring, tilted her chin upward to him, and received his eager lips. Paul was lost in the sight and scent of her and stood oblivious to friend and family. The fiddle was joined by guitar and banjo as the wedding party and crowd swept across the field to the barn to satiate their hunger at a table of fried chicken, butterbeans, fresh creamed corn, fried okra, buttermilk biscuits, sweet tea, and peach pie.

As some ate, others danced and the band played:

"Roosters crowing on Sourwood Mountain

Hi, ho, diddle-ah day

So many pretty gals you can't count 'em

Hi, ho, diddle-ah day

Roosters crowing on Sourwood Mountain

Hi, ho

So many pretty gals you can't count 'em

Hi, ho, diddle-ah day

My true love lives across the river

Hi, ho, diddle-ah day

Four more jumps and I'll be with her

Hi, ho, diddle-ah day

Roosters crowing on Sourwood Mountain

Hi, ho

So many pretty gals you can't count 'em

Hi, ho, diddle-ah day

No alcohol for the Methodists and Presbyterians, but they risked the flames of hell to dance. However, as they danced and the stars appeared, men of both persuasions snuck away one by one to the back of the barn, supposedly to relieve themselves but more often to satisfy their thirst for something other than sweet tea.

In the wee hours of the morning, Paul and Pearline slipped off to the old honeymoon cabin by the creek, breathlessly revealed themselves to each other and reveled in the joys of flesh upon flesh until long after the rising of the morning sun.

CHAPTER ELEVEN
The Kill

Pearline and Paul walked slowly back up the same side of the creek hand in hand. Though they were newly married, they already possessed the comfort of two people who had grown up as friends in a small rural community. They knew each other's people and most of the families that shared their county. They had gone to school together, celebrated community events together, buried folks together. They had done everything but church together. Pearline's family were all devout Presbyterians, but Paul's had shed Calvinism upon their arrival in the New World and embraced the less arduous path of lapsed, occasional Methodists. As they reached the connection to the path back to Pearline's folks' house, Paul stopped, causing Pearline to stumble.

In the brambles on the righthand side of the path, hordes of flies droned, dipping in and out of the deeper vegetation below. As the couple slipped forward, they sensed death, but it must have been a recent one because there was no accompanying stench of decay. The source of the blowflies' delight lay heavy in the grass. The large body of a headless buck was warming in the morning sun. Pearline sensed Paul's rising rage as his jaw tightened, face flushed, and respiration increased. She sensed the source of his rage too.

"What a waste!" Paul shouted into the sunlit air. "Who would kill a deer this size and leave the whole carcass to rot in the woods? He just took the head as a trophy and left the rest of the beast for the vultures rather than a family."

Paul stooped to search the chest of the buck for a bullet hole, mystified as to how they had not heard a shot in the fog of the creek bottom. He shook his head and stammered, "Oh my God. He didn't even shoot the animal. He attacked it like some kind of puma! Look at the cut on its leg where he first snared it. Look at the stab wounds up and down the deer's side where he let it run lame, stabbing it over and over again. He took pleasure in bleeding the buck down."

Shivers ran down Pearline's spine. Paul just stared and shook his head.

"What kind of beast could have done this?" said Pearline.

Slowly, Paul's head stopped shaking and his eyes focused and widened.

"Dred ... Dred Mabry."

DRED

CHAPTER TWELVE
Beginnings

DRED MABRY MIGHT well be the sheriff and most powerful man in Anson County, but plenty of people around still remembered that his grandmaw had been a dime store whore. She had spread her legs for gold to survive the War Between the States and had finally gotten herself bred by a deserting son of a bitch. He left her two gold coins for her troubles that he said he stole from a dead officer from South Carolina.

Dred's mama and daddy had been sharecroppers, poor White trash no better off than darkies. For most of his growing up years, he had chopped his share of cotton for Mr. Jack Westbrook, but he had begged his way onto a job at the gin and worked his way up the ranks. Then he had bought his own cotton farm and finally had bought the gin. Every single White peckerwood cotton farmer in Anson County had voted for Dred when he ran for sheriff five years ago. Even some of the poor but high-minded Elliotts had voted for him when they realized they would be taking their cotton all the way to Laurinburg if he turned them away at Huntley Gin and Lumber in Peachland. People often surrender their principles when push comes to shove.

Dred liked to say, "I never could figure out people who was poor, half-breed trash but acted like they was some kind of king or queen of England. That is Paul Elliott and his kind. Noses in the air, farming a burned-out cotton farm and tending a bunch of scraggly-assed peach trees. What a goddamned bunch of fools. Not a darky on the whole place, just some half-witted White boy. Paul Elliott may have survived the war and be some kind of a hero, but he will be old and dead before his time trying to beat life out of that dead horse of a farm. And when he is dead and gone, I will take the only thing on the Elliott farm worth having—Pearline Elliott. Now that is one damn fine woman. How she ended up with an Injun with a stick up his ass like Paul Elliott I will never understand. I remember when that girl got tits when we was still at Peachland Elementary School. My pecker used to stick straight up in the air under my desk every time she walked down the aisle and the smell of her reached my nose. I would fuck that girl like a racehorse given half a chance, time, and opportunity. All it ever really takes is time and opportunity."

Dred Mabry was a crude but patient man.

PAUL

CHAPTER THIRTEEN
War

PAUL'S STRUGGLES WITH the farm had not been the only way that he had underestimated his hardships after the official end of the war. At first, he had simply been grateful to have survived with no noticeable harm, especially as he watched the mute form of Rory Faulkner loping from task to task about the barnyard and in the fields and orchards each day. The angry, scarlet gash in his head stood as a stark reminder of the price he had paid to end all wars and to save a virtual stranger, but for Paul his own injuries were slow to take shape and even slower in revealing their hideous dimensions.

The first sign of problems came months after the ex-soldier's return, when Paul, Rory, and his bird dog, Bonnie, were in the back pasture quail hunting. When the men finally stumbled upon a covey of the elusive birds and Bonnie came to point, Paul motioned the dog to advance. The birds exploded in all directions. Their flight was accompanied almost immediately by the thunder of Rory's shotgun.

When the gun boomed, Paul thought that Rory had turned the barrel on him as his target. The explosion reverberated in Paul's head and buckled his knees almost to the ground. His head throbbed and his heart pounded until he regained part of his senses and saw Bonnie bounding back over the broom straw with a limp quail clenched softly, but firmly, in her teeth. Paul broke into a sweat as he realized that he had not shot himself and Rory had not shot him either. In fact, one shot had been fired and the recipient was in his dog's mouth. What the hell had happened?

He had bird hunted with his daddy since he was eight years old, and nothing like this had ever occurred. Rory just kind of looked at him quizzically, confused about why Paul was sweating on a crisp November day. Paul pulled himself together and shouted at Rory and Bonnie that that was enough hunting for one day. Then he stomped off, leaving his confused companion and best bird dog exchanging confused glances with each other as they slowly brought up the rear.

The hunting episode would become the first, but by no means the last, event that would eventually make it crystal clear to Paul that he had brought home another unexpected, and certainly undesired, souvenir from his time in service to his country in France.

CHAPTER FOURTEEN
More War

Over the course of the next year, Paul felt large portions of his world slowly crumble like the clods of red dirt that washed down from the fields into the creek bed. Disturbing dreams, not of war but of storm, entered into the quiet peace of his sleep. Pearline began to carry circles under her eyes in the morning from riding the waves of his distress in the night as Paul tossed to and fro in their bed seeking comfort and oblivion.

"Paul, honey, what in the world is wrong? You seem to be plowing all night as well as all day."

"Pearline, I'm just worn out from working. It's planting time," Paul mumbled sleepily.

He wasn't lying. He was as confused as Pearline about what was going on during the night. Most nights brought the same dream. The sky darkened, thunder rumbled, and the wind rose until a twister appeared in the west headed straight for the farmhouse. Paul frantically closed the windows, bolted the door, and cast his six-foot frame and broad shoulders against it, bracing as the pressure intensified to the point of impact and explosion. Then he sat bolt upright in bed waiting once again for his heart to still and the beads of perspiration to be reabsorbed into his body and damp bed covers. Pearline was a sound sleeper, so he did not have to stumble for words as to why a grown man was sitting up in bed like a small child who had had a bad encounter in the night with the boogeyman.

Pearline did not know about the hunting incident. Though she slept through many of his nightmares, she began to notice his fatigue throughout the day, the decrease in his appetite, the slow disappearance of small jokes and hearty laughs, and finally the decline in their coupling less than a year after their marriage.

For the first few months of their union, Paul and Pearline had rutted like deer in the fall, often and with great enthusiasm. But as Paul's state worsened, his unrest at night and exhaustion from the day's work began to take their toll. As much as he loved to rut, by nightfall he just came to crave a good night's sleep just like he craved a delicious meal or a period of relaxation during the day. Pearline accepted his excuses for everything else, but as a young bride she was rightly hurt by what she was doing or not doing that had made a virile soldier and farmer fall to sleep on her after less than a year of marriage.

Paul began to drink coffee at dinnertime and get himself started at bedtime just to stay awake and perform his husbandly duties when Pearline crawled into bed beside him, fragrant and soft. Shame became Paul's constant companion as his cock would not take flight as it always had at Pearline's slightest touch. Often now, it had not even risen when he got up to take his first piss of the morning in the slop jar by the bed. What kind of man was he becoming?

In desperation, he began to slip around to every old medicine woman hidden away in the recesses of nearby backwaters searching for a powder or poultice to restore his manhood. All his efforts were slowly making him a poorer man but not a better one. All the while, it had not even crossed his mind that his plight had anything to do with his time at war. Like so many soldiers believe as they leave the battlefield for the last time, Paul had thought, *The war is over. We won. I get to go home. This is over by God.*

Much to Paul's surprise, about six months into marriage, he had competition for the slop jar in the morning. On the third day of

Paul awakening to the sound of Pearline upchucking in the morning, he broke out in a sweat for a completely new reason: His bride was pregnant. By fall, he would have a new reason to struggle with sleep as the father of a rambunctious baby boy named John Rudolph. They would always call him by his first and middle names.

JOHN RUDOLPH

CHAPTER FIFTEEN
Baptism

JOHN RUDOLPH WALKED the side of the red dirt road, headed to Great Aunt Minnie's. Word had come that she had a surprise for him, and as close as it was to his birthday, his hopes were high for good news. He needed some. His bottom still smarted from the licking his daddy had given him when he told what was believed to be a fib. Even though he was not a churchgoing man, John Rudolph's daddy had a Baptist hatred for anything he thought was a lie or even smacked of a lie. Well, enough of that for today.

Today was the day before his birthday, and ever since he could remember, Great Aunt Minnie had never let him down. One year it had been a ball glove, another year a checkerboard, and last year, best of all, a slingshot. John Rudolph had been the terror of the county for almost a year now, sending every bird and squirrel in sight into a panic with any stone, marble, or even pecan that he could strap into the slingshot and fire. He reached into his back pocket, withdrew the weapon, loaded it with a piece of quartz, and sent it tearing through the weeds ahead just in case some animal lurked up the road in wait for him.

After about fifteen minutes, the heat of the afternoon began to catch up with him. John Rudolph felt the top of his bare head and the back of his neck begin to warm, and within minutes he could feel small drops of perspiration slide down his bare upper body within his overalls. Since he was just going to see family, he had left the house barefooted, bareheaded, and barebacked. The only things between him and nature were his underwear and overalls, but even at that, nature is cruel in the South on a summer afternoon. Within fifteen more minutes, John Rudolph was looking for a good stand of trees and a creek for a drink of water and maybe even a little wading.

Before he ever quite saw what he was looking for, he heard a sound off to the side of the road. After a few minutes, he knew exactly what it was—a group of darkies singing. At an early age, John Rudolph had learned to call Black folks "darkies." His daddy had beat the fire out of him the only time he ever remembered using that other word. Since his grandmaw was an Injun, his daddy had had to fight more times than he could count after some other country boy had called him that word. To White folks, darkies and Injuns were all Black. It was one of the many rules that a ten-year-old had to figure out in Peachland, so he just called Black folk "darkies" and Injuns he just called "Injuns" to be polite.

Within a few minutes, the singing became louder and more beautiful. Another thing that John Rudolph had never been able to figure out was why Black folks sounded so good when they sang together and White folks sounded so bad. He didn't have a lot of experience in churches, but he had been to Peachland Methodist a few times when some of his daddy's people had died. He would usually sit there in misery either freezing his butt off in winter or fanning the heck out of himself with a paper funeral fan in summer, dodging the occasional wasp that flew in through the full open windows. The worst part was when they started to sing. Good golly. It didn't matter how many of them you packed into a church, only a few could sing good and the rest sounded like barking dogs, cats with their tails caught in the door, or rusty lumber saws. It always surprised John Rudolph that the dead person didn't hop up and make a run for it. He sure wanted to. But a few times, Daddy would drive the wagon down to New

Apostolic Missionary Baptist Church on Sunday, and they would park under a tree in the dirt and listen to the Black folks sing.

Sometimes, the music would be so beautiful that the boy would feel like laughing, shouting, or even crying. Even with the place packed, they all sounded like one big voice. Not a dud in the whole bunch of them. Even though they would have never thought about going in, the preacher would send a deacon out to them and a few other Whites parked in the yard and pass the plate to all. They weren't in the business of helping White folks gyp them or the Lord out of His due on Sunday. Other than sneaking music off the Black church or burying his dead relatives, the boy never went to a church or a Sunday school of his own on Sunday. No reason given. It's just the way that it was.

As John Rudolph drew closer to the music, it kind of got inside of his head. Before he knew it, he had scrambled down the roadside through a considerable patch of briars to the creek bank. There he saw about fifty darkies, all dressed in white robes, no more than thirty or forty feet down the creek below him. Some of the men stood waist deep in the muddy creek, and before John Rudolph knew what was happening, they grabbed one of the men by the nose, plunged him backward into the creek, and shouted, "I baptize you in the name of the Lord Jesus Christ."

Poor John Rudolph nearly passed out and fell into the creek. He had never seen a baptism, and for a second he thought that he was witnessing his first murder. When they let go of the fellow, all the womenfolk burst into singing, clapped in rhythm with each other, hallelujahed, and praised the blood of the Lamb. John Rudolph peed a little bit in his shorts. But the music went on, the people began to speak in some other language, the clapping increased in complexity, smiles grew larger, hands rose higher, and before the boy even knew what was going on, he realized that he wanted to be part of it. For the first time in his life, he wanted to be a darky and feel what these people felt, sing what these people sang, and love what these people loved.

Within seconds, John Rudolph was on the bank with a bunch of startled Black folk who suddenly became quieter than they had been since he first heard them on the road. A few of the men waded closer to where he stood on the creek bank, exchanging mysterious looks of dread and terror among themselves. Slowly, the men parted, and the black-skinned, white-robed apostle of Jesus waded forward, looked down into John Rudolph's excited, little uplifted white face, and in a deep sonorous voice proclaimed with authority, "Suffer little children and forbid them not to come unto Him."

Before John Rudolph knew it, a couple of Black women grabbed him by the shoulders, popped open the buckles on his overalls, dropped his drawers, and slid a small, white robe over his head. Next thing he knew, he was dog paddling in the creek with darkies all around him singing and maybe a water moccasin sliding by headed south. In seconds, his nose was pinched and he was fully plunged into the murky depths of Lanes Creek.

"I baptize you in the name of the Father."

Down he went.

"The Son."

Deeper this time.

"And the Holy Ghost."

Scraped bottom on the last plunge.

My Lord! How many gods do these folks have and how did a ghost get thrown into the mix? he wondered. Each time he went under, he panicked a little more because it seemed that the darkies held his little white body on the creek bottom longer than they had for any of their own people. But suddenly, John Rudolph burst through the cold, muddy water into the sparking light of day, spitting water like a bass and heaving in the life-giving afternoon air. His final surfacing was followed by the most and loudest hallelujahs of the day, people raising their hands and their voices in praise of the Lamb who was slain. Within minutes, the darkies gathered their belongings, then pulled the robe off John Rudolph and left him on the banks of Lanes Creek in his birthday suit. Retreating rapidly from the scene of the crime, their voices faded into the afternoon air.

John Rudolph sat naked for a moment, unaware and unashamed. He felt strangely renewed and more alive than he had ever felt in his ten short years. Slowly, he worked his shorts up around his skinny waist, rehitched his overalls, shook the water from his damp head, climbed up the banks of the creek, and continued his journey to hopefully retrieve his second birthday present of the day.

CHAPTER SIXTEEN
Sunshine Cake

As Miss Minnie Kelly had gone about the considerable chores of her day, she had fortified herself from stashes of blackberry wine hidden throughout her old farmhouse. One bottle sat behind the mantel clock in the dining room, another was stashed under the upside-down bucket by her well on the screened-in back porch, and the third really wasn't a bottle at all but the whole inside of her butter churn on the sleeping porch. A small dipper leaned against it. She hadn't churned her own butter in years.

Life could have been easier if she had allowed the fellow from the Rural Electric Association to hook her up to the electricity, but she wasn't about to let some stranger come nose around in her house. No telling what they might find. Them devils might get their hands on her five gold coins hidden since the War Between the States, her Chinese checkerboard that her sister had brought her all the way from Charlotte, or the neatly wrapped Daisy BB gun waiting to be opened. The last time one of those copperheads had come calling, she had kicked open the front screen door and unloaded two barrels of birdshot on his scrawny ass as he had hippity hopped up the driveway. She did not need to be electrified. She had a Victrola for music, a loom for weaving, an icebox and woodstove for preparing food, a T-model Ford for transportation, and a double-barreled shotgun for the REA. What else could anyone need?

Now her way of life was a choice, especially in modern times, but who could begrudge an old lady with rheumatism a few sips of blackberry wine as she went about the hard life of chopping wood, drawing water, and hand-cranking a cantankerous automobile. She would sail out into the yard, chop a little then drink a little. Sprint into the kitchen, cook a little and sip a little. Float to the porch, weave a little and indulge a little. For an old lady, she ran a lot more smoothly than the Ford out in the shed. The only problem was she had a hard time gearing down at night. Most nights, she would turn back her kerosene lamp and be out by eight, but she was often wide awake by two in the morning. For years she had fought it, but now she would just sit up, put on her slippers, and head to the kitchen to fire up her stove. Cooking in the wee hours of the morning was practical. It cut down on the buildup of heat during the summer months. As she rose in the dark this morning, she was a woman on a mission.

Thursday would be her great-nephew John Rudolph's tenth birthday. His ninth year had not ended so well. His daddy had caught him in a lie this week telling tales about stories that the idiot boy on their farm had told him when everybody in the county knew that idiots don't talk much less tell stories. His daddy had whipped him something fierce with a cotton stalk, and everybody knowed that there ain't no worse whooping than with a thorny old cotton stalk. Paul ought not to have done that. John Rudolph was a good boy. He just got him an awful big imagination. It weren't her right to tell her nephew how to raise his boy, but she did intend to raise John Rudolph's spirits by fixing him a special birthday cake to go with his new BB gun.

A peddler from Wadesboro had sold her six bottles of a new fizzy drink called Sunshine Cola. She didn't care nothing about electricity, but she was fond of a fizzy drink every now and again. Just the other day, she had seen a recipe in her Women's Home

Missionary Society newsletter about a Coka Cola cake, and she didn't see no reason in the world why she could not substitute one of her Sunshine Colas for a Coka Cola. Her Kelly people were just not one to leave something alone. They were bold and curious about new things. Now, for a while she had considered a blackberry wine cake, but people could be queer about such things, especially with all the temperance fanatics running around.

Miss Minnie sailed down the hall, taking a quick nip in the dining room on the way to the kitchen. Within minutes, she had red flames going in the firebox of the stove, banishing the early morning chill. After lighting a lamp, she rummaged through the icebox and lined up all her wet ingredients on the countertop. Next, she stood on her tippy toes and retrieved the dry goods from the pantry and lined them up beside the wet ones. By the time she had mixing bowls, utensils, and ingredients in order after the short stop in the dining room, it was nearly three in the morning. She sifted flour and other dry goods into her mixing bowl and broke in several dark orange hen's eggs and deposited some store-bought butter and fresh milk from her own cow, Mary Louise.

As she stirred the batter to a silklike satisfaction, Minnie caught a glimpse out of the kitchen window of a rising full moon. She experienced the overwhelming urge to kick off her bedroom slippers like a girl and stand barefoot on the now warm pine floorboards of her kitchen, so she did just that. Nothing could be better for the human soul than to stand barefoot in the kitchen at three in the morning, stirring cake batter and watching the moon. Well, one thing could be better. She reached into the icebox, retrieved one of the Sunshines, took a small slug from it, and poured the fizzy, yellow soda into her golden batter. The mixture gave a sigh and rose as if in tandem with her own joy.

Minnie stirred the mixture once again, shuffled her bare feet on the worn floors, stared out the window, and softly sang several bars of "Harvest Moon Over Carolina" as she slid the magical mixture into her hot wood oven.

CHAPTER SEVENTEEN
The Outhouse

JOHN RUDOLPH LOVED treats like being dipped in a creek but hated daytime, summer duties like trips to the outhouse. As long as he just had to pee, it was easy. He could do it in the slop jar by his bed at night in the winter or summer, but sometimes in the summer he would slip out on the front or back porch in the night, climb up on a porch chair, and pee over the banister to see just how far he could make it go. After holding it one night for an extra hour, he had actually hit the fire bell on the wooden post about six feet from the porch. He was young, had a great stream and a good aim. During the daytime, he peed anywhere he wanted to around the farm as long as he didn't have an audience. He peed in the barn, behind his mama's lilac bush, on the plow, and in the corn patch. Like a dog, he worked his way around the place, marking his territory, but he made sure never to pee by the well or in the creek. Even a boy doesn't want to drink or swim in piss.

Going dookie was a whole other matter. Nobody really wanted to dookie at night in a slop pan and then have to smell it till the sun came up, so in the winter you just put on your coat and made a run for it to the outhouse. Huffing and puffing, you broke records doing your business and bolting back for the house and the comfort of your still partially warm covers. There was no competition for the outhouse at night in the wintertime, but summer in the daytime was a different story. The outhouse swarmed with flies, hate-filled red wasps, and dirt daubers bouncing dangerously against the walls and roof of the inside of the oppressively hot, stink-filled shed. It was a real chore to concentrate and make doo when every grunt brought a wasp bouncing off your head or exposed back with your overall straps dropped and your britches around your ankles. After getting stung once last summer, John Rudolph had tried to do his business in the yard, but when his daddy eliminated the dogs, foxes, or possums as the culprit, he had beaten the tar out of his son. John Rudolph would take his chances with the wasps.

As he approached the outhouse in the middle of the afternoon heat, he realized that he had been outmaneuvered and would have to hold it for a while. The door to the shed was closed tightly, a clear sign of a customer in line ahead of him. Plus, through the cracks in the walls, he could hear a man's voice mumbling. In the quiet of the summer afternoon, John Rudolph could soon make out his words and became entranced by the story that they spun. The only thing that he could not discern was the identity of the speaker's voice, but his words began to imprint in the boy's mind.

RORY

CHAPTER EIGHTEEN
Silence Breaks

Rory Faulkner sat in the oppressive heat of the outhouse fully clothed. Sweat slipped down his entire body as his lips began to slowly move. The last sound he had remembered making had been on the battlefield as he cried out in searing pain lying across the body of Paul Elliott. Cry after cry had come until the body beneath him began to reanimate, and then nothing else came from his mouth. Not the next hour. Not the next day. Not the next year. Silence. All around him sounds came at him, but until today he answered nothing back in reply. During the past hour, he had felt his lips begin to move and a force beginning to take form within him to make words. The force had slowly increased to the point that Rory thought he might explode, so, in desperation, he had ducked into the outhouse for privacy. Then the words came:

"A red-tailed hawk rose, gliding round the pine before resting on a branch. A cottontail came from its hiding place and nibbled on wildflowers. Then a rattlesnake appeared over the rim."

When the words finished, he sat in stunned, sweat-soaked silence. He did not know where they came from. He did not know why he would ramble about a snake and a hawk after years of silence. He sat relieved by the expulsion of the story, but after the outburst silence descended once again. No more words came. Rory slowly rose from his seat and burst out of the suffocating shed into the bright sun and refreshing air of the afternoon. As he came through the door, he took no notice of a dumbfounded boy standing in shocked silence just around the corner.

Every month or so, the scene would repeat itself. Rory would feel the urge to speak rising once again within him. On two more of those occasions, he was unaware that he had a witness. Once, John Rudolph had come upon him swimming in the creek just in time to hear Rory saying as he surfaced, *"You little fool, Vancie. Instead of looking for a man to come along with a buggy load of fancies, you had better be looking for a man to come with a pocket full of silver!"*

John Rudolph had little curiosity about girls, but he did kind of want to know about this one. Sadly, there was no one to ask. Except on the rare occasion when John Rudolph caught Rory talking, the farmhand sat completely mute at family meals and as he went about his work tasks during the day. Well, at least until one day. A few weeks after the episode at the creek, John had walked into the barn and caught Rory storytelling again as he pitched hay into the loft:

"It would be a long, hot day because a hay wagon pulled into the barn on Main Street in Saluda with Josiah's work for the day."

Rory had accidentally given his young spy two more clues—another name, this time a boy, and a place, but sadly one that John Rudolph had never heard any of the grown-ups mention. A month or two later, John Rudolph got his last clue and sadly not nearly enough of one to begin to solve the mystery.

Rory's bedroom really wasn't a bedroom at all, just an old bed stored in the barn that Grandma Jule had reluctantly allowed John Rudolph's daddy to set up in the corner of his room. Most nights, Rory was a pretty good roommate and slept soundly. John Rudolph even felt somehow safer having the strong workman in the corner of his bedroom to keep the boogeyman far away. However, on some nights, Rory moaned and tossed and turned. These were what the boy called war nights. On one of those nights and only one of those nights, the moaning suddenly turned to words. John Rudolph could tell that his roommate was in the grips of a full-out nightmare:

"Jagger ripped his belt from his pants, and the leather strap struck James like a rattler across his backside."

Rory shot straight up in bed and caught John Rudolph staring at him in open-mouthed terror. The man silently pulled the covers over his head and turned to the wall, promising himself that there would never be another witness to his outbursts. He kept his promise. John Rudolph never heard another word from the farmhand in daylight or in sleep for over a year. Long after Rory's breathing had regulated and he had begun to snore softly, John Rudolph lay in bed wide awake asking himself over and over, "Did he say Jagger, or did he say Dagger?"

PAUL

CHAPTER NINETEEN
Cows

PAUL HAD NEW problems come spring. Every time he turned around from chores and a hard day's work, he discovered that one of the cows had gotten out of the pasture and was on the run. Since returning from the war, he had fought yet another battle trying to keep the cows on their land. First, almost every single fence post on the farm had to be replaced from age and rot. Since he couldn't afford precut posts from the lumber mill, he had to fell trees and cut the posts himself.

After finding a particularly good stand of locust trees on a ridge above the pond, he recruited a sharecropper friend named George to spend weeks with him cutting the trees down, sawing them in six-foot sections, and loading their crop in his old mule-drawn wagon. Then hole after hole had to be dug fifteen feet apart with rusty, old post hole diggers. Next, a post was dropped in, one foot down and five showing. Finally, holes were refilled, dirt tamped and on to the next one. All this played out under a blistering cloudless Carolina sky. After all the homemade preparation, the last, most painful stage happened. Paul had to go to Wadesboro and withdraw enough of his hard-earned and scarce cash money to buy staples and rolls of barbed wire to finish the job. With thick gloves, he and George rolled out miles of the wicked wire, set a staple, stretched the wire with the come-along and crowbar, and finally finished the stapling.

Every fifty yards or so as Paul sweat into his brogans and unwound the wire, a barb would penetrate his gloves, draw blood, and leave him swearing like a two-faced Baptist preacher at a whorehouse. Each time, George would chuckle softly and say, "Now, Mister Paul, you keep a talking like that and the only thing you are going to be good for is to be one of those 'Piscopalians. Them people down at your daddy's church ain't going to take you back if you get a mind to go or have a relation drop dead."

Paul would just grind his teeth and soldier on until break or lunchtime. With the Depression grinding on, lunch options from Pearline had fallen off and most of the time now consisted of spring water, store-bought crackers, and tins of sardines or Vienna sausages. Sometimes, Paul would also abscond with leftover breakfast biscuits, which filled the stomach of a hard-working man better than a whole tin full of crackers. After weeks of sweating, digging holes, stretching wire, and swearing oaths fueled by buckets of spicy sausages and greasy fish, the pasture fences were all replaced. Paul beamed with pride.

"Well dang, George, there's the post I was looking for," he said as he dropped one in the hole and tightened the wire. "The last one."

George smiled a slight smile, showing a small gap in his row of yellowed teeth. "Yessuh. We finished till the Lord puts us back to work."

Within a week, George revealed himself to be a prophet. A thunderstorm rolled across the arid red earth, cracking tree limbs from oaks and tossing the heavy debris down randomly on their finished work. For days afterward, Paul and George walked miles of fence lines, lifting limbs, tightening wire, and retamping now shaky posts in red mudholes. Also, as the rain revived grass on the farm, the hungry cattle, affirming that the grass is indeed greener on the other side, began destroying the fences in sections. First, they would press the lowest strands of barbed wire to the ground with two thousand pounds of pressure in a hoof. Then they would stick their thickly carpeted necks in the hole, lift the strands above into the sky, and step lightly through the now considerable hole in the barricade. Paul did not know a lot of Bible, but the part in the beginning about God cursing Adam and the earth sure rang true. He eventually realized what wise, old George had long known—fences are for happy cows. There is no fence on earth that will keep a hungry, curious, horny, or frightened heifer or bull in its place. They might as well be buffalo.

About once every two weeks or so, Paul would have fugitive cows on the loose. About every other time, much to his chagrin, they would head straight down the road to the Mabry place. All his other neighbors had cows too and were sympathetic to their wandering ways, but since Dred Mabry had claimed heart issues in the war and had his daddy buy him papers, he had not served. Instead, with most of the able-bodied menfolk gone, he had cajoled and intimidated the old folks and overworked womenfolk into electing him sheriff.

How someone unfit for battle could be fit to guard the county, Paul had never understood; but when he left for France, Dred was a redneck ne'er-do-well. When he returned home, Dred was one of the richest and most powerful men in the county. Since he was so busy as sheriff, he leased out his considerable lands to tenant grain and cotton farmers. He had no use for time-consuming cattle and absolutely no tolerance for any of them wandering onto his lands and tearing up his fields. He had put the word out at his general store that any stray cow on Mabry land was a dead cow. So, although Paul was not scared of Dred Mabry, he was fond of his cows and not up to a nerve-rattling encounter with a grown-up version of the schoolyard bully that he used to cockfight with all too often as a boy. Any word of an Elliott cow loose on Mabry land sent him in a hurry to retrieve his field hand, Hank, and then his cows before the biggest jackass in the county showed up spoiling for a fight.

Thirty minutes after the cows had made a run for it, Paul found three of his best heifers deep in a stand of pine trees square in the center of Mabry land. Wasting no time, he put Hank out of the truck to keep the cows from crossing the road to more Mabry land on the other side. He hoped Hank could turn them south, back down Lower

White Store Road to Elliott territory. Paul's job was to ferret the stupid beasts out of the pines and get them to him to head them home. Two of the cows cooperated readily and started trotting back out of the pines toward Hank. The third, of course, proceeded deeper into the heart of Dred's domain. Paul swore and lit out in hot pursuit after her, cursing the entire animal kingdom with each beat of his heart and stride of his long legs. He was brought up short by a high, piercing cry. He stopped, trying to figure out what could be in such distress. Then a word formed in his mind and on his lips: "Hank."

He ran back down the trail toward the road. Immature pine branches and the occasional cedar limb or briar slapped him in the face, leaving specks of salty blood and aromatic resin dotting it. Gasping, he emerged from the woods, climbed the roadbank, and landed before his worst nightmare. Dred Mabry stood with one foot on poor Hank Cason's chest as he lay on his back in the tar of the blacktopped road. The sheriff's rifle pointed down with the barrel between the old man's eyes. While Hank pleaded for mercy, Dred Mabry raised his eyes and coolly asked Paul Elliott, "This your clod buster?"

Paul felt panic wash over him. He continued to sweat as his heart raced. In his youth, he could have taken Dred in a fair fight, but now the fight was not fair. Paul had two enemies before him: one the rogue force of the law in Anson County and the other the forces of shellshock, which assaulted him in both his mind and gut. He labored to still his pounding heart and fought for a clearness of mind, but all the while the forces of chaos threatened to deprive him of breath and leave him crumpled on the ground in his friend's hour of need. Suppressing all hatred, Paul struggled to steady his quivering voice as he responded to Dred's taunt.

"Now, Dred, you know Hank Cason. He and his wife, Scotia, live in the cabin down the road from your farm. He is an old man who minds his business, works his farm, and doesn't do any harm."

"Well, his business put him on my land, and I ain't gonna have no White trash trespassing on my property."

Paul's anger began to eclipse his body's attempts at panic. "Dammit, Dred. He is on the road not on your land."

Dred smiled slyly, spitting on the ground beside Hank's head.

"Any goddamned road in Anson County that passes through Mabry land is Mabry land. I put out the word about people letting their cows get in my fields and eat my crops. Hell, while you was in the Army, I had a rogue Negroid getting in my corn, and I put out the word on him. The vermin came back one time too many, and I shot his ass dead. Didn't even have a charge much less jailtime. I don't serve the law. I *am* the law in this county. Killing another field hand today won't change that."

The old man shook beneath him, and Mabry continued, "But now if you want to trade me that sweet wife of yours, I can give you this cracker back. I've had a thing for her for years."

Paul's eyes narrowed like a puma's as he felt every muscle in his body tense for a pounce. The only thing that restrained him was a vision of Pearline and Scotia grieving over his body and Hank's body in the church cemetery. Reluctantly and with great effort, Paul slowly changed course. "Tell you what. Two of my cows are halfway home. It's getting late. I will leave the third heifer with you. She's yours. Just let the old man go."

Dred cracked a big smile and slowly lifted his foot off Hank's chest. "Well, that ain't what I really want from what you've got, but since you want the old man, it will just have to do for now."

Hank stumbled, gasping, toward the shotgun side of the truck while Paul eased around to the driver's side with murder in his heart. As the two of them pulled away, Dred shouted behind them, "Now you gents have a good day!"

Paul sped back toward his own farm with one sure thought in his mind and heart.

With the Lord God as my witness, I will have to kill that son of a bitch someday.

CHAPTER TWENTY
Attack

Paul told Pearline about what happened to Hank out on the road and why they were one milk cow short.

"Pearline, he is crazy. Butchering harmless animals. Hurting innocent old men. Killing unarmed trespassers on his land. All of that scares me, but what scares me more is that he talked about you, in an evil way. I have you, Mother, Rory, and John Rudolph here on this farm. None of us are a match for him on our own, especially if he catches us unaware. Stick to the house and yard. Stick together and for God's sake, be careful. I have got to find a way to deal with him, but I need time. There is something twisted and warped in the soul of that man. He is dangerous. Promise me you will be careful."

"I promise, dear. I am more frightened of him than you are. He has made me uncomfortable ever since we were in school. I will be careful. I promise."

For several weeks, the house seemed under siege. Pearline and Paul tried not to spread fear to Rory or John Rudolph, but they were both prone to wander, so they at least tried to make sure that they were together. Rory was wounded but had not forgotten his marksmanship training from the Army. John Rudolph was young but like most Southern boys carried a small squirrel gun almost everywhere he went and was almost always accompanied by some of the yard dogs. Jule was another story. She could not be managed or wrangled. By nature, she knew no fear. They would just have to take their chances with her.

The family settled into its new routines and turned its attention back to the ever-present work that surrounded them. One bright morning, Pearline rose, helped Jule with breakfast preparation, and then took the scant remains of biscuits and red-eyed gravy to the yard for one of the penned dogs. Bonnie had come into heat a couple of days before, and Paul was bound and determined to not have one more mouth of any description to feed. Champ and Scout had not been happy with this decision and had spent the last two days barking, whining, and humping against the fence. Pearline pulled the wooden peg out of the latch and entered the pen. Showing great submission and happiness at her appearance, Bonnie cowered and wagged her tail furiously. As Pearline stooped to pet her, Bonnie rose, tipping Pearline over, and shot out of the slightly ajar gate of the pen.

Clambering back on her feet, Pearline pulled her skirt up a bit and lit out after Bonnie, frantically calling her name. Fortunately, the male dogs were off looking for rabbits somewhere. Pearline knew exactly where Bonnie was headed. She loved a morning romp in the creek, and she was making a beeline in that direction. Pearline would never beat her there, but she needed to get to the spot before the dog finished her bath and wandered on to greater mischief. Red-cheeked and damp with perspiration from the humid morning air, Pearline arrived just in time for Bonnie to exit the creek and begin shaking. In a second, Pearline pushed her damp hair back from her eyes and grabbed the startled dog by her collar.

Turning to drag Bonnie back to the house, Pearline felt something grab her right arm like a vise and pull her backward into a bear hug of hair, muscle, sweat, and man stench. Bonnie bolted for home. Dred Mabry whispered hotly into her left ear, "Why good morning, Mrs. Elliott. I have been waiting a long time for this."

Pearline could not thrash, kick, bite, or breathe. Dred was a powerful man and held her like a constrictor. She could not move, but her terror mounted as Dred began to make small movements, slowly repositioning her against the trunk of a hickory tree. As he walked her, he breathed his putrid breath against the back of her neck. Screaming was not an option. He had clasped his huge, beefy hand across her small mouth. Once he got her pressed firmly against the tree, she began to scream inside because she realized that with his spare hand he was beginning to inch her skirt up her leg. Her greatest horror came next when she realized he was growing in anticipation against her backside. No man other than Paul had ever lain with her, and Paul had never shown anything but love and tenderness to her. This was other, a profane violation, and she was suddenly filled with simultaneous impulses to both vomit and faint.

As she became dizzy and the woods around her began to blur, a sharp sound cracked and then reverberated down the creek bed. The first retort was followed by another and then another, like a string of firecrackers on Independence Day. The vise around her loosened, and she fell into the mud of the creek bank gasping for air and crying hysterically. Her attacker retreated into the forest soundlessly. She looked up expecting to see Paul in hot pursuit of Dred Mabry, but all she saw about twenty-five yards down the creek was Rory and John Rudolph with uptilted guns shooting into the trees oblivious to her plight. Occasionally, they burst into happy laughter and bounded into the brush, retrieving a twitching gray squirrel.

Silently, Pearline rose shaking and carried her secret home with her. She hid her assault and torn muddy dress for a day to keep her husband from being killed; but before she could get it to a washpot, Paul found it. Now, it was his time to shake. Softly, so that the others in different corners of the house and porch would not hear him, he muttered, "Now, I have to kill him."

DRED

CHAPTER TWENTY-ONE
Holocaust

DRED MABRY LAY soundly sleeping in his big mahogany bed. The spacious two-story white farmhouse was silent except for the sound of clocks ticking in bedrooms, hallways, and parlors throughout the house. His destitute mother had longed for a mantel clock when he was a boy, so as his wealth grew, Dred had filled his home with clock after clock as an expression of wealth and a scant amount of sentiment. His maw and paw were gone now, and his two brothers had taken off for better cotton prospects in Alabama. There was no Mrs. Mabry. Dred had no use for a woman other than to satiate his hungers and that he could do at Miss Ruby's whorehouse out on the Wadesboro Road. He was alone, but he was master of his horses, dogs, field hands, crops, considerable lands, and a strongbox of folding money, silver, and gold under his bed. That was the way he liked it. Paying enough taxes to keep the Feds off him and no spying eyes of accountants and lawyers.

Most nights, he slept soundly like a dragon on his hoard, but tonight was different. Deep into the night, he awakened to an acrid odor floating into the window with the cool night breeze. The room was not pitch black as it should have been on a moonless night but had taken on a faint orange glow as though under the spell of a rising harvest moon. Rubbing sleep from his eyes, Dred stumbled to the window to shut out the unpleasant smell.

Arriving there, he experienced horror for the first time in his life. Small orange spots dotted his dry, grain-ripened fields over dozens of acres. Not only were there spots of fire, but they darted wildly about, creating lines of fire and after minutes, zones of fire, growing and merging into a mounting holocaust.

The greatest horror was that nothing stood between the inferno in the fields and his house, outbuildings, and livestock—no pond, creek, or gully to serve as a firebreak. Dred had planted winter wheat right up to the edge of his yard to maximize his profits. Grabbing his clothes and several bags of cash from beneath the bed, he ran downstairs and out the door. The force of the heat in the yard was jarring and made him pull up for a moment on the porch. Smoke swirled about him and a torrent of small, red embers rained down on the house. Animals screamed in terror as his hired hands ran about the yard freeing coon dogs, poultry, and horses from the barn. An old community fire bell stood silent, mounted on a post in the yard with the cord whipping about in the hellish breeze. Nothing could be saved, not the fields, livestock, barn, house, silver, or gold.

Grabbing the mane of one of his frenzied stallions tearing through the barnyard, Dred threw himself, part of his remaining clothes, and two bags of cash onto the horse's back and fled for his life. His field hands fought on for a while and then fled for their own lives. Tearing up the red dirt of his driveway, Dred thundered toward the main road. Tears streamed from his blackened face and burning red eyes. Venom surged through every muscle and vein in his body. Clenching the horse's mane, he spewed his wrath as he rode, "Goddamn you, Paul Elliott. Goddamn you."

CHAPTER TWENTY-TWO
Destiny

WHEN DRED PULLED his horse up at the end of the Elliotts' driveway, one lone window stood out illuminated downstairs. Paul Elliott sat at the kitchen table poring over bills at the end of a hard day at work. He was still trying to burn off rage after finding out what had happened to his wife. Pearline had told him that Dred had tried to kiss her and that she had torn her dress escaping him, but Paul knew better. Presbyterians are bad liars. It had taken every bit of his self-restraint to not grab a gun and head to the Mabry house to let fate run its course.

The only thing that had kept him home had been the harsh realization that if he died, everyone he loved would die a slow death in poverty. They were barely hanging on as it was. He had taken out a second mortgage on the farm a few months ago, and if they didn't have the best peach and cotton crop that they had ever seen, the farm would be lost anyway. As he sat sorting through bills, his hand shook from leftover rage and the ravages of shell shock.

What were his chances of outgunning a professional law enforcement officer who had used his gun more than any good cop should have? Every man, White, Black, or Red in the county was either terrified of him, bought off by his money, or silenced by his power. He knew that he would never have a fair hearing in court over what had happened to Hank or to Pearline, and he also knew that men like Dred Mabry don't stop. They eventually have to be stopped. Dead ends appeared every way Paul turned.

He got up from the table and walked to the kitchen cupboard to get a BC Powder to go with his coffee. Between the stress, anger, and overwhelming odor of someone burning brush nearby, his head pounded. He was glad Pearline had gone to her mother's for the night to help with some canning. Rory and John Rudolph had been sawing logs upstairs for a couple of hours. The house lay quiet except for the pounding in his head as he pored over the bills one more time.

Dred slipped around the house quiet as a cat. All the dogs had been kenneled down by the barn after the escape yesterday. He had the yard to himself as he walked up to the back screen door. His revenge would be quick and simple. No drama, no words. He had his pistol but was holding it by the barrel, unloaded with the grip up. He would not butcher him here. Just knock him unconscious, drag him to his horse, take him deep enough into the woods where they would not be heard, and then take him apart piece by piece. Paul would beg for mercy he would not receive. The family he would leave to nature and the Depression. He just wanted the man who destroyed his farm now; all other cares were lesser concerns.

Paul's last sight was the flash of a smirking, familiar face in the mirror on the mantel. His head, which had been pounding, suddenly exploded. He fell into darkness and oblivion.

CHAPTER TWENTY-THREE
Hank

HANK CASON ROCKED slowly on the porch of his decaying cabin. Scotia had gone to see her people a week ago, so supper wasn't much to speak of. The old man had eaten a quick meal of cornbread and buttermilk before retreating to the comfort of his rocking chair and the occasional breeze. Each time he rocked, he winced a little. Even after several months, his brittle, broken ribs had not healed completely from Dred Mabry grinding his shiny black boot heel into his chest. For comfort, he reached slowly to retrieve his family Bible from the small table between his rocker and the porch swing. Straining through the thick lens of his bifocals and thumbing gingerly through the dried cracking pages of the ancient book that had crossed the sea with his ancestors, Hank found his new favorite passage once again. He read it to himself now at least once a day:

Then Samson went and caught three hundred foxes; and he took torches, turned the foxes tail to tail, and put a torch between each pair of tails. When he had set the torches on fire, he let the foxes go into the standing grain of the Philistines, and burned up both the shocks and the standing grain, as well as the vineyards and olive groves. Then the Philistines said, "Who has done this?" Judges 15:5-6

"I have done this," murmured the vindicated old man. "I have done this to the Philistine."

Hank closed the book and resumed his rocking as the breeze kicked up a little.

JULE

CHAPTER TWENTY-FOUR
Recovery

THE NEXT EVENING, Jule Elliott stood at the kitchen sink, pumping water out of the hand pump and washing her supper dishes. Paul sat at the kitchen table drinking the last of his coffee. His head still ached from yesterday's blow. His mother had taken needle and cotton thread to it and doused it with rubbing alcohol to the point that he thought he would lose consciousness again. Her ministrations had saved his more delicate wife the trauma of having to piece her own husband's head back together.

Pearline had taken to her bed for most of the day to recuperate from finding Paul at the table with blood gushing everywhere. She was still puzzled by her husband's account of Dred Mabry being gone when he woke from the blow. It was not like Dred to back off in a fight. He was a sorry excuse for a man, brutal and not prone to mercy. Jule had appeared the next day after reporting she had been gathering clay for making her pottery. She had set to work further doctoring Paul. Later, she fed Rory and John Rudolph, who had not even awakened from sleep upstairs during all the furor last night. The old woman had stoically and silently floated about the house and yard all day, preparing food, sweeping, drawing water, and playing doctor. Pearline never knew what to make of her. Even as Paul's mother, the Indian in her kept her apart from all of them, even her son.

As Paul returned his cup to the sink, still somewhat dazed, he mumbled, "I called down to the store and jailhouse this morning. Nobody has seen Dred. As a matter of fact, they started looking for him when he didn't show up this morning. Not a sign of him at what's left of his farm or anywhere else around town. It's not like I miss him or anything, but I would just like to know where he is so I can be ready for the next time he shows up." Paul set his cup in the sink and said, "Mother, you are making a mess."

Jule replied, "I've been washing dishes my whole life, boy. I don't need any help from you."

"No, Mother, your feet. You have red mud on your shoes and have tracked it all over the braided rug."

Jule looked down and muttered, "I went to the creek this morning to dig clay to make my pots. Mind your own business, Paulie."

The old woman washed her son's coffee cup, dried it with a cloth, and set it up on the shelf.

CHAPTER TWENTY-FIVE
Moonlight

A MOTHER SHOULD not lie to her child, but Jule Elliott had lied to hers. The mud on her shoes had not come from the creek bank while digging clay. It had come from her ride back to Nanih Waiya last night. She had arrived on her faithful mule near midnight and had forced the animal to carry her all the way to the top. The moon rode full at its zenith, obscured only occasionally by the passing of a wispy cloud over its yellow face. The mount lay silent and mysterious, and her ancestors pressed their faces down from the stars nearly close enough for her to touch.

Rain had come earlier in the day, so her heavy shoes pressed into the damp earth, planting her like a tree in the moonlight. Wind, Deer, Wolf, Holly Leaf, Bird, Raccoon, Crawfish, and Bear encircled her, neither affirming nor scorning her but rather just accompanying her. They all stood silently with her in her mission. An hour later, it was complete, and her feet were even muddier. She was an old woman, but the suffering of her days had made her strong. She tamped down the last clods of red earth in the waning moon and prepared to remount her faithful mule. Her only witnesses to her visit would soon disappear into the heavens when the day dawned. Her work was done.

How could he have thought that she would allow it. She had nearly lost Paul to another senseless White-man war. The flu could have taken him like her husband, Jubal, but the ancestors had asked mercy to the Creator. She had birthed him, nursed him, anointed him, prayed for him, fed him, and worked like a dog with him. But she would not lose him, not to a crazy White man. She had felt nothing when she caught the crazy demon in the kitchen gloating over her son's prostate body on the floor. She had felt nothing when she took her ax and split his head open with one swipe.

Strength had come from her ancestors to clean up the mess, drag him to the barn, and with the hook and pulley used to hoist hay bales, lift him onto the back of her waiting mule. She might have awakened Rory in the barn to help her. He would not tell, but this death was for her lost people. This death was for wounded Mother, Nanih Waiya. This death was for Paulie, the only part of her people spared to her. The blood would fall on her and no other. Untying his body and dropping him into the hole, the last of Dred Mabry that she saw was his white, exposed skull glowing softly in the moonlight. Her son would see him no more. He would torment her son and daughter-in-law no more, nor any other innocent. He would molder in the red earth of Town Creek until the Creator drew him into soil, purified his remains, and fed the roots of the wildflowers that crowned this sister of Mother in the springtime. Jule did not wipe the red clumps of earth from her feet before leaving. She did not feel unclean but wore the earth on her feet as she rode her old mule home, arriving at her house with the sun.

PAUL

CHAPTER TWENTY-SIX
Water

AFTER SEVERAL WEEKS of no news about Dred, Paul let his guard down a little and went back to farming. After the fire and decades of bad blood building up in the county over Dred's corruption and brutality, the prevailing sentiment seemed to be that he had just taken his cash and hit the road like a carpetbagger. Most believed he would start over among the unaware in a new place.

It was time for Paul to be a farmer again. Once he got back to the field, he had no problem remembering that God had cursed the earth shortly after He had made it. Even on the days when he did not believe in God at all, he had no problems believing in the curse of the earth. He had been behind his aged mules, Hennie and Henry, since before the rooster had crowed, trying to escape as much of the heat of a Carolina summer day as was possible. However, by midmorning he could smell the ripe stench of his own sweat. Most of the gasoline-powered tractors that were scattered around the county sat idle, their owners too poor since the crash to even fuel them up.

Paul thought sarcastically of the twisted blessing it was to have never had the money after the war to buy one of the new-fangled machines. When many of his neighbors had had to go back to farming with animals, they were still the only way that Paul and his family had ever known. He slapped the reins of the mules, and the plow share cut through the red clay soil, leaving sticky balls of earth in two straight lines on either side of the furrow. Traveling for a few dozen yards without striking an obstacle temporarily boosted Paul's spirit.

All morning long, he had struck rocks, pieces of rusty iron, roots, and in the bottomland of the creek even shards of what appeared to be old Catawba Indian pottery. The slowing of his plowing every few yards to reset the plowshare had been excruciating. On one occasion, Hennie had nearly delivered a hindfoot print to his forehead as he forgot in his frustration to mind her range. By the time he took a quick lunch of a tin of sausages and biscuits, the blazing sun had scorched his forehead and gnats and no-see-ums had found their way into his most private parts. It had been a day of uninterrupted misery.

By midafternoon, a plan had begun to take shape in Paul's mind. Before the war, his daddy had found a couple of acres with several springs and a small branch, which made the land unfit for any kind of farming, in a low-lying section of the homeplace. With the help of some day-laboring workers from Greasy Corner in Wadesboro, a small dam had been built across the branch in just a few weeks. Paul's daddy had had no formal education, but he knew about land and how nature worked. He had understood that the backed-up creek would eventually fill in the low spot and make a small pond. He also had understood that the springs would keep it filled even in the driest of weather and provide insurance as a dependable year-round water supply for the crops and the livestock.

Today, when Paul looked down the hill to the pond, he saw one heck of a place to skinny dip at the end of hours of suffering. By about five, temptation broke him. He didn't even take time to lead the mules to the barn. He just tied them up in the shade and ran to the banks of the water hole. Stepping from the blistering sun beneath the branches of a huge oak tree, he snatched off his putrid shirt and, hopping from one foot to another, shed his boots, socks, work pants, and finally underwear as he stepped gingerly into the edge of the cool water. Small frogs leapt in a frenzy left and right of his advancing naked frame. Cold, slick mud slipped through his toes as he waded up to his knees. He gasped as he felt his cock and balls pull closer to his body as he lowered them beneath the surface of the spring-fed coldness of the waters. With a last plunge, he dove beneath the surface, leaving the sweat, filth, heat, and hitchhikers on his skin floating in a thin sheen on the surface. Several small bream scattered before him as he dove deeper in the pond, resurfacing long enough to take in another gasp of the scorching afternoon air.

Within minutes, the cares and torment of his day leached from his farming-tanned body into the surrounding coolness and greenness of the waters. His euphoria drove him more deeply in a newfound quest to touch the bottom of the pond in its deepest most secret parts, visited only by its biggest catfish and an occasional ancient snapping turtle. Now, Paul had forgotten not only his day of plowing but his years of eking out an existence for himself and family on a used-up cotton farm. As he groped about for the pond bottom, he even forgot his memories of France, death, and the recent torment of Dred Mabry. Finally, after a quick trip back to the surface, he dove one last time with filled lungs. Within moments, he found the heretofore-elusive pond bottom and waved his hand about in its dark depths. He was certain of his success as the icy waters of the underground springs seeped out of the mud around his exposed, refreshed flesh.

With the grail found, he could float peacefully back to the surface, dry himself in the sun, reclothe himself, and head to a much more substantial supper than his poor excuse of a lunch. He upended his frame for his return home. Suddenly, a wave of panic shot through him as something bit into his left ankle. He twisted about, terrified that a giant snapping turtle had him by the foot and would not let go until it thundered. Then he whipped about in a frenzy as the thought of a nest of water moccasins animated him with terror. However, whatever had him did not strike again. As he jerked his right leg, his captor stretched, bit into his flesh, and then slowly retracted. Paul's panic grew as the pressure in his chest mounted.

Thrashing about, the identity of his attacker finally came into focus. He remembered a story about his daddy being in such a hurry to finish the pond that he had not removed an old section of barbed wire fence. In despair, Paul realized that he was ensnarled in part of it. The harder he pulled his leg, the more deeply the wire cut into his flesh. All the wire he had crawled under in France. All the bullets he had ducked. All the shrapnel he had dodged, and now he was going to die in the bottom of the pond on his family farm.

It might be days before they even put together the fool thing that he had done and dove down to find what nature had left of his decaying body. His last thoughts were of Pearline and the keening of a woman who had believed her man to have returned to her from the ravages of war. As his mind darkened, he ceased his struggles and looked up at the lengthening rays of the sun dancing on the sparkling surface of the waters far beyond his reach.

CHAPTER TWENTY-SEVEN
Déjà Vu

Slowly, Paul opened his eyes, feelings clumps of earth pressing into his back as he marveled with pride that the dome of heaven looked remarkably like the late afternoon sky of North Carolina. Slowly turning to one side, he suddenly rolled up in a start like a possum in the midst of two simultaneous realizations. One was that the ugly-assed, stupefied face of Rory Faulkner was staring down on him on the banks of the Jordan River. The other was that he was naked as a jaybird and that his dick was flapping from side to side like a bass as he rolled about in Glory Land.

"Dammit, Rory Faulkner! What the hell are you doing staring down on me buck nekkid!"

Rory, of course, said nothing. Paul jumped up bare-assed, scrambling about for his clothes as he blushed in the realization and humiliation that Rory had not only pulled him out of the bottom of the family pond in his birthday suit but that he had saved his life again.

"Dammit, Rory, this crap has got to stop. The first time was kind of heroic, but this is just humiliating," Paul said as he pulled on his underwear and shook red clay from the back of his head.

Rory stared back in silence, water still dripping from his hair and the hems of his work jeans. Paul worked frantically to reclothe himself and repair his fractured dignity. As his breathing slowed and his mind cleared, he looked into Rory's whipped-dog face. Once the boy had come to an awareness of Paul's distress, there had been no hesitation in his response. Paul may have been caught with his pants down, but Rory had dived into the pond nearly fully clothed. Later that night, Paul would learn that Pearline had sent the boy out to find him with a bottle of freshly drawn well water to combat the effects of the long day's heat.

Rory had come over the hill just as Paul surfaced for his last dive and was still high enough on the hill to see and understand the burst of air bubbles a few moments later. Like a water spaniel responding to the signal of his master, Rory had run down the remainder of the hill, kicking shoes in opposite directions as he dove into the pond. He had found Paul's limp body on his second dive, tearing his hands to shreds as he pried the barbed wire from Paul's mangled ankle, then locked Paul's neck in the crook of his arm and stroked with the other arm toward the algae-dappled surface of the waters. On the bank of the pond, he had pressed water from Paul's lungs and forced in air as he sputtered back to life. Now he sat, knees drawn up to his chest, as Paul's profanity rained down like summer hail.

Paul did not come fully to his senses until he saw Rory's damaged hands. The sudden awareness of the rawness of Paul's ankle brought him up short. The other thing that cut him to the quick was that from the perspective of his full stature looming over Rory, he could see the outline of the shrapnel scar in Rory's still wet, blond hair plastered tightly to his skull. At that moment, the full extent of the sacrifices of the idiot boy sank into the depths of Paul's wounded soul. At the same time, the reality of his near drowning overwhelmed him, and Paul did what he had wanted to do a thousand times in the trenches of Europe: He dropped to his knees and vomited the remaining watery contents of his stomach onto the bank of the pond. Spitting the last vile drops of it from his mouth, with tears in his eyes, he put his arm around the shoulders of the vacant-eyed, shivering man and said, "Come on, Rory. Let's go home."

Paul had spent his last day as a self-made man. Whether it was Rory's bravery on the battlefields of France, his mother's brutal instinct to hold the farm together, or Pearline's prayers, something wanted him to live. Pieces came together in his mind and heart. A spectral human image with the wounded head and battered hands of Rory Faulkner and the wounded feet of himself arose from his long-discarded childhood memory. The old story, much to his shock and dismay, had found and broken him at last. Next Sunday, the Presbyterians would need a new roof on their church when Paul Elliott walked in on the arm of his beloved wife.

RORY

CHAPTER TWENTY-EIGHT
Awakening

LATER THAT EVENING at supper, to the great shock of Jule, Paul, Pearline, and John Rudolph Elliott, Rory Faulkner spoke. First, he quietly prayed a blessing over their food. He then lifted his head, looked each of them in the eyes one at a time, and said, *"All the goodbyes had been said. James and Josiah stood by a canoe on the Green River. James would leave Saluda. There were few things left to be settled."*

Then, after these strange words, the man blurted, "My name is not Rory Faulkner. My name is Isaiah Buckland."

John Rudolph smiled broadly in long-awaited triumph while his grandmother, mother, and father stared thunderstruck in stupefied silence. For months, John Rudolph had tried repeatedly to tell his parents about their field hand's spasms of storytelling. Repeatedly, they met his attempts with scorn and contempt, banishing him to the barn and fields for additional chores to sweat the sin of lying out of his soul. Today, he finally stood before his parents fully vindicated.

"Isaiah Buckland."

The healed mute rolled the words slowly about in his mouth as though tasting some long-forgotten food from childhood and trying to decide if it had been abandoned or simply unavailable for a very long time. At first, there was only the name. After a few moments, images emerged of a distant place, high, deep, and cool. It was a world so unlike the vulcanized cotton fields of the Piedmont that he questioned whether it was all just a dream. However, other images in addition to the forests emerged in his mind in rapid succession: a long, twisting road, a cabin on a hill, and finally the faces of his mother and father, James and Geneva Buckland. For a moment, their images seemed to disappear behind a veil of mist as his eyes welled up with tears.

"I have to go home now. Please forgive me, but I just have to go home," Isaiah blurted in pain and desperation.

Paul stepped forward cautiously in a state of his own pain. Trying to adjust to the sight and sound of a voice coming from his friend's mouth, Paul stammered, "But, Rory … I mean Isaiah, this is your home."

Isaiah sat in silence. As Paul looked down upon his shell-shocked friend, the images of Rory throwing his body upon him on that distant battlefield in France came to his mind. Almost simultaneously, Paul recalled the gurgling and sputtering of his lungs as Rory dragged his limp body from the farm pond and willed life back into him. Paul's eyes filled with mist of their own as Pearline squeezed his hand.

"I … Isaiah, do you even know where to go?"

For a moment, the man sat in silence. All his memories of the last few moments had been of images, but now he reached deeply within the shrouded depths of his past and mined a single word from the darkness: "Saluda." After a pause, he said, "If someone can get me to a place called Saluda, I can find my way home from there."

Two days later, Isaiah found himself a hobo on the boxcar of an old freight train crossing the red clay of the central Piedmont headed west. By midafternoon, he stared out of the open car door in wonder as the Appalachian escarpment rose before him like a massive blue curtain of tree and stone. Isaiah stared in a slack-jawed stupor. Nothing in his recent life had prepared him for mountains. The red clay fields, peach orchards, dusty roads, and poverty of the Piedmont required no stretch of the imagination to picture them just rupturing from the drought-cracked earth. What lay before him now spoke of miracles and a place that had descended from some otherworldly realm. Though this was the land of his birth, it seemed as though Isaiah was seeing it for the very first time as cooling air and new fragrances excited his nostrils.

There had been no money for a trip home. God knows Isaiah had none, and the Elliotts were land rich but as poor as Isaiah when it came to cash money. Their poverty had in no way diminished their generosity as they carried Isaiah in the back of the old hay wagon to the train tracks near Wadesboro. Depositing him there, Pearline had pressed the handle of a basket of food into his trembling hand.

For someone going home, the pain of parting with the Elliotts had greatly exceeded Isaiah's expectations. Pearline wept softly as she said her last goodbyes to the man who had returned her husband to her from the River Styx not once but twice. Paul then stepped forward and in an exceptional display of affection, hugged Isaiah strongly for longer than is comfortable for any Southern farmer. However, much to his surprise, his greatest pain had come in saying goodbye to the boy. John Rudolph had been the one who had led Isaiah like Mentor through the seven layers of hell back to the land of the living. Isaiah softly placed his deeply calloused hand on the top of the boy's head, looked into his small, sad face, and said, "Now, John Rudolph, don't you cry. The good Lord only gives us all a certain amount of time together and you and me was lucky enough to have time to finish our story. Every time you miss me, you just think of Josiah and Vancie, waterfalls, lightning bugs, and a poor man's supper. After all, all that we really ever have in this world is story."

Despite his admonition, the boy had cried and so had Isaiah after he leapt onto the speeding train and caught his last glimpse of the Elliotts as the train rounded the first bend in the tracks.

Suddenly, Isaiah was jolted back into the present moment by the huffing of the engine as gravity bore down upon the train in the beginning of its assault of the mountains.

CHAPTER TWENTY-NINE
Home

THE OLD FREIGHT train strained as it inched its way up the Saluda Grade, the highest railway incline in the eastern half of the country. Soon, Isaiah could glance down and see the world that he had known for the past three years shrink and recede out to the hazy rim of the horizon. He now rode alone up the grade except for the company of a red-tailed hawk that circled about the train, finally landing on the outstretched branch of a weather-beaten fir tree. Isaiah peered forward, alert for the first signs of the village of Saluda. Finally, he caught a glimpse of the station in the distance. He gathered his meager belongings, tensed his legs, and jumped into the wild grasses on the now level sides of the tracks. Falling with a thud, he rolled twice, landing on steady feet and quickly dashing for cover. The last thing in the world he wanted when he arrived in town was to be beaten about the head by company railway men with blackjacks. The Depression had hardened the railroad companies to the ways of freeloaders.

Cutting through the woods, Isaiah picked up the last leg of the road to Saluda. Making it all the way to the high country today was still going to require some luck in picking up a ride, but for now he was content to walk and attempt to gather his memories of coming down to town from the high mountains with his parents when he was a boy. As he reached the edge of Saluda, the reality of how little things had changed jolted him. When he was a child, there had been eight stores of various types "downtown." Now, with the Depression and a fire, there appeared to be seven. With the exception of the loss of the old livery barn that his grandfather had been so strangely fond of, the serpentine arch of downtown had changed little. The old brick façade of Pace's mercantile still dominated Main Street. The Paces had kept the store going for nearly three generations ever since its original founding by a Hill fellow.

As Isaiah walked the short length of downtown, horns blared as cars swept by, annoyed by the slower pickup trucks operated by farmers who had come to town to supply themselves and their families for the coming week. A handful of children emerged from Pace's, transfixed by the hard candy and sodas that they held tightly. All Isaiah needed now was a little luck and a stray vehicle heading north. He had no desire to linger in Saluda amidst all the Saturday racket and run the slight risk of having someone recognize him. Fate was with him as he flagged down a farmer in an old pickup truck who reported that he was on his way to Flat Rock. That would put him within a few miles walk of home.

Isaiah hopped into the hay-covered bed of the truck feigning the need for fresh air to avoid an awkward conversation with the old driver. They pulled out into the road, and Isaiah slowly relaxed as the speed of the truck increased as they left the hubbub of Saluda on market day. His last glimpses of the village were of a sign to Pearson's Falls, another dilapidated one for a place once called Orchard Trace, and a marker on the bridge over the Green River for the old ferry crossing.

Isaiah's anxiety heightened as he leapt from the back of the pickup, said his thanks, and began the last few miles of his walk uphill to the Buckland homeplace. Four generations of his family had now eked out a living on the top of this ridge in the upper heights of Balsam Mountain. Isaiah's heart beat like a drum as he realized that he had no assurance that his family remained here. The Great War, the Spanish flu, and the Depression had swept millions of people and a great deal of the world of his childhood away like the sins of John Rudolph in the muddy waters of Lanes Creek.

What was the source of his faith and hope in the late afternoon of this day that any of those whom he loved remained? Isaiah had no name for his hope, but his pulse quickened as he topped the last ridge before the homestead. He caught his breath at the sight of a curl of smoke rising from the chimney of his cabin home in the gloaming of the day. Before he could even question whether the smoke rose from his own people or carpetbaggers, the form of his mother looked up from the gathering of her wash on the line by the side of the cabin. Neve Buckland held her hand in salute over her eyes, shielding them against the last rays of the summer sun as it westered over the ridgeline behind the form of a man on the hill. Isaiah knew her moment of recognition of the apparition of her long-dead son when a high-piercing cry reached his ears as the woman fell to her knees.

Geneva Buckland cried out as women have done since the time of mother Eve. She cried out for the piercing of her heart by the child of her womb. She cried the cry that women have cried for all time over the men of the earth. James Buckland bolted from the old woodworking shop and came to the aid of his stricken wife. By the time he reached her, lifted her to her feet, and looked up, he stared into the eyes of his dead boy. All blood drained from his face, and the force of life abandoned his own legs. He might have fallen had it not been for the strong arms of his own Lazarus as Isaiah wrapped a muscular arm around each of his aging, grief-worn parents. As he held them tightly, through the open doors of the woodworking shed he saw a nearly finished wooden replica of himself as a boy, glowing richly in the very last rays of the setting sun.

Epilogue

Isaiah's mother and father had squeezed him until black and blue, trying to allay all fears that he would evaporate into the evening mist. His father then took him by the hand and led him into the cabin. In the small back bedroom of the downstairs, Isaiah drew in his breath realizing the last shred of his highest hopes of reunion.

The ancient form of Josiah Buckland lay propped up in his bed with his long rifle mounted on the wall above his white head. The statue of Isaiah's long-dead grandmother, Vancie, great with child, was ensconced in the corner, where it had remained all of James's life and Isaiah's life. Isaiah quietly approached the now milky eyes of Josiah Buckland. Reaching into his pocket, he retrieved the small gold pocket watch sent off with him to war and pressed the cool form of it into his grandfather's calloused hand. Instantly, a flash of recognition escaped the old man as he fumbled for the hidden latch. He pressed it, and the back cover sprang open as it dropped into his lap. Like a child reaching for his mother, the patriarch reached out and pulled the face of the prodigal Isaiah close to his own. With his yellowed hands, he traced each line and crevice of Isaiah's tear-stained face. As the smile broadened on the old man's ancient visage, he glanced down at the watch now unreadable to him with his eyes, but with a full heart he whispered to the boy, *"J.B. loves V. K."*

Somewhere in the now dark night of the homestead, all the fireflies blinked as one and the haunting hoot of an owl echoed through the depths of the forest where a beautiful young girl danced, her long wait for her love nearly complete.

BLUE SEA:

WILD HORSES

Prologue

WHEN THE FIRES started, some of the field hands fled. After Mr. Dred tore off on his big horse, Buck, the rest of them ran. All but Robert. He stood there with his hands in his overall pockets, sweat pouring down his face. The sweat came from the mounting inferno beginning to encircle the house and the rising panic and indecision growing in his gut. He had seen Mr. Dred mounting Buck. The sheriff had thrown two sacks over the saddle, surely containing the bulk of his cash money, but there had been no time for the heavy mounds of gold coins in the strongbox under the bed. Several times while the kitchen maid, Bertie, had mopped the hall or entered Mr. Dred's room to empty his slop jar in the morning, she heard the plink of metal coins as the master of the house had risen from his knees in his nightshirt, slapped the lid of the strongbox down, clicked the heavy lock, and kicked the chest under the skirt of his bed. No word was spoken to Bertie, just a quick, hate-filled glance that clearly said, "Tell my secret, and I will cut your damned throat."

For a long time, she kept her tongue; but one night too full of liquor in Robert's bed, she had bragged, "Mistuh Dred's rich. Richer than any of us even thought. Richer than ole King Creeshus or the Bank of Peachland."

After she and Robert had satisfied each other, she sleepily described what she saw the Mister doing with the box under his bed. By morning, as far as Robert could tell, Bertie remembered nothing of her secret telling from the night before.

CHAPTER ONE
Crime

Now, Robert stood conflicted. For the time being, the strongbox lay unguarded. The dragon had fled his lair surrounded by flames. The field hands and house servants had fled. Bertie was long gone. There would be no witnesses. The only question was whether he could move fast enough to outrun the fires, the vengeance of Dred Mabry, and the wrath of a righteous Baptist God in the Great Judgment. Though Robert felt paralyzed from fear, he became aware that his feet were moving slowly and then very quickly. He fetched the two remaining mules from the barn, hitched them to a wagon, rode to the root cellar, loaded the wagon with provisions, and then parked the wagon close to the front steps of the Mabry home. He tightly lashed the reins to the porch banister. The heat, smoke, and advancing flames had filled the mules with panic, so he did not have long. The smoke from the fires had already penetrated the stairwell and hallways of the big house. Coughing violently, Robert took the stairs two by two and kicked back the Mister's partially opened door. Getting on his knees, he grabbed the handles of the old chest and heaved it toward him.

"Dear Gawd in heaven, you done tricked me. This thing's gonna bust me open trying to git it down the stairs."

Robert Carter was young and had muscles like ropes, but he felt the veins popping out on his forehead as he carried the strongbox to the stairs. The young fieldworker struggled as he negotiated the steps. He tried not to break his spine as he leaned backward or pitch himself head first to his death if he leaned forward. He made it to the landing and down half of the front porch steps. Finally, in one last Herculean heave, he tossed the chest the rest of the way into the back of the wagon. Gravity was his friend; but from the cracking sound as the strongbox landed, he thought that it might break through the wagon and land on the ground. Despite his fears, the oak slats held. The mules screamed as the chest crashed. Robert grabbed the reins and lunged onto the buckboard seat.

As he jumped, he tossed a flaming branch back onto the porch to help Mother Nature. The house had to burn. Making one last circle, he threw another flaming limb into the barn. The barn had to burn too. He had to leave debris, ashes, doubt, and confusion to erase the evidence of the crime and to slow down Dred Mabry as long as possible. Now, Robert had to run far and fast, leaving little proof of his whereabouts because one day a force more deadly than rabid dogs, hornets, and a watery pit of moccasins would follow him, torture him, and make him beg for the flames of hell before cutting his throat. Only a childhood of deprivation and abuse and the rank stupidity of youth could ever have tempted him to defy an evil White sheriff in Anson County, North Carolina. It was too late now. Dred Mabry's house exploded in flames behind him, and Robert Carter lashed the backside of the two mules until blood ran as the wagon headed East.

CHAPTER TWO
Down East

ROBERT TRAVELED EASTWARD and mainly at night for several reasons. Very few Black folks lived in western North Carolina. Farther west, he would draw more attention. The eastern part of the state was filled with his kind from past days of slavery and current days of tobacco. Most of his people remained poor, so seeing a Black man driving a mule-drawn wagon was nothing special down east. Nor was seeing one traveling the sides of the roads at night to avoid the growing stream of White people in new cars and trucks as the Great Depression finally drew to a close. For a week, Robert had settled into a pattern.

When the sun came up, he took to the pine woods, preferably near a creek or stream on the most desolate stretch of road he could find at the end of his day's journey. After settling the wagon into a grove of trees, he would pitch the oilcloth covering over the back to fend off the bloodsucking horseflies that densely populated creek beds in the South. After replenishing water supplies when available, Robert would build the smallest fire possible. Then he would roast a potato or two, open a can of beans, and make a pot of coffee. The mules nibbled grass and rations of grain from the back of the wagon. Pretty poor fare for a rich man and his animals on the run, but it filled their bellies and comforted them for the beginning of sleep.

Most of the time, the retired field hand slept well. Occasionally, the moan of a car whizzing down the road in the distance or the faraway bark of a dog interrupted his sleep, but he quickly found oblivion again. The tarp created a bit of cool and shade from the summer sun. His conscience did not bother him in the least, and he could not yet imagine Dred Mabry on his trail. All were ingredients for a good sleep.

As the sun waned in the west, Robert rose, broke camp, and hit the road as darkness fell. Most nights were the same. The movement of the wagon kept some of the mosquitoes at bay. Nameless stars that had guided some of his people to freedom sparked. Various stages of the moon shone down. When the rains came, he pulled up his jacket collar and backed himself up under the edge of the overhanging tarp. Eat, sleep, ride; eat, sleep, ride. Day after day. No work for the first time in memory. The good life had already begun. He softly sang "Follow the Drinking Gourd." Robert rode on, only this time east instead of north.

> *"Follow the drinkin' gourd*
> *Follow the drinkin' gourd*
> *For the old man is comin' just to carry you to freedom*
> *Follow the drinkin' gourd*
> *When the sun comes back, and the first quail calls*
> *Follow the drinkin' gourd*
> *For the old man is waiting just to carry you to freedom*
> *Follow the drinkin' gourd*
> *Well, the river bank makes a mighty good road*
> *Dead trees will show you the way*
> *Left foot, peg foot, travelin' on*
> *Follow the drinkin' gourd*

Well, the river ends, between two hills
Follow the drinkin' gourd
There's another river on the other side
Follow the drinkin' gourd
Well, where the great big river meets the little river
Follow the drinkin' gourd
The old man is waiting to carry you to freedom
Follow the drinkin' gourd"

CHAPTER THREE
Bright Lights

WHEN HE LEFT Peachland over a week ago, his first thought had been to flee to Wilmington. Many Black folks lived there. If Mr. Dred ever caught up with him, he might be able to board a ship and put a big part of the world between himself and the murderous sheriff. As he slowly approached the city, he realized his mistake. Lights loomed on the eastern horizon, and cars and trucks increasingly clogged the roads even at night. Water became brackish and foul from waste disposed of in the waterways. The sweetness of the country air that Robert had always known faded. Too little privacy, too many eyes, and too much change.

Late at night on the outskirts of Wilmington, Robert turned north. Maybe New Bern. Smaller city but still with opportunities for escape by water. Days later, as Robert approached the beautiful port city, he panicked again. He was running low on supplies. He had bought a few things at lonely country stores, but his meager pocket money was running low. He had little education, but he knew that a poor, young Black man couldn't walk into a store in downtown New Bern and hand a White man or woman a gold coin. Every counter in those stores shielded an ax handle or a gun for just such occasions to slow him down until the police arrested or killed him. What was he thinking? The gold might as well be rocks for all the good it was doing him.

He needed a small place off the main paths where he could pass a coin to one of his own kind for a case of liquor and then trade the liquor for other things. It would take a long while to slowly and discreetly turn the gold into wealth. It would be years in fact, but he was young and had lots of years ahead. Later, his new wife could help him. Never two coins to one person. Never too close together in time or space. But what place? Looking up, he saw a sign on the side of the road—"Beaufort, 67 miles." Pulling out an old map he had found on the side of the road, he looked at the dot that was Beaufort. Small. Isolated. On the water. Maybe a job fishing for cover. Boats for escape. Robert Carter shouted into the dark, cracking his whip over the heads of his two jack mules, "Come up, Pap. Come up, Hap. Beaufort it is."

CHAPTER FOUR
The Coast

AFTER NEARLY TWO weeks on the run, Robert was anxious for his first sighting of Beaufort. The sleepy little fishing village was finally just a mile or two away, but before Robert rode around town, he had an errand to perform. The first part of the errand would be the fulfillment of a lifelong dream. The young man had never seen the ocean, but the salty musk of it had already begun to register in his nose and excite his senses.

For two long weeks, the landscape had flattened to the grade of an old cast-iron skillet. Oak trees had disappeared, replaced almost exclusively by pines. The red clay of the fields back home had transitioned to yellow and then white sand. All the changes had been slow and subtle, but Robert sensed the nearness of dramatic change. In addition to the sting of salt, the wind increased in force and unfamiliar birds thickly populated the blue sky above. The road was now just a sandy trace heading in a straight line through wax myrtle, yaupon, and scrub brush straight toward the sea.

The fugitive waited for the loud crash of the waves he had heard about as a boy, but the loudest sounds remained the whistling of the wind and cries of the white birds. Finally, Robert reached an enormous expanse of water with small waves lapping along the shoreline. His disappointment in the waves was the only thing that tempered the stories from his boyhood. The rest of the scene of water sparkling with sunlight was glorious and filled Robert's lungs with brine and his heart with wild optimism.

What he did not know was that in approaching the ocean from the west in North Carolina, the first expanses of water are more often bays or sounds rather than the full flood of the Atlantic. The small islands scattered near and far in the sound formed a protective barrier from the wildness and at times wrath of the cold, bluish-gray waters of the Atlantic. What Robert saw was parts of the sound at North River and a collection of small islands hoping to survive the next storm or hurricane. None of that mattered to the weary traveler. In some strange, exotic sense, he was home.

Now, it was time for the second part of his errand. He could not risk taking Dred Mabry's strongbox into Beaufort. As a Black stranger in town, a policeman or any other White man might want to search his wagon. He just couldn't take a chance. Like the Ole Black-Bearded Man he had heard about from his grandfather, Robert had decided to bury his treasure too. He had muscle, a shovel, and gold. All he needed was a place. It couldn't be on the mainland. Too many people might notice the telltale signs of a recently dug hole.

It had to be one of the small islands in the shallow waters of the sound. Scanning his options, Robert chose the nearest one to the shoreline. It had some vegetation to hold the sand in place until he could move the treasure to a more secure home. With his hiding place in sight, he slapped the backsides of Hap and Pap and drove them against their instincts into the clear, shallow waters of North River Sound at low tide. Though the water never rose above the height of the wheels on the wagon, its driver had to repeatedly beat the rumps of the ornery mules to force them forward across the hundred yards or so of the channel. Both his team and Robert breathed better when the wagon reached solid ground again. The sensation of sitting high in the wagon surveying water in all directions was disorienting, and he fought for equilibrium before hopping down on the ground.

It was late afternoon and would take some time to create a hole deep enough to bury the chest. The state's newest pirate set straight to work. Gravity made unloading the chest far easier than loading it. With the strongbox quickly on the sand, Robert began excavating a massive hole in unstable earth buffeted by scorching sun and unbearable humidity. He just thought he had sweated in the red-clay cotton fields of the Piedmont. Any exertion on the coast brought trickles of liquid streaming down his back, chest, and the inside of his thighs. Occasionally, he paused and let the ever-present wind dry his body liquids. As soon as he started to shovel again, the pumps resumed, irrigating his entire body. He had no watch, but the lowering sun told him when enough would have to be enough. It was time to drop the strongbox into its new home. But first, he had to have a look.

Taking his shovel blade, he struck the massive lock, sending sparks flying. Again and again, the blade dropped until the old lock finally hung open in defeat. Snatching it from the chest, he threw back the lid and gasped. Brilliant loose coins of various denominations and dates lay scattered across the bottom of the bare portion of the chest. Multiple cloth bags of coins and a smaller chest of what might be bars filled the remainder of the box. Robert gasped with glee, scooping up handfuls of the loose coins with shaking hands and filling his overall pockets. Soon, he had captured all the loose treasure. The rest would have to wait for another day. His young heart was already pounding from exertion and excitement as the sun neared the horizon.

He resealed the chest with a new lock from his wagon and dropped the key into his pocket with the coins. Then it was time to refill the hole and make a run toward Beaufort. Robert needed to see if he might find a room with some of his last silver money before darkness fell. He wanted to celebrate his victory in a bed tonight.

Completing his work and remounting his much lighter wagon, Robert turned his mules toward the mainland and slapped them sharply across their rumps. With a bray, Hap and Pap bounded back into the water. However, after a few yards, the driver knew something was wrong. The wagon wheels sank much deeper and much more quickly into the waters of the bay. Struggling for control, Robert beat the beasts more fiercely. For a few more yards, the pair reluctantly forged forward. Then without warning, both screamed in unison. The mules reared up, cracking the wooden guides to which they were lashed and tipping the wagon and its driver into the deepening waters of the sound. As coastal folk say, Robert was a dingbatter, an inland dweller unfamiliar with the rise and fall of tides and the intricacies of their dance with sun and moon. He would have been doomed even if the wagon had not landed on him, pinning him to the sandy bottom of the bay.

He shared another trait of the dingbatters that was incomprehensible to the High Tiders of the coast: He could not swim. To people of the sea, he might just as well have never learned to breathe. In a couple of minutes, his last breath bubbled to the surface of his rippling, watery grave. Within hours, the motions of rising and receding waters worked all the glittering coins in his pockets out and scattered them across the shifting sands of the sound. Finally, within days, the crabs released the last morsels of flesh from bones, both large and small, and settled back satisfied for a time into the muddy bottoms of nearby tidal creeks.

CHAPTER FIVE
The Coin

TRISTAN MCCLURE'S TEETH clicked together as his beat-up red Schwinn bicycle hit another pothole on the sandy backroad to the sound. It was a sorry excuse for transportation for a boy in the 1970s. All he could hear was the clicking of the jokers out of a new pack of playing cards that he had attached to his spokes and the occasional cry of a gull overhead. Sounds were not his problem. He was pedaling like the devil to get ahead of the funk of his pubescent body after another shift at the fish factory. The stench of sweat, BO, blood, and fish guts hung one turn of his pedals behind him, nipping at his backside as he rode straight-legged, butt-off-the-seat down the old, unpaved coastal path. As he pedaled, sweat stung his large blue eyes, flecked with gray.

Just around the last bend, the first refreshing sight of the sparkling waters of the back sound at North River came into view. Whitecaps danced across the grayish-blue sheen of liquid that stretched out to the first of the barrier islands and beyond. He would have loved to have taken a mullet skiff out to baptize himself in the cold, pounding surf of the Atlantic in Onslow Bay on one of the island beaches, but there was no time left of the September afternoon. The backwaters of the sound would serve his purpose. Reaching the edge of its water, Tristan's bike went one way and he another. Landing on his feet with one motion, his putrid, previously white T-shirt flew up into the sun-filled air. With another motion, his stained, fringed jean shorts and underwear came down. He danced for a moment in the intoxicating salt air, shaking his mop of brown hair and small white ass in the sun and air of the afternoon.

Hopping across the prickly ground cover of the shoreline, the boy painfully pulled a sandbur from his naked right foot before leaping into the cleansing waters of the North River estuary. He dove toward the shallow bottom, swishing about for a bit before bursting through the surface like a dolphin in search of breath. The water was now deep enough to tread and float on the surface of the bay. Though Tristan's teeth chattered a little from the coolness of the water, the sun beamed down on his hair plastered to his head and illuminated his torso dangling down into the opaqueness below. Even with the murkiness of the bay, he was pleased to see how brown most of his body had become over the course of the summer. Only his midsection stood out in pale contrast, highlighting his dick and tufts of dark hair dancing in the water. Someday, he might even have a six-pack like his Uncle Marcus if he worked at the shad factory long enough. Tristan was still skinny as a rail but was growing tauter each day. Glancing around, he reached one hand down and pleasured himself, emboldened by the isolation of the bay and the pleasing sensation of moving water.

When he finished, the boy took one last cleansing dive to the sandy bottom. His eyes were wide open and stinging. With his whole body stretching upward, his field of sight was open to take in every weed, rock, and shell that lay below. Nothing in particular caught his fancy until the lengthening rays of the afternoon sun struck something that sparked. Reaching downward, Tristan dug his hand into the sand and mud until it closed around something small, hard, and thin. Stroking upward as best he could with one hand opened and one closed, the boy reached the surface. As he treaded water, he shook his clenched fist in the brine to remove all the detritus except the captured object.

Opening his fist in the last red rays of the sun, Tristan took in a sharp breath as his hand was set ablaze.

"Gold," the boy whispered in childlike wonder.

Tristan had rarely ever held a silver dollar. Never in his wildest dreams did he believe he would see a twenty dollar gold piece much less grasp one in his fist. After savoring the sensation for a moment, he swam to the shallows, splashed one foot after another to shore, and shook his naked body before gathering his clothes. Shorts, shirt, and shoes on, he mounted his bicycle renewed in body and spirit and headed back to civilization in Beaufort.

CHAPTER SIX
Beaufort

If Beaufort had been located a hundred miles inland, it would have been a pretty, but ordinary, town. Its age as a colonial settlement with British soldiers in its graveyard and neatly planned rows of charming white clapboard houses would still distinguish it, but the sheer magic of Beaufort was its proximity to the sea. A two-block walk could take a citizen or visitor from a quiet street deeply shaded by oaks to the blinding light of the waterfront punctuated by the pungent smell of marsh and the piercing cries of seabirds overhead.

The view was soon to get dramatically better on Front Street, much to the dismay of the long-term populous of the village. After more than two hundred years, change was coming quickly and dramatically to Beaufort. It had escaped many of the forces of history that had swept the nation, but it was not to escape the current call for "urban renewal." Locals blamed the inland dingbatters who now wandered into town at an ever-increasing rate. Sometimes, they crashed into local shops in their bikinis and cutoff jeans, reeking of suntan lotion and shocking and embarrassing the morals of older denizens.

Although the list was not quite complete, flyers hung like toe tags in the morgue on most of the buildings on the east side of Front Street. Casualties so far looked like they would include Bailey Jewelers, C.D. Jones Grocery, A&P Food Store, City Grocery, Bank of Beaufort (later

Rumley's nursery & feed store), Carteret Hardware, Pender Grocery Co., Jeff's Barber Shop & Dora's Beauty Shop, Beaufort Hardware, C.B. Hill Grocery, Bell's Drug Store, Mathis Café, S.W. Davis & Bro. Seafood, Eudy's Barber Shop, Ramsey Grocery, W.V.B. Potter's fish house, Davis Fish Company, Biggs Shoe Shop, Ideal Dry Cleaners, and Way's fish house. In earlier years, the older folks watched with pride as their fishing village grew in a slow, organic fashion. Now, many of them had lived long enough to anticipate with horror the amputation of much of what brought familiarity and comfort to their aging souls. All in the name of progress.

In fairness, the handwriting had been on the wall for more than a decade. Most of the fish factories that had brought stench and dollars to Beaufort for decades were long shuttered. Only one remained—the Beaufort Fish Company. So, in essence, the village was slowly, but gracefully, dying. The younger members of the town council faced the truth with gritted teeth. Most of the money in North Carolina lay inland in uglier, burgeoning cities like Charlotte, Greensboro, and Raleigh. Those folks had no taste for menhaden but could not get enough of their weekend jaunts to the coast. Tearing down one side of downtown Beaufort would give them what they longed for—an unobstructed view of Taylor Creek and the open vista of the sea and Shackleford Banks.

Though painful, opening Beaufort to the sea held the prospect of an influx of local tourists, hippies, and Yankees who would make the remaining cash registers ring and save the town from a slide into genteel poverty. Tristan McClure knew nothing of these things as he pedaled back into town in the dusk. He had been delivered to Beaufort at the turning of the tide.

CHAPTER SEVEN
Marcus

THE HOUSE THAT Tristan returned to that evening was a strange one. Once upon a time, it had been a home before his grandpa and grandma died, leaving his teenaged Uncle Marcus as its sole surviving occupant. Tristan's dad, long gone, had deeded his portion of the property to his baby brother to keep a roof over the boy's head and assuage his own guilt regarding his unwillingness to return to the confines of Beaufort. Life as a trucker had provided all he needed for himself and Tristan and kept him safely away from the ghosts of his hometown. After all, Marcus had already left school and taken a man's job at the Beaufort Fish Company. He was too old and wild to be parented by an older brother and could fend for himself.

That turned out to be only partially true. Marcus did survive but fared better than his homeplace. With his mother, father, and older brother gone, within a few years the house was in a state of steady decline. Shingles blew off in hurricanes and nor'easters. Paint peeled. Weeds flourished. The roof leaked. His mama's well-tended roses failed, and the dwelling fell increasingly under suspicion of occupation by poor White trash. After his mama's passing, her china, needlepoint samplers, and other lady things ended up at the local antique or junk store at the end of most months. They helped replace the cash that Marcus had spent on a hell of a lot of Pabst Blue Ribbon for himself and his friends. His crowd took over the house on weekends to drink, listen to Led Zeppelin albums, and have sex. During the wildest of those times, Tristan would retreat to his room upstairs, lock the door, and lay waiting in his sweltering bed for everyone to pass out or for the cops or dawn to arrive.

Weekdays were far quieter but just as lonely. Tristan never spoke with his uncle on weekday mornings. Marcus awoke in the bedroom directly across the hall from his own at four. His hairy, well-muscled body emerged in his jockey shorts each morning underneath a harsh, bare lightbulb ignited by a string hanging in the air by his bed. He then staggered tight-eyed, like a mole, toward the bathroom at the end of the hall to pee, clearing his throat and scratching his butt on the way. Though he cleaned up well for the ladies, he looked like the creature from the black lagoon at four in the morning. Within an hour, he would dress, grab something out of the fridge, and be on the docks for a man's day of work either on a boat or in the fish processing plant.

Gone were Tristan's grandfather's days of sea shanties and sailing ships. Marcus worked in a mechanized world on an old WW II mine sweeper refitted to capture menhaden by the thousands and disgorge them into a factory that would reduce them to oil and fertilizer in short order. Machinery had destroyed the old ways in the fishing industry on the coast, logging on the slopes of the mountains and cotton farming in the Piedmont. Silence was replaced by noise, the individual by the collective, and the bond between human and earth by the tyranny of efficiency and the bottom line. Five days a week and more often six, Marcus was just a cog in a machine belching the stench of dead fish and money into the air that hung over the venerable village of Beaufort.

Once the screen door slapped shut downstairs, Tristan was on his own. He had to rise as a young teen each morning, trying to remember his father's voice and the fainter voice of his mother. In past days, they had provided his instruction for dressing, hygiene, nutrition, and punctuality to get himself to school on time. Later in the day, he would arrive at the fish plant for a few hours to work, clean up, and pay for his impact on expenses at the house. Except for an occasional buck or two tossed back to him by Marcus for a hot dog or movie, he surrendered his wages to his uncle on Fridays for the good of the cause and the bottom line of the Pabst Blue Ribbon company. That, in part, was why feeling the weight of the coin in his pocket in the lulls of the day was intoxicating. For an orphaned kid, it was the only thrill in an unending series of soulless days and often sleep-deprived nights.

CHAPTER EIGHT
Parents

Tristan had not always been an orphan. He too had once had parents like the kids in his class. His memories of his mother, Carol, were now more faded because she had passed first when Tristan was only six. By first grade, the box on his permanent record for "mother" read simply "deceased." Like most boys, he thought of his mama as beautiful. Details were few now, but he was sure that her eyes had been cobalt blue like the sea. She would have said that they were blue like the mountains in North Carolina. That was where Tristan's daddy, David , had found her before cajoling her to marry him and settle in Beaufort.

She did marry and come to Beaufort, but she never settled. The coast would always remain alien to her. She loved Robert but never made peace with the constant wind and screeching gulls of his home. The worst part for her was the ocean itself. Having only waded in creeks as a child, she found the depth of the ocean and its storms terrifying. She refused to learn to swim and retained a morbid fear of drowning.

Carol had no way of knowing that her peril lay within rather than without. In her late twenties, she began to cough incessantly. After folk remedies and local doctors failed to provide relief, Robert took her to Wilmington for care. The diagnosis came quickly and with devastating impact—cancer. Oddly, lung cancer. Carol had never smoked. Her doctors just said that it was more complicated than people realized. From the start, there was little time and even less hope.

Within months, Robert watched his beloved young wife age and shrink in the hospital bed that had been set up in the downstairs living room. Having recently lost his own parents from age-related illnesses, he was not prepared for the unrelenting ravages of cancer. In the last stage of her disease, women were hired to sit with Carol as Robert tried to keep working at the fish plant. That brought a tragedy of its own.

One day when he returned home, Carol weakly announced that a much-treasured piece of jewelry that had belonged to her grandmother and other women in the family before her was missing. Robert interrogated the healthcare workers and ransacked the house without success on either front. Screaming in frustration, he fired all the women and tried without success to console what remained of his wife. All the while, his younger brother, Marcus, kept silent watch and greater distance from his crazed, older brother.

As is typically the case with children when adults are caught up in their own troubles, Tristan was often forgotten. Extended family and neighbors would feed him and then exile him to the yard to "protect him" from what was happening inside. Tristan only vaguely remembered the funeral. His next memory was of his father pulling up in a truck one morning, quickly loading him and a few possessions, dropping the key to the house on the table, and hitting the road. Life for the next seven years consisted of endless cross-country trips with his daddy trying to make a living as a trucker and escape his demons.

That continued until the day they jackknifed on ice in Oklahoma. Tristan survived, but his father did not. His last memory of his dad was of him writing the name and address of his Uncle Marcus on a sheet of paper for the social worker at the hospital. A couple of days later, after crossing half of the country on a Greyhound bus, Tristan stood on the porch of a house he barely remembered. He repeatedly rang the bell. The door was finally opened by his wide-eyed, angry uncle.

"Welcome home, butt wipe," he growled in greeting.

CHAPTER NINE
Iris

NOT EVERY DAY in Tristan's life that first summer was uneventful. A few weeks later, on Sunday afternoon at about two, Marcus walked through the front screen door in swim shorts and shirtless, brushing dried sand from his ankles and chest on the parlor carpet. Snatching his knock-off Ray-Bans from the top of his head, he shouted, "Damn, it's hot out there!"

Dropping the swimsuit at the foot of the stairs, he mounted them two by two, spewing words as he went. "Hitting the shower. Iris decided to clean up out back. She'll be in in a minute. Fix us a sandwich!"

Tristan was tired of Marcus treating him like a maid. He would get around to the sandwiches to keep the peace, but first he wanted to say hello to Iris.

It's a sad fact of life that tools like Marcus end up with the hot girls. Iris Hill was certainly no exception to the rule. She was gorgeous. Even though she had grown up on the wrong side of town and had a drunk for a daddy, she had stayed in school and even worked part time. She toiled as a barmaid at the Handle Bar to earn back part of the money that her father left there most nights. She was tough but had a good heart. Way too good for Marcus. Tristan would only take a few minutes to hang out with her as she hosed off, and it would fortify his spirits for kitchen duty.

As he rounded the back corner of the house, he realized his error. The garden hose lay in a pile by the abandoned vegetable garden. The sound of water came from within the rusty, corrugated walls of the seldom used outdoor shower. There was no door, just offset walls of tin. From one small spot in the yard, he could see Iris's sun-dappled figure inside. His whole body went rigid, and blood pounded in his ears. He had never seen a naked woman before, certainly not one like this. Iris stood with her blond hair plastered back on her head and to her long nape. Her perfectly rounded white buttocks faced him, framed in contrast to the tanned flesh on the other sides of her tan lines. For just a second, she pivoted to the side and Tristan saw a quick flash of darkness below. At that moment, he thought he would lose consciousness, and a few seconds later he nearly did.

A force from behind hit him like a linebacker, knocking the breath from his lungs and catapulting his face and torso into the grass and sandburs of the backyard. Pain shot through his entire body. It grew much worse as his attacker flipped him over, punched him in the face, and spat in rage, "You little pervert. What are you doing leering at my girlfriend, you piece of crap? I take you into my house, and this is what I get!"

Marcus raised his fist again, but it was caught midair in a vise. Iris had bolted from the shower wrapped in a beach towel and captured Marcus from behind. One hand held his wrist, and the other gripped the back of his long hair.

"Stop it, you big ape. What the hell is wrong with you! He's just a horny kid, you stupid bully."

She steered him a few feet away from Tristan and released him when he stopped struggling. His body relaxed and his breathing slowed, but hate blazed in his eyes as he glared at his sobbing nephew. Iris had quickly moved to comfort the boy as Marcus bellowed, "Shut up, you pansy."

Fire lit up Iris's eyes as she glanced back in anger at her boyfriend. Softly, she said, "Tristan, you are a good kid."

The boy bristled despite his tears. Continuing, she said, "In the future, if you need any help in being a perv, just ask your Uncle Marcus. He is the king of the pervs and one messed up, twisted dude. Kind of cute on a good day but still really messed up."

Now, Marcus bristled.

Iris continued, "You guys make quite a pair. Tristan, take a little bit of good advice from me. If you see another naked woman before you finish puberty, just drop your eyes and turn your back instead of gawking at her like a bullfrog."

Tristan stopped his sniffling and blushed. He pulled himself together but only for a moment. Suddenly, he saw Marcus smile broadly and lunge forward into the grass beside him.

"Well, blow me down. What do we have here. Lose something, nephew? Finders keepers, as they say."

Tristan sat transfixed in horror as his uncle lifted his shining coin up into the glare of the afternoon light. Despair and rage swept over the boy.

"Give it to me! It's mine."

"Where would a punk kid like you get a twenty dollar gold piece, you little liar? By the way, do you know that these things are illegal?"

Suddenly, Tristan was the liar. "My daddy gave that to me. You know, your dead brother. It's the only thing he left me."

Tristan played the family card, dead card, and orphan card one after another, trying to dislodge his treasure from his uncle's strong, clenched fist. It did not work. Marcus stood resolute until a more resolute presence demanded, "Give the boy his coin. It may not be his, but it sure as hell is not yours. Give it to him, or you will be using that hand for the only pleasure that you will see for the rest of the summer."

The uncooperative girlfriend card worked. Marcus threw the coin at Tristan. Still fuming, he shouted, "It's yours ... for now. But you are still a liar, and someday you're going to tell me where it really came from and whether there is any more. I work too hard in a shitty fish factory to keep a roof over our heads. I will be damned if you are going to prance around here with gold in your pocket while I work myself to death. We'll settle this later."

Iris took Marcus by the arm and dragged him around the house for some cooldown time upstairs. Later, when he came down for his delayed sandwich, he seemed much better. The now tamed beast ravenously ate three sandwiches instead of one, and for the time being made no further mention to Tristan of the coin.

CHAPTER TEN
Miss Kitty

BY AGE ELEVEN, Iris Hill had decided that she descended from at least fourteen kinds of trailer trash. By name, she could work down the list of pot growers, drug dealers, hookers, pool sharks, moonshiners, and bookies in multiple generations of her clan. Hers was a family of carpetbaggers and scalawags. By sixteen, she was working a shit job to make up for the shortcomings of her drunk father and pill-popping mother.

Her boobs came in early, so she had been pinched, butt-slapped, and groped by every low-life creep in the county. Some girls it would have broken, but it all just made her angry and tough before her time. Not one biker in the Handle Bar had ever seen her cry, but a few had felt her right knee crack them in the nuts when things had gotten really out of control.

Life came into focus for her one night while watching *Gunsmoke* in middle school. Good thing that the show was in black and white because nothing on their small TV at the trailer park was in color, not even the NBC peacock or the rest of *The Wizard of Oz* after Dorothy left Kansas. Miss Kitty Russell was her favorite character on the show. Miss Kitty wasn't just a whore—she was a whore wrangler, a madam. Still, people respected her. She ran a successful business, was strong and Marshall Dillon was sweet on her. Most of all, Miss Kitty was a good woman. With all her baggage, she chose to be good. Being good is a choice, so at the ripe old age of twelve, Iris Hill decided to be good. It was her choice.

CHAPTER ELEVEN
Shackleford Banks

It took all of a week before Marcus resurrected the issue of the coin.

"Alright, punk, where did you get the gold?"

Tristan had been rehearsing this conversation in his head for days.

"On the beach at Shackleford Banks. It washed up on a wave. No others in sight. I looked for a couple of hours."

Marcus squinted slightly and pounced. "Seriously, you expect me to believe that you went to Shackleford in my johnboat after only pissing around in a boat on your own in the shallows in Taylor Creek. Give me a break. Come on. Fess up!"

Tristan said calmly, "Of course not. I went to see Old Pete, who used to run the mail route around here and Harkers Island in his boat. He said no boy from inland could live in Beaufort and stay a dingbatter. I needed to go to deeper waters on the banks, see the Atlantic from the beach, and start earning my stripes as a High Tider. Pete took me."

Marcus's eyes smoldered. "Listen, you little ape. You can sail to Africa if you want to, but trust me, no little landlubber like you will ever be a High Tider. For generations, the real men in our family busted their asses hauling nets, facing down hurricanes, and spitting and pissing into the wind. No little candy ass like you will ever be a High Tider."

Marcus punctuated his last sentence by spitting a stream of chewing tobacco juice onto the porch and the end of Tristan's Keds.

A couple of weeks later, he was more conciliatory. "Hey, kid, it's time for you to earn another of your 'High Tider' stripes." Marcus winked. "Me and Iris are headed out to Shackleford to surf fish. The drum and blues are running. I don't want you to be a complete embarrassment to this family. It's time for you to learn how to fish. Meet me and Iris down at the dock about eight on Sunday morning. I'm going to see if that thick head of yours can soak up some real education."

On Sunday, Tristan pedaled his bike down to the dock. Marcus had picked up Iris in his beloved candy-apple-red Dodge Charger. By the time Tristan arrived, the two of them had loaded a small backpack with water, a couple of beers, leftover roast beef sandwiches from the tavern, and bait into an old battered crab boat borrowed from a friend. Next came the fishing gear and last a long mystery object in a small canvas bag. Before Tristan even asked, Marcus unmoored the craft and shouted, "None of your beeswax, nephew. Jump in!"

Tristan leapt and awkwardly landed against Iris. She smelled like lavender soap and suntan lotion. He looked straight ahead to keep his eyes off her bare legs and thanked God that she had on a T-shirt with sleeves and that he had on a light, but long, windbreaker.

"Hey, handsome, ready for an adventure?"

Her voice made his flesh tingle, and he focused on it to steady his stomach as the water whitecapped a bit and the boat bobbed up and down. By the time they arrived on the backside of Shackleford, even Iris's voice and occasional pat on the knee were barely enough to keep Tristan from losing his breakfast. As he bounced, he wondered how the men of Beaufort went to sea every day, sucked up millions of shad, emptied crab traps, gathered oysters, and took tourists out into the Gulf Stream deep sea fishing. For someone from inland, the whole nature of life lived here in the lulls between nor'easters and hurricanes was unnatural and insane. At they neared the island, the water finally became nearly calm or "slick cam" as the old-timers say.

Landing on the back of the barrier island, Marcus and Iris stepped out onto dry land, and Tristan stepped into another world. Hundreds of gulls and terns gathered over their small craft, hovering and diving in search of food. Now, Tristan understood why their lunch and bait was so snugly secured in the knapsack. The birds were insatiable. In their small brains, boats equaled food. The trio gathered their belongings and distanced themselves from the crab boat.

Within moments, they were engulfed in the largest dunes Tristan had ever seen. They followed a well-defined path, which Iris said had been laid down by the wild horses on the island. The horses were said to be descendants of precolonial Spanish mustangs. Tristan's heart soared. He appreciated the beauty of Beaufort, but Beaufort was placid on a good day and downright boring on a bad one. Shackleford, just a short boat trip away, was exotic and wild. The few trees that survived were bent from the buffeting of the wind, and down between the dunes the only sounds that came to their ears were those of birds and the growing hiss of the surf in the distance.

Tristan's heart pounded in anticipation and nearly burst when they topped the last dune. With little warning, the wild, gray, whitecapped Atlantic stretched to the horizon. Marcus and Iris seemed unaffected, but Tristan stood for a moment, transfixed and a bit dizzy from the sheer scope and scale of the open sea. Marcus barked back at him, "Sheez, keep up douche and stop dragging my fishing gear in the sand. What is wrong with you?"

Tristan tried to pull himself together, but in a moment his efforts were foiled. A high shrieking sound erupted down the beach, and a small herd of the wild horses of Shackleford Banks thundered from the dunes. They sprayed surf from beneath their hooves as they approached, passed, and then disappeared into a stand of trees on the north end of the island. Tristan was stunned by what he had just seen but even more worried by what was unfolding in front of him. Having already baited his hook and cast his line out into the surf, Marcus planted the handle of the rod into the damp sand. Without instruction, he motioned for Tristan to do likewise with the other large rod. Then he emptied the contents of the canvas bag onto the sand. Tristan had no idea what he was looking at. It looked like a broken robot from *Lost in Space*.

"What the heck is that thing?" Tristan asked with a sense of growing dread.

"A metal detector. What did you think?" Marcus slyly replied.

"A metal detector? What does it do?"

"Well, let's say your nephew found a gold coin on the beach and said that he couldn't find any others. This little baby would do two things: Help him find others or possibly serve as a lie detector to confirm his uncle's suspicion that the little bitch just might be lying," Marcus droned on with a treacherous smile.

"So, here is how it's going to go down. You're going to mind my gear and do your best job of baiting your own hook and catching our supper. If you need any help, I'm going to leave Iris here with you to swim and babysit. Now, you're going to give me your best guess as to where you found that coin. I'm going to take my friend here, put on my earphones, and scour the hell out of this beach until lunch. Then we're going to do it all over again this afternoon before we go back to Beaufort. For your sake, it will be a safer trip home if you have our supper ready and I have some souvenirs jingling in my swimsuit pocket."

Tristan scanned the beach and pointed Marcus north toward where the horses had retreated into the forest. Marcus pulled off his shirt and dropped it on top of the jacket Tristan had already shed in the growing heat and humidity of the morning. Lowering his ever-present shades, Marcus strapped on his headgear and strode slowly north, waving the pan of the detector first left and then right. Even from a distance, Iris and Tristan could periodically hear Marcus swear as he extracted a fishing lure, bobby pin, or pocket change from the damp sand.

After Marcus was finally out of earshot, Iris made sure that Tristan knew what he was doing. "Tristan, try to understand, there is some good in him, or I wouldn't be with him," Iris said as she and Tristan sat. "First, Marcus lost his mama and daddy. Then your dad took off for years and died. All these things have bent and nearly broken him. Hurt and hate look a lot alike. You can't believe or accept it, but at some level he cares for you even when he treats you like trash. Otherwise, he would have turned you away. You remind him of them. You remind him of everything he has lost. He grew up too fast in a silent house that dissolves a little more around him every day. I won't defend the meanness, but it's more complicated than it looks."

She fell silent for a while as the fish began to strike, and Tristan fell a little more in love with a woman who could even see good in his messed-up uncle. Over the next hour or so, he realized that Marcus had lied about some things to get him to Shackleford, but he hadn't lied about the drum and blues. One after another, they pulled them from the pounding surf until they realized they had way more than they needed for supper. It was nearing noon and was blazing hot with no shade in sight, so Iris decided it was time for a swim.

Right in front of Tristan, the young woman peeled her T-shirt over her yellow mane. When finished, she had even more clearly exposed the two most perfect breasts the boy had ever seen. Iris then dropped the shirt onto the pile of clothes on the beach. Tristan only thought that wild horses were going to be the highlight of his trip. He found himself trying to commit her breasts to memory for sleepless, humid nights ahead this summer. As he ogled her, Iris bounded into the surf in her shorts and sheer halter top.

Tristan dropped his T-shirt on the growing mound of clothes, exposing his white, shallow chest. Despite his shame, he quickly followed Iris, seeking her company and waist-deep water as soon as possible. Blushing fourteen shades of red, he caught up with her. For a while, the two just laughed, chatted, and bobbed with the waves. Tristan faced north in fear of the ever-approaching figure of his uncle as he strode nearer. Iris faced south. In a few minutes, she began to snicker softly and then laugh out loud. Tristan froze in horror, fearing that the descending water level after a passing wave had revealed his growing secret. He didn't know much about God, but he had an idea that having a boner for your uncle's girlfriend would get you an express ticket to hell. The boy bobbed downward as Iris pointed down the beach and loudly said, "Look!"

Tristan did an about-face, wiped the stinging salt water from his eyes, and tried to see what had Iris so amused. As his vision cleared, he first just saw a guy and girl approaching. What was so funny? Iris encouraged him to wait. Slowly, details came into focus. First, bobbing bare breasts on her. Then, something else bobbing on him. Dark circles of hair adorned the nether regions of each. They strolled in a state of blissful innocence that rivaled that of Adam and Eve in the garden as they neared, and every detail of their undress came into crystal-clear focus.

"Dear God in heaven, they are both buck naked," Tristan squeaked.

Iris doubled over in a spasm of uncontrollable, painful laughter.

"Yes, they are," she whistled.

"What do you think they want?" Tristan whispered as the two strangers swayed directly in front of them.

"Well, sport, the only thing we have are our swimsuits, and they sure as hell don't seem to have a lot of interest in those."

As Iris and Tristan emerged from the surf, revelations came in waves. Once they got within a dozen yards of the couple, the sickeningly sweet, unmistakable smell of weed enveloped them all. Tristan gagged a little at the unfamiliar smell, and Iris just uttered softly, "Mystery solved."

Their other revelation was far more alarming. In their revelry in the ocean and fascination with their newfound friends, Iris and Tristan had foolishly lost track of the tide. Their pile of discarded clothes, lunch, and the stringer of their fish left in a tidal pool on the beach were nowhere to be seen. Fortunately, Marcus's beloved fishing gear had been planted deeply in the sand, or there might have been a double murder that day. Still, he would be furious, and he was. A loud bark suddenly came at them from behind and made them both jump.

"WHAT THE FUCK!"

Between sunburn and rage, Marcus looked like he could burst into flames. "I leave the two of you in charge of our stuff for a couple of hours to come back and find that you have traded the ocean our lunch, supper, and clothes for two scrawny, naked, baked hippies."

In response, Adam and Eve swayed and sang, "We are stardust. We are golden, and we have to get ourselves back to the garden."

Marcus's forehead veins throbbed. "Holy shit!" Gathering himself, he looked at Iris and flatly announced, "I have the metal detector. Grab the rods. We have to get off this island and back to Beaufort. Now!"

Iris replied, "Now? But why? First, we have to help these two find their boat or camp or something. We can't just leave them here!"

"Fuck 'em. There's a squall line headed this way. If we don't leave now, that crappy crab boat will not make it back. There's no shelter on the island. We will get fried by lightning on this beach."

Iris looked around. The sky remained blue, but she noticed a slight increase in the wind speed. Looking at Marcus's eyes, she saw that he had set his rage aside. In fact, she saw something she had seldom seen in his eyes—a tinge of fear. Respecting the instincts of a fisherman, she trusted in what he could see and feel rather than what she saw. Quickly, she grabbed one rod as Tristan grabbed the other but insisted that Adam and Eve come with them. After assuring Marcus that they would find a way to explain why his Southern Baptist buddy's boat reeked of pot, they all headed out.

Marcus led the way through the dunes. Iris and Tristan followed, each guiding one of their naked gender counterparts with their spare hand. By the time they reached the boat, the skies had begun to darken. The trip across the bay was harrowing. Since they did not have a scrap of clothing to spare, their new friends rode the waves in their natural state. Tristan had never seen a naked man and woman side by side, so when he wasn't throwing up overboard, he broadened his education in comparative anatomy.

Iris tried to calm Marcus, but at one point, Eve asked him if he was a follower of the blessed Dead. Flatly, he responded, "No, Princess Pubes, but I can proclaim with certainty that I would be more than grateful if the two of you horndogs were dead."

Lightning ripped through the heavens and thunder boomed as their boat scraped against the dock in Beaufort. The last that the three saw of Adam and Eve were their butts as they shimmied up the dock ladder. The pair strolled blissfully away through the raging storm toward the unexpected residents of Front Street in downtown Beaufort.

Marcus did not speak to either Tristan or Iris for a week, but several times Tristan caught him glaring at him with smoldering eyes.

CHAPTER TWELVE
Ma'am and Old Pete

AFTER A WEEK of Marcus's hate-filled stares, Tristan decided to cover some of his tracks with his uncle. The business about going to Shackleford with Old Pete was just a bold-faced lie and failed attempt to keep Marcus from knowing where his gold piece had really come from. At best it had bought him a little time but not much. He had chatted with the old Black man down on the docks in Beaufort about Pete's early life net fishing for shad in small flotillas of wooden trawlers, a far cry from the hulking metal, refitted mine sweepers of today.

Pete and his Black counterparts, though scorned on land, were revered at sea for their extraordinary stamina and bravery in corralling huge schools of shad. Singing the old shanties, the crews set to sea guided only by a lookout perched precariously in the crow's nest on top of the ship's mast. Old Pete had been one of those lookouts, and the citizenry of Old Beaufort remembered and respected him for his skill in helping fill the nets of their small fleets and the accounts of the Bank of Beaufort.

In an unprecedented move, they lobbied for Pete to be rewarded, in his old age, with the job of captaining the local mail boat, a role never held by a Black. He was responsible for "calling the mail over" or distributing it throughout the watery community. Boats were more natural to Old Pete than walking. He was part of a very small group of Negroes who had grown up on the fringes of Ocracoke Island, and the people proudly bestowed the moniker of "O'cocker" upon him and his wife. She was known in the village as Ma'am. After retiring from his captaining work, Old Pete and Ma'am had settled on the mainland in a small, unpainted house on the outskirts of Beaufort. Attempting a reworking of his narrative about Pete would only require a ten-minute bike ride out to his house.

Tristan pulled up into Ma'am and Old Pete's sandy, oak-shaded yard to find Ma'am sitting out on the porch. She was pinching the heads off a small bowl of shrimp. A basket of shelled butterbeans that would be added to the meal sat at her feet.

"Hey dah, little fern'ner, Ma'am ain't seen you in a month of Sundays. What you wanting today?"

"I want to see Old Pete, Ma'am. Is he home?"

Ma'am's blue eyes sparkled with love and mischief beneath her furrowed brow and rows of silver hair.

"Dat ol' fool be to the back of the house. He sot out here with me till I got plum mommucks. He 'bout drove me crazy with his nonsense about curing the warts. Ev'r since he stopped calling the mail over, people been coming here to the house for him to say his mumbo jumbo over them, take their corder coin, and make the warts be gone."

"Does he have the power, Ma'am?"

"The old fool says he does. Most of the time he cures them and makes me quamished to the stomach." She laughed. "Go 'round and see what he can fix for you."

As Ma'am sat down the finished shrimp, to Tristan's shock she began to sing one of Pete's old shanties:

"Young man, I pray you to take warnin'
Be ker'ful what you do and say,

Remember life is very short,
And thar's a judgem't day.

The book of life it will be brought,
The Judge he will unfol',
And ever'thing that you have done,
Is there writ down in gold."

The word "gold" hung in the air and unsettled Tristan as he beat a hasty retreat, fleeing the old woman's plaintive song. Clearing his head, he slowly approached Old Pete out back seated on a stump. The aged man was mending a small shrimp net with his gnarled hands.

Looking up, Pete hooted, "Greetings, lil buck. What brought you all the way out here to find an old man fumblin' with a net that's a getting the best of him? Pull up that old tar there and take a seat."

Tristan dropped the tire down beside the old man to buffer his behind from any sand fleas in the parched yard, then he cut straight to the chase. After settling the business of getting Old Pete to entertain the possibility of a future fishing trip to Shackleford, Tristan turned to the deeper reason for his visit.

"Pete, you've lived around here about as long as anyone and know these waters like the back of your hand. I love pirate stories and stories about buried treasures. I have heard all the stuff about Blackbeard and Beaufort, but the other day I heard a strange one about some kind of treasure hidden back in the bay at North River. You ever heard of such a thing?"

The old man slowed his mending of the net and did not lift his eyes from his work. "Nosuh. No stories about no pirates and the sound. Never did."

Tristan shifted on his tire in agitation and growing guilt. There was just something really low about trying to milk information out of a crippled-up old man, Black or otherwise. He wasn't as interested in the gold itself as how it might change the way that Iris saw him. Or at least that's what he told himself.

Slowly, the old man said, "Now, if you ar' talking gold but no pirates, that is another story. O'er the years, a handful of gold coins has been found back there. Always one or two at a time. My pap told me they dragged a skeleton and busted up wagon out of that water. Had to be a dingbatter. No Hoi Toider is that foolish around the water. May even have been a Black man. Months after the bones wuz found, posters went up in Beaufort from the law inland looking for a runaway farmhand wanted for arson. Offered a big reward, but nuttin' come of it. Must have been a crazy man. Ain't a thing in that sound but spits of land way out now after so much washing away of the shore after the hurricanes. No more stories I know about."

Lifting his eyes, the old man stared at the boy till the boy squirmed.

"Well, just let me know when you want to go out to the banks someday. Thanks, Pete. Take care."

Tristan strode across the yard and around the house. He felt Pete's and Ma'am's eyes drilling holes in him as he fled on his bike and pedaled out of the yard and down the road. He felt more guilty than he ever had in his life. Lying to Marcus was one thing, this was another.

Ma'am's words looped through his brain as he pumped the pedals:

The book of life it will be brought,
The Judge he will unfol',
And ever'thing that you have done,
Is there writ down in gold.

As light failed, the luminescence of water fire rose in the marsh, the glowing gases further haunting Tristan on his journey home.

CHAPTER THIRTEEN
Josh Treadway

MOST OF THE time, Josh Treadway wore long-sleeved shirts to hide the fading track marks on his arms. Growing up in an upper-class enclave like Myers Park in Charlotte had provided a lot of perks. As a boy, he had access to tutors, tennis lessons, and eventually some of the best heroin in the city. Heroin had arrived in great abundance in the South in the '70s along with heavy metal, Vietnam, civil rights eruptions, and *Star Wars*.

Privilege saved him from military service, but his indolent self-absorption had put a target on his back for heroin addiction. High-dollar rehab out of state had saved his life several times but had done little to address his damaged soul. In a weak moment when he was trying to stay away from his old crowd, Josh had agreed to go to the Charlottetown Mall with a cute girl in his chemistry class.

There, instead of hitting the record store or movies across the street, she steered them through the door of a place with a sign over the door that read "Salt Cellar." At first, Josh panicked as they plunged into darkness and loud music. He could feel his sobriety draining from his body. As his eyes and ears adjusted to the darkness and sound, a different type of panic settled in. There wasn't a single chair in the room. Young people, some holding hands, were scattered about in circles on a carpeted floor in a room illuminated solely by lights from a small stage. One long-haired guy in a tie-dyed T-shirt held court with a microphone reading Scripture passages from a jean-covered Bible. Soft music swept over the room from a couple of acoustic guitar players strumming backup.

"Holy shit," Josh mumbled inappropriately as he suddenly realized where he was.

Jesus freaks were the other thing that had arrived with heroin in Charlotte in the early '70s, and he had just been drawn into a nest of them by a hot girl. Before he could bolt for the door, she pulled him down into one of the circles. Things got fuzzy after that. The preacher read, cheesy music swelled, and at some point a "donation plate" made from a Kentucky Fried Chicken bucket was passed around. Only one other thing happened after the bucket. Enveloped by a cloud of love, Josh Treadway wept uncontrollably and changed irrevocably.

The next day, he announced to his distraught parents that he was going to the coast to try to find a new life. Over the next few days, he hitchhiked east, arriving by chance or Providence in Beaufort. Finding a lot of evidence of beer and little of heroin, he settled into a rented trailer on the outskirts of town. A few days later, he walked into an open door at St. Paul's and took a job that would have horrified his parents if they had not recently disowned him. He had never been happier in his short life.

CHAPTER FOURTEEN
St. Paul's

TRISTAN SPENT THE following week trying to escape himself, but it really didn't matter how much time he spent swimming, biking, fishing, or working. He still felt dirty after the sneaky way he had tried to take advantage of the old man's goodness. Feeling guilty was an unfamiliar experience for Tristan. In comparison to Marcus, most of the time the boy felt like a saint. Around town, people referred to him as "the nice kid" or "that sweet McClure boy." Truth was Tristan had not felt nice or sweet lately. He had no real vocabulary of God. Faith and forgiveness, for that matter, were as foreign to him as a country club or a bagel. Yet, several times a day the church bells pealed through the lanes of Beaufort as they had since before the Revolution. Most times, they went unnoticed, but occasionally a village matron would pause and look skyward or an older gentleman would stand silent and doff his hat. Vestiges of the holy still lingered over the town in the shuttered storefronts on Sunday, or cars pulled to the sides of the country lanes that surrounded town when a funeral procession passed. Holiness lingered, yet waned.

One day, Tristan could stand himself no longer. He pulled his bicycle up to the privet hedge beside old St. Paul's and slipped in the side door in the last hours of a summer afternoon. No one appeared to have seen him. Miss Edith Barry stood silently in her front yard across the street watering her hydrangeas as he passed, but she only gave a weak wave of acknowledgment and did not lift her eyes from her task. Once inside the church, Tristan's eyes adjusted to the waning afternoon light as it filtered through the miasma of stained glass that adorned the sanctuary.

A huge star-shaped window filled the high part of the back wall, and other rectangular windows lined the sides and front of the space. Many of the forms on the windows were foreign to his eyes, but he clearly made out a crown, a tall cup, and an anchor in several of them. The anchor especially fascinated him. Even in the most unexpected places in Beaufort, the sea always followed you. In fact, the entire worship space of the building looked like the hull of a great wooden ship turned upside down. The blinding colors and geometry of the great scissored rafters made Tristan feel a bit off balance. He could use an anchor right now in so many ways.

Tristan was uncertain of his mission. He knew about prayer but had no idea how to do it. A Catholic girl at school had told him about lighting candles, but he saw none. So, he just sat down in the front pew and listened to the buffered sound of a car passing occasionally or the distant whir of a lawnmower. After a few moments, he felt no forgiveness, but he did begin to doze. His nap abruptly ended.

Without warning, a door opened outward into an interior hallway and a ladder poked through the door followed by a rather shabby-looking, young guy dressed in paint-speckled jeans and a faded *Godspell* T-shirt. The intruder was tall with broad shoulders and a shaggy sun-bleached mane. Tristan and the workman quickly exchanged awkward apologies for interrupting the other. After that, the stranger identified himself as Josh, the church sexton.

The boy mumbled back, "Hi, I'm Tristan, and um, I have no idea why I am here."

The rock and roll sexton simply replied, "Well, dude, while you're working on that one, can you steady my ladder while I stand on top of it on my tiptoes and try to change out some of these danged burned-out lights?"

For about thirty minutes, the two of them worked together in silence. When the task was completed, Tristan sat down again on the pew. Meanwhile, Josh lay down on the carpeted floor in front of him to stretch and take five before he moved on to his next task somewhere in the church. After a couple of minutes, the scruffy hippie opened his eyes and said, "So, are you done? Did you find what you were looking for?"

Flustered, Tristan sputtered, "Hard to say. Not sure what I'm looking for."

"Good one," the sexton volleyed back.

"But in my experience, when a young guy finds himself in a church on a summer afternoon, he's got to be looking for something. If you don't know what you want, do you know maybe who or whose you want to be?"

The question struck Tristan as a bit odd, deep, and strangely too personal for comfort. Shifting uncomfortably, he fired back, "Well, I guess at some point, I want to be my own man."

Josh closed his eyes again, exhaled, and said, "That sounds heavy and exhausting. You may want to leave that here. I find that I need help being a man. Sometimes even help from Jesus."

Josh was a nice guy, but something rose up in rebellion inside Tristan to what the janitor had said. Tristan got up from the pew and mumbled, "Nice to meet you, Josh."

"Likewise, dude," the sexton said, rising to perform his next task.

Tristan bolted to his bike. Just as he had fled to the church, he fled from it.

CHAPTER FIFTEEN
The Old Burying Ground

TRISTAN HAD BECOME familiar with his new home in Beaufort, and most of the time he now pronounced it correctly. "Bo Fert, not Bhew Furt" he had heard uttered from pain-contorted faces in town as they corrected him for the millionth time. However it was pronounced, the town was beautiful, especially pedaling west down the middle of Ann Street on an October evening. Of all the streets, Ann was the crown jewel. Most houses had porches and picket fences. All were equipped with swings from which the house's occupants caught up on town gossip as other citizens of the village strolled the deeply shaded sidewalks.

At points on the long avenue, the live oaks stretched out limbs, joining hands with their counterparts on the other side of the street. On some blocks, white and pastel wooden cottages were graced with not only one sweeping front porch but occasionally a second-layered one, above which housed beds for especially humid summer nights. In spring, azaleas blazed along the entirety of the street. Summer brought the perfume of well-tended roses mixing with the salt air and rotting fish wafting in from Front Street and the Beaufort Fish Factory.

Now, in the last days of October, Tristan rode his bike through a tunnel of evergreen live oak dappled by the reds, yellows, and oranges of maples and the occasional dying elm. Throwing his arms out in freedom, he rode down the now abandoned Ann Street. Neighbors' cars sat parked along its sides and their butts at their supper tables as they feasted on fish and the last remnants of dead summer vegetable gardens. In rapid succession, Tristan passed the intersections of Pollack, Queen, and finally Craven, gliding to a slow stop in front of the entrance to the ancient, revered block that housed The Old Burying Ground between the watchful towers of Ann Street Methodist and First Baptist.

Maybe it was the nearness of Halloween or the last rays of day filtering through the oaks, but Tristan felt captured by an unseen force as he reached the four hundredth block of Ann. For several minutes, the boy sat in silence on his bike, balancing from one foot to the other as darkness fell and bells tolled the hours of the dying day. No one waited at home for Tristan. Marcus was out on the town. No supper would grace the table or perfume his entrance to the house when he finally pedaled back into the ill-kept yard. So, he sat indulging his impulse, curiosity, and vague fear as night fell.

Suddenly, Tristan's fear rose as he spotted the bobbing glow of an old lantern on an outstretched arm weaving its way through the graveyard. Beaufort was an ancient village overpopulated by ghosts, so possibilities for the identity of the interloper were endless. Couldn't be the baby said to have been buried in a cask of rum after dying at sea. Too tall. Or the faithful British soldier buried upright facing his king across the Atlantic. Too short. Just one lanky fellow with a long, outstretched arm weaving among gravestones, dormant azaleas, and the low-hanging, massive branches of ancient live oaks.

Tristan breathed deeply and chuckled in relief. Last week, his teacher had told his class that costumed interpreters wandered the streets of Beaufort during holiday periods, providing local color for the tourists. In exchange, visitors provided their all-important dollars to the town. Maybe this one could satisfy a bit of his curiosity about pirate lore after a few months on the coast walking about with a gold coin in his pocket. Clenching his teeth against the dark, Tristan dismounted his bike and pursued the receding light through the maze of the old cemetery. Fast as he was, within moments he stood huffing behind the slender figure of the man. Barking into the night, Tristan spoke a little too loudly.

"Excuse me, sir, what do you know about pirates?"

Slowly, the figure turned. He lifted the lantern to better illuminate his pursuer. In the process, he lighted his own frame, revealing a middle-aged man with a lean face. His most prominent features were his bony cheeks, sharp chin, and brow crowned with salt-and-pepper oily hair. In character, a baritone voice boomed out, "Why, boy, what a curiosity of a question for this late hour. What would lead thee to believe that I would have knowledge of such things? I am a Christian man, an honest man of trade whatever ye might have heard from the local populous. They often speak ill of me as a 'privateer,' whatever meaning such word might bestow. Why seek ye word of pirates at such a late hour?"

Tristan squirmed at the oddness of the man's speech and his own growing uncertainty. He didn't know whether to play along in character or to just be himself. In desperation, without thinking, he reached into his pocket, drew out the coin, and held it out. The gold sparkled beneath the glow of the lantern sputtering in the soft night breeze. In horror, Tristan realized his potential peril. He was alone in the dark of night in a graveyard with a stranger. Of all the crazy things he could have said or done, he had chosen to reveal his secret for the first time since the fumble with Marcus. Despite the cool of the evening, small beads of sweat broke out on his forehead.

"My God. What have I done?" he said without thinking. He could hear his own heart beating as the stranger's eyes widened and his mouth gaped open slightly.

The actor leaned downward and spoke. "I say, I have not seen one of these in a great long time indeed."

The old man's face revealed delight and profound sorrow. Slowly, he spoke, stretched his finger out toward the coin, and then hastily withdrew it. He folded his hand within the lapel of his worn military frock. Softly, he said, "Lad, let me tell thee a mite about the pretty that ye hold there. As long as ye hold on to the yellow, ye will not have to seek knowledge of the pirates. The longer ye hold to man's curse, the ways of the pirate will come to thine own young heart. Trust the words of an old man who came to such knowledge far too late in years."

A single bead of salt water trickled down through the furrows of the man's age-spotted cheek. "If the village folk ask thee how ye came to the possession of such dreadful wisdom, tell them it came from the withered lips of Cap'n Otway Burns of the good ship *Crissie Wright*."

With great weariness, the old man turned and retreated slowly toward the inner depths of the Old Burying Ground. In great confusion and awkwardness, Tristan didn't move. No sound issued from his lips until the old captain made a sudden turn to the right in the distance. At that moment, a bit of quarter moon slipped from behind the autumn clouds and revealed a lantern bobbing through the cemetery unsupported by arm and unaccompanied by a costumed bearer of the light.

Had the neighbors of Ann Street not been preoccupied with evening TV, dirty supper dishes, and bedtime routines, they might have heard the high-pitched wail of a barely teenaged boy and mistaken it for the terrifying keen of cats winding up for their nighttime battles to the death. The only other sound in the stillness of Ann Street was the frantic clatter of pedals as a solitary figure headed east at a strangely frantic speed, wishing he had followed the sexton's advice.

CHAPTER SIXTEEN
Shave and a Haircut

About once a month, Tristan left the world of boys and briefly visited the world of men at Jeff's Barber Shop down on Front Street. Not a woman in sight, just three barber chairs, WWII veterans, jazz on the radio, and the scent of lime aftershave. A long leather strap hung from each chair, waiting to sharpen a pearl-handled straight razor for the umpteenth time.

All the old guys had a ritual that took about an hour: Remove your hat and cigar, lean back, and have steaming towels applied to your salt-and-pepper whiskers. As this happens, listen to Frank and Ella as another old guy in a white, waist-length shirt etches a stainless razor around your lathered face, carefully avoiding the jugular. Finally, after the shave comes a severe military haircut, Vitalis, and the redonning of hat and cigar.

The whole process happened every two weeks and only cost a couple of bucks. This made Jeff's an affordable place for shopkeepers, business owners, plumbers, and lawyers to hang out and talk weather, fishing, football, and government away from the interference of the womenfolk. For most of them, it was the best hour of their week.

For boys, the routine was a little different. They got a fifteen-minute cut that would qualify them for the draft and a slight adjustment of the conversation out of consideration for their more delicate ears. If they were really lucky, they also might get to see Jeff shear an unsuspecting hippie from out of town that had wandered in unaware of the house cut.

Today, however, was different for Tristan. As he settled into the worn leather chair, Wayne, one of the head barber's assistants, greeted him. Then, the owner of Beaufort Fish, Mr. West, walked through the front door. He removed his hat and cigar and was seated in the slightly less worn chair beside him.

"Afternoon, Jeff. Why, hello there, Mr. McClure. How is your work going down at the plant?"

Tristan froze. He'd had no idea that Mr. Sam West knew who he was. Tristan responded softly, "Hello, sir. Fine thank you."

His boss's next statement nearly knocked him out of his chair.

"Usual, Jeff. Short on the sides and a little longer on the top. By the way, my employee here is looking a little shabby. I can see that beard of his coming in heavy now. Give Tristan the works on me."

Tristan knew the status of his facial hair. He prayed for more than peach fuzz every morning. Before he knew it, Wayne spun his chair around to the sink and wrapped piping hot towels around his tender face. As the steam rose, he felt every muscle in his body relax. More importantly, for the first time since returning to Beaufort, he felt like a man and one who belonged there. He could no longer see Mr. West, but he felt his kindness and generosity. Wreathed in steam, Tristan heard him say, "Son, I have a little business proposition since we are both here—man to man."

CHAPTER SEVENTEEN
Sam West

THE WEST FAMILY occupied the oldest and most revered graves in Beaufort and the grandest house on Front Street. The house's porches rose like layers on a wedding cake. The uppermost floor was topped with a widow's walk from which the Wests could look to sea in search of their fishing bounty returning to port. As their wealth had grown over the centuries so had their influence in Beaufort, at least until fairly recently. After many years of prosperity, the fishing industry was in a state of freefall. Overfishing, pollution, and environmental regulations had shuttered dozens of processing plants up and down the Atlantic coast. The current head of the family, Samuel Thomas West, held sway over a fragile, endangered means of livelihood.

Unlike some of his ancestors, Sam West's grip on Beaufort was soft. He still chaired the board at the Star Hill Golf Club, presided over the Rotary, and signed the checks of many of the workers in town, but his guiding ethic was one of "noblesse oblige," the obligation of the nobility. This life perspective had been drilled into him by his grandfather and reinforced by both his father and the headmaster at his boarding school in Virginia: It is the responsibility of the privileged to extend generosity and kindness to the less fortunate; in short, an incarnation of the biblical principle "to whom much is given, much is required." Sam West did not chafe under his yoke. His responsibilities were in accord with his personality and character. Though he had the power to terrorize his town, his life was one of service to the people of Beaufort.

Declining profits, keeping up appearances, and Christian charity were beginning to take their toll on the West family. His wife, Marylee, despite Sam's pleas for a bit more frugality, still flew to New York a couple of times a year to "resupply her wardrobe" for activities at the Beaufort Women's Club. Sadly, his oldest son, Barrett, had developed an early taste for good Kentucky bourbon. Like his grandfather and many gentlemen of the South, his brown breakfast was impacting his productivity in managing a growing financial crisis at the plant. For now, Sam West's façade of genteel wealth still held in town. His bankers showed the utmost propriety and held his secrets close and well—perhaps too well, because every day someone dropped by looking for help to sponsor a ball team, cover a medical bill, or bail a loved one out of jail. Even in trying times, Sam West's response was much more often yes than no. In fact, the only time he said no was when he knew that a visitor was just outright lying or not willing to put any of their own skin in the game. Even then, his words were usually, "Well, do this. Then come back, and we will talk."

Occasionally, Sam would trudge up the many stairs to the widow's walk and gaze out across the village of Beaufort. From his topmost porch, he could see smoke rising from the Beaufort Fish Company, the church spires of town, familiar houses occupied by people with familiar needs, and the growing preparation for the elimination of a large part of Front Street. The wrecking ball would arrive soon to clear the view from downtown to Taylor Creek and the sea.

He might have been able to stop it if he had tried harder, but soon the Wests would not be the answer to all the town's problems. An infusion of cash from inland would be needed to prevent the suffering of future generations. Sam braced himself against the railing of the widow's walk for the wave of destruction and change that was coming. The last thing that he saw from the walk that day was a vision of his ancestors rolling over in their graves in the Old Burying Ground. He hoped they would not rise up and haunt his deteriorating sleep. After all, though a powerful man, he was just a man. Sighing deeply and squaring his stooped shoulders, Sam began to descend the many stairs back to another day of service to the village.

CHAPTER EIGHTEEN
Dante's Realm

THE RUSTED, HULKING metal framework of Beaufort Fish Company loomed into sight as Tristan rolled off the end of Front Street and into the parking lot on his small Yamaha motorcycle. The company owner had shown mercy on Tristan, who was now sixteen years old. He had encountered the boy downtown one day on his old bicycle, which he had clearly outgrown, pulling up to the barbershop. Bumping his pay a bit, Mr. West had kept the "raise" until one of his son's unused motorcycles was paid for. This arrangement also kept Marcus unaware for a while of the extra dollars in his nephew's pay. Tristan now had a mode of transportation that better matched his age and deepening voice.

Even after a couple of years at Beaufort Fish, Tristan still approached the building in awe. In the lighter part of the menhaden season, the complex curled around the end of Front Street like an old dragon in repose. Smoke, steam, and stench leaked from every orifice, darkening the bluest sky by day and emitting a fiery, ominous glow by night. Day or night, the putrid odor of several million pounds of decomposing, oily fish enveloped everything both close to and far from the plant. Sunday was no different. Even though he and Marcus were the only employees on an extra cleanup shift on Sunday, the six previous days of cooked fish still hung in the air.

Tristan coughed and gagged a bit as his lungs reacclimated to the fetid cloud surrounding him.

On a regular workday, one or both of the old mine sweepers would be pulled up next to the plant, their bulkheads teeming with countless pounds of menhaden. The Native Americans of the coast called menhaden "inside out porcupines" due to the hundreds of bones concealed within their skin and scales. Only the most patient of fishermen had the skill to clean the shad by hand, and only a handful of those held enough passion for the fish's flesh to think it worth the time or effort. The vast majority of the billions of menhaden that teemed in the Atlantic were destined for an inglorious future as industrial fertilizer. Not a glamorous fate, but under the right conditions, fish processing was still a profitable venture for the handful of families still plying the trade.

The economics of the menhaden industry were above Tristan's pay grade. He was only there to man a broom and hose. During the week, more skilled professionals would man the huge hoses that sucked the fish from the ships, animate the presses, fire the boilers, and extract the oil for shipment and sale at the end of the whole bloody, smelly process. On a day when the plant was in full operation spewing smoke and fire, it was hard to believe that the tree-lined lane of Ann Street, the Old Burying Ground, the businesses of Front Street, and the dunes of Shackleford Banks lay just a short distance away. Beaufort was a mystery and contradiction within the boy's mind.

As Tristan stepped from the bright light of day into the cavernous semidarkness of the outer shipping docks, his eyes and brain struggled to adjust. Short of the light filtering in through the dock doors, the only other source of illumination was a few bare lightbulbs encased in decades of cobwebs. Tristan felt like a mole. In the emptiness of the bays, he could hear the repetitive scraping and see the dim, shirtless form of his uncle removing muck with a flat-ended shovel on a section of the floor. For better lighting, Marcus had an old miner's light attached to a hardhat on his head.

"Hey, butt wipe!" he shouted from the dim interior of the plant.

Tristan responded flatly, "Hi, Marcus."

Fortunately, the two of them would not have to work near each other today. As a creature of the light and air, and a victim of claustrophobia, Tristan would sweep and hose the portions of the bays in what passed for light. Ever at home in the darkness and closeness of the interior spaces, Marcus would scrape and hose the areas where blood, guts, and slime collected from the beginnings of the great slaughter process. Each was well suited to his task.

Tristan set to work and only occasionally noticed the light on the top of Marcus's hardhat bobbing about in the darkness. The monotonous rhythm of the work gave him time to feel his gratitude for what he referred to as "The Great Silence." For almost a year after Marcus's ill-fated trip to Shackleford with his metal detector, he had tried every trick in the book to wheedle more information out of Tristan about the source of his coin. Sometimes, that involved profanity, pain, and threats of violence and death. At other times, the carrot came out and he promised reward, eternal gratitude, and domestic tranquility. When all his efforts failed, he even tried to enlist Iris's aid, but she would have nothing to do with his ploys. Then an uncomfortable, but welcomed, silence descended. That had now lasted for months. Tristan rested in the peace.

From the corner of his eye, he saw the bobbing light on Marcus's head retreat into the second chamber of the cavernous factory. Several minutes later, the solitary light retreated farther into the heart of the darkness.

"What the heck is he cleaning that deeply in the plant on a shutdown day?" the teen mumbled.

Fifty to a hundred yards into the darkness, the light suddenly plummeted downward toward the floor. For what seemed like an eternity, Tristan heard nothing but the popping of metal as it cooled within the structure and the faint hissing of steam slowly escaping from small orifices throughout the building. Then faintly, but distinctly, he heard an unmistakable, "Help … help me, Tristan."

Then nothing. Dropping his broom, Tristan ran toward the distant light, but after a few dozen yards he slowed. He felt a cold sweat begin to dampen his forehead, chest, and limbs, and his heart began to beat more strongly. He slowly realized that his fear of darkness and closed-in places was hijacking his mind. He paused, breathed deeply, and focused.

"Just keep your eyes on the light. Just keep your eyes on the light," the boy whispered.

With hesitation and fear, his body reanimated. After finally crossing about three quarters of the distance to Marcus, Tristan's mind began to play a trick on him. The light seemed to rise and veer sharply to the left. Focusing his faculties, Tristan followed the light but his anxiety rose as he realized that he could no longer see any light behind him. He had never ventured into the center of the factory, which was devoid of windows and obvious controls for any artificial light that might provide illumination. His only hope was to reach his uncle and use his light to find their way back to the loading dock.

"Just trust the light."

But in a small flash, all light disappeared.

"Marcus! Marcus, where are you?" Tristan screamed as panic washed over him.

Or at least he thought it was panic. The real panic began a minute or two later. The temperature began to rise sharply as did his paralyzing fear. He could hear a gurgling noise nearby, and at the same instant an acrid odor of fish oil enveloped him.

Oh, dear God. Someone has released boiling oil into the transport channels, the boy thought as his brain numbed.

He was drenched with sweat, his heart ran away, and it became harder and harder to think. He froze. The oil lay enveloped in darkness in channels somewhere around him. One false step and he would plunge into boiling oil that would peel his flesh from his bones. No longer in control of his faculties or bladder, the last blow assaulted his ears. Someone had turned on the presses that crushed millions of pounds of menhaden to pulp each day. Now, he could be crushed or boiled. His knees weakened, and Tristan dropped painfully to the floor shrieking, "Marcus! Marcus! Help me. PLEASE HELP ME!"

As if in response to his plea, the equipment ground to a violent stop. Slowly, the gurgling sound began to still to a slight trickle. The temperature dropped with Tristan's pulse. Then, complete stillness and silence followed. From the unfathomable darkness, a voice calmly, but slyly, spoke, "Ask and you shall receive."

Every hair on Tristan's body rose in response.

"Marcus, is that you? What are you doing? Get me out of here!" his spent nephew shouted.

"What am I doing? What am *I* doing? Well, getting your attention, you little prick. Getting your undivided attention. Now, let's revisit our little chat before our goose chase to Shackleford and back in a squall. So, one last time. Where did you find that coin, you little turd? I will give you one shot before I pull all the handles to fire this place back up."

Fear and panic broke Tristan. Without hesitation, he told his uncle every detail of finding the coin and of his conversation with Old Pete. He then promised on his life to forsake treachery and serve as Marcus's guide and servant. He was defeated. He had been betrayed by his own kin.

CHAPTER NINETEEN
Storm

Even with weather warnings on the radio and storm flags flapping in the breeze the next morning, Marcus insisted that it was time to retrieve the gold.

"I am not giving nature one more chance to tear that island apart and wash any more treasure into the Atlantic. That gold will pay to get me and Iris to the Florida Keys and set me up with a charter boat for deep sea fishing. I have worked my last damned day in a stinking fish factory. We are out of here. I will give the house and this pissant town to you before we head south. If you cooperate, I will also give you enough money to set you up for quite a while. Just get me to that island," Marcus barked as they unloaded shovels from the back of his Charger. With so little warning, the only boat Marcus had been able to beg, borrow, or steal was a small, barnacle-covered trawler.

"I tried to tell Iris on the phone this morning about my plan, but she kept telling me that I was out of my mind. So, I hung up on her. She'll sing a different tune when we get back. So will all the high and mighty folk of Beaufort who have looked down their noses at the McClures for generations."

Marcus fumed as he tossed things about the deck. He then fired the sputtering engine to life and pulled away from the dock on Taylor

Creek. Turning the boat toward the sound, Tristan saw Iris emerge from her old Mustang in the parking lot with both middle fingers pointed in their direction. Though they were already too far from the dock to hear her in the wind, her message was pretty clear.

The trip to the sound was not far in miles, but it was torturously slow on a foul weather day in a piece of crap boat. Despite the weather, Marcus set his jaw and kept the old tug on course, navigating wind, current, and tide with the skill of an experienced seaman. Shortly after lunchtime, the two queasy sailors arrived in the open waters of the sound on the North River. The shoreline around the bay was jagged from erosion. It had been assaulted by dozens of storms since the treasure had been deposited on the island almost fifty years before.

The real question was whether the shoreline was the only land feature that had receded. No one kept track of the dozens of little no-named islands that dotted the sounds and bays up and down the North Carolina coast. They were all subject to the vagaries of nature as the coast creeped out into the Atlantic and then receded deeply inland time and again as ages passed. The coast and its Outer Banks were a blur that vacillated between solid and liquid states. There was no way of knowing if the island most reachable from the shore at low tide fifty or more years ago still existed without exploring the best prospects.

The island they were looking for might be on the bottom of the sound and require scuba gear as well as a boat. Marcus and Tristan were not even sure how they would know when they had found their destination, but they had little time for mistakes. Although early in the afternoon, the sky looked more like evening. Far in the east, a rain curtain was shaping up, indicating the formation of a squall line. Time was running out.

The survey of the first two islands was quick and unfruitful. Too flat. Water would wash right over them later in the day. The third choice showed more promise. A small hillock bumped up the center of the spit of sand and vegetation. Marcus glided the boat up to the island and tied it to a large root from a tree hanging on to the sand for life. Jumping up to full height on the prow, he studied the patch of sand intently to find some clue.

"Come on. This is crazy!" Tristan shouted. "Let's get this boat back to Beaufort while we can. We can try again tomorrow or the next day!"

All of his uncle's knowledge of the sea and good sense that he had displayed getting them off Shackleford Banks last year seemed to have abandoned him. He was a man obsessed. Suddenly, Marcus cried out, and Tristan realized he had found what he was looking for. Marcus spotted one small area covered by grasses and small plants but nothing larger. If a chest was buried there in the sand, it might be preventing larger vegetation from taking root. There was only one way to find out.

"Grab your shovel, bitch," he hollered at his nephew.

Pressing their way through chest-high myrtle, yaupon, and brambles that pierced and tore at their bare arms and legs, they began to dig. Within moments, their shovels struck something hard. Marcus dropped onto his knees and clawed with his hands like a dog. Within seconds, he exposed rusted metal straps and howled with delight.

"Treasure, my boy. Treasure!"

Dancing a jig, he retrieved his shovel and extricated the rest of the large trunk from its grave. At about the same time, the squall line arrived. Rain pelted them like ball bearings, and the wind nearly knocked them from their feet. Lightning flashed and thunder boomed. There was no time to flee, so the two squatted to the ground, hugged their knees, and tried to provide little target for the lightning bolts as they exploded above and around them. In minutes, it was over. The wind lessened, and the roar of the thunder retreated westward. Regaining his sea senses, Marcus more sanely announced, "That's not the last of it. The tools to open this thing are back on board. Let's get this crate on the boat. We can crack into it on the way back to Beaufort." A big dopey grin spread on his face.

The grin did not last long. The chest was so heavy that even with one of them on each end, they thought they would rupture themselves before they covered the short distance back to the trawler. Arriving soaked in rain, sweat, and blood, they heaved the chest over the side of the boat and prayed that it would not crack the decking on board. Coming out of the vegetation, they had seen the first vestiges of a new squall line forming in the east, far darker and more menacing than the last.

"It's okay, kid," Marcus said, smiling more broadly. "We can make it. I'm feeling lucky today."

Tristan's heart fell as he unmoored the craft and it began to crawl toward Beaufort in a mounting wind. After making about a third of the trip back, Marcus could no longer wait to see his treasure, though the sky had grown pitch black. Giving the wheel to his nephew, he retrieved a handful of tools stowed below deck, then he assaulted the locked strongbox with chisel, hammer, and fury. After a handful of well-directed blows, the lock dropped from the box.

Snatching the heavy lid upward, Marcus squealed with glee, at least until he opened the first bag and poured its contents into the bottom of the chest. "Silver dollars," he said as his face fell. Pausing, he gathered himself as he said softly, "Oh, the good stuff is in the box inside not the bags."

He grabbed the lid of the interior chest and jerked it open only to be confronted by small bars of a dull metal used for making shot for antique guns. Its original owner was not quite as wealthy as might have been believed. Marcus's entire body shook as his face contorted.

"LEAD! LEAD!"

His pronouncement was followed by a clenched fist shaken at a dark, sickeningly green sky. What then issued from Marcus was the longest, vilest stream of profanity that Tristan had ever heard. His tirade was answered by a burst of wind that struck the vessel like a sledgehammer. The old trawler spun in a circle, nearly casting Marcus overboard and snatching the wheel of the vessel from Tristan's trembling, inexperienced grasp. The teen pancaked onto the deck. An enormous wave that crashed over the vessel tossed him and Marcus like flotsam and jetsam from one end of the craft to another. Before they could regain their footing, the wind rose to the volume of a banshee and another wave cracked over them.

In a flash of lightning, Tristan stared upward from calf-deep salt water and caught the empty, dream-dashed eyes of his uncle. They stared outward into the maelstrom of the sea. With one great heave, Marcus tossed the iron chest with all its contents overboard into the darkness and spray. Though, perhaps only in Tristan's imagination, something in the boat seemed to right a bit. Plowing through water, wind, and cracking lightning, Marcus lunged toward the wheelhouse on the boat. Grabbing the wheel, it spun loose from his strong, seasoned hands as another wave nearly rolled the boat over. Water rose on deck.

There was little left to throw overboard. Though no words were exchanged, Tristan could see in his uncle's eyes the dawning realization that for the first time in his life, he was not in control. The sea was in control. Whatever lay behind the sea, wind, and waves was in control. In a fit of futility, Marcus threw every remaining object that was not bolted to the deck into the ocean. In response, the wind howled as the boat took on more water from another rogue wave.

Finally, Marcus staggered upward and looked at his nephew. For the rest of his life, Tristan would try to decipher that face. Defiance? Despair? His last insult or something entirely unknowable? He could never decide, and his uncle provided only one clue. Staring deeply into his nephew's eyes, Marcus mounted the rail of the boat, spread his arms, threw himself backward, and shouted into the howling gale, "Blood! He is my blood!"

He disappeared into the darkness.

Tristan lay silent and stunned in the flooded boat. There was no longer anyone to speak to. The storm surged around him. He had no prospects of rescue and no skills to rescue himself. There was only the waiting for the last wave.

From somewhere inside himself, he felt an impulse, an insane one. Rising to his feet, he shouted into the dark maelstrom that threatened to envelop him, "Help! Help me!"

Then falling back into the cold salt water, he laughed. He did not know why he shouted or why he laughed. He just did. The storm raged on, and then it did not.

The sea began to still, and the wind began to quiet. He lay in a nearly swamped vessel in open water with a dead motor. No other vessel or land mass was in sight. He had no food, water, working radio, or means of navigation. After a long time, water lapped softly both against and within his vessel. Stars slowly emerged, and Tristan searched for figures or animals within them but found none that he recognized with certainty. His uncle and the "treasure" now lay on the bottom of the Atlantic, and he would most probably join them before dawn.

For now, there was silence—deafening, profound, and painfully prolonged silence. Like the embryo that he had once been, he lay in salt water and darkness. All through the night, he lay there, slowly transitioning to a state of unknowing, subject to the whims of waves, currents, tide, and wind. Just silence, and then very slowly … presence. Though adrift from all his own kind, Tristan realized that he was not alone. In fact, he somehow knew that if he let his new companion draw near, very near, he would never be alone again. His last conscious thought was the slight movement of his mouth forming the single word, "Yes."

When light finally came, he was awakened by the church bells of Beaufort pealing the morning hour close at hand.

CHAPTER TWENTY
Lazarus

THREE DAYS LATER, a man's body was found on the beach on Harkers Island clutching an old life belt. He was taken to the hospital in Morehead City. After treatment by the doctors there, Marcus McClure was expected to make a full recovery.

CHAPTER TWENTY-ONE
Purchase

TRISTAN STRODE NUMBLY down Front Street, eyes down and bloodshot. The trauma of the previous week hung on his young frame like a plague. Images of storm, madness, Marcus's plunge, and the word "blood" assaulted him by day and haunted his sleep at night. It could have been him. It should have been him for starting the whole thing. In the midst of Marcus's betrayal, from what deep recess in his brain had his last impulse emerged to save his nephew? Blood—that word so entwined in human history since the days of Cain. That triple-edged tool used to convey the precious liquid that sustains us, the emblem of the first murder and all since then, but lastly, our ancient word for family. Life, death, family. What had Marcus intended in that moment? One of them, some of them, all of them, none of them? Words obscured, but acts revealed. Tristan lived. Marcus dove into the sea.

"Blood."

The other word that burned his brain this morning after the last few months … gold. Tristan painfully fingered the single coin in his pocket that had set all the darkness and evil in motion. Gold—the stain of humankind. How many had died in its name? How many armies launched, cities sacked, oaths betrayed? Tristan burned with Adam's stain as he neared the last block of the village. When he reached Iris, he would throw it into the sea. But had it been safe there before? Out of the corner of his eye, he saw the last shop on Front Street as he raised his head to turn for the dock. A small hand-lettered sign dangled above the entrance: "Bailey's Jewelers."

The morning sun created a bright reflection off one of the objects in the display window. As Tristan approached the glass, he saw that the reflection emanated from a small, gold, rose-colored ladies pocket watch. The teenager stood transfixed by the watch, and an impulse suddenly overwhelmed him.

Within minutes, he had traded his accursed twenty dollar gold coin to a very happy shopkeeper for the slightly dented pocket watch. A token for Iris, if not of eternal love at this point, at least of undying friendship, kindness, beauty, and perhaps a small movement toward healing and forgiveness. He made one more stop to buy a small basket of fruit at the docks from a stand marked "Elliott's Peaches." There would be no potable water on the island, and he had forgotten his canteen. He would need something to keep him going out there after skipping breakfast. Reaching the docks, Tristan gently rattled the watch in his pocket inside its new giftbox, set the peaches gently into his boat, and stepped down into the skiff for the short trip to Shackleford Banks.

CHAPTER TWENTY-TWO
Wild Horses

TRISTAN HAD MADE the trip to Shackleford before, so he got there without any trouble. As he approached the back of the island, he saw Iris's boat tied to a small scrub in the marsh grass. He pulled up and secured his skiff next to hers. From there it was only a five-minute walk through the dunes to the Atlantic side of the island. As Tristan topped the last dune, he lost all shelter and found himself buffeted by the blunt force of the ocean wind. His brown hair blew madly in the gale, and his shirt flapped about his torso. At about the same time, a few of the feral horses shot from the dunes and thundered down the beach, screaming wildly and freely. The noise was ancient and primal and brought Tristan to a full state of alertness from the haze of his morning slog through Beaufort.

He only thought the wind and horses had taken his breath away. About fifty yards down the beach, he caught his first glimpse of Iris since the horrors of the past week. She stood ankle deep in the surf. The breeze tossed about her blond hair, and her peasant skirt swirled about her. In the east, a faint rainbow lingered from a remnant of yet another storm far out to sea. If ever a nearly seventeen-year-old boy loved a woman, Tristan loved this one. The sight of her broke his young heart and took his breath away. Turning, she emerged from the surf and walked rapidly toward him. Tristan descended the dune and headed toward her, but as they neared, their gaits slowed and eyes dropped. The sorrow of recent days hung between them like a dark cloud. No words came.

They veered toward shelter at the foot of the dunes and flopped down side by side. The awkward silence continued for a long time. They just looked to sea, seeking comfort in the endless crash, hiss, and retreat of wave after wave.

Iris finally broke the painful silence. "You know, people say we come from the sea."

The boy softly replied, "I don't know where I come from. My mama died when I was a baby. Daddy was a trucker and damaged, so we just hit the road. Everywhere was home, and nowhere was home. He told me that Mama's people had come from some Podunk town up in the mountains; but of all the places that we went, we never went there. Before he died in a truck accident, he left instructions to send me here to Marcus. I don't know why he did that. I think Marcus hated me because my father chose me and made a run for it. Dad left his baby brother holding the bag. In the past, I never believed in God taking care of me, so I just tried to make the best of bad situations. Hard to believe Daddy didn't have better options. If he did, I don't know what they were, and at this point I don't care. Even with all the pain, I still don't know where I come from, but I want to be here."

Tristan's voice dropped to a whisper. "I want to be here because of you."

Iris shifted uncomfortably in the sand and said nothing for a long time. Finally, she spoke.

"Tristan, you're a teenager, and I am not. After last week, I don't want to think about a relationship for a long time. Marcus and I are over, but we still have unfinished business."

Tristan nodded in understanding and agreement.

"I heard Sam West went to see him at the hospital," Iris mumbled. Iris looked intently at Tristan and asked, "Are you going?"

"No. Too soon."

Smiling slightly, Iris joked for the first time in a long while. "Heck, who knows, by the time I'm ready, you might not be jailbait."

Tristan blushed a visible shade of crimson, shyly reached into his pocket, and handed her the small box.

"So, what is this?" Iris asked warily.

"Just open it."

Slowly, she unwrapped the package until the watch lay coolly in her palm.

"It's lovely, Tristan, but why?"

Slowly, he responded, "Don't take this wrong, but last week was ugly. The last few months have been dark. When I saw it shining in the sunlight, I was just drawn to it the way I have been drawn to you. I'm not stupid. I know I'm still a kid to you, but even kids have feelings. Even kids can love."

Looking back at Tristan, Iris knew that she held his vulnerable soul in her hand like a small bird. One false move would damage him. Leaning over in sincerity and with more love than she had ever felt for any man her own age, she kissed the boy lightly on his sunburned cheek. Making eye contact with him, she said, "Yes, they can."

Squeezing the watch tightly, she realized that the lid had sprung open. As she peered into the back plate of the watch, Tristan asked in the startling, lower range of advanced puberty, "What does it say?"

Iris whispered, "*V.K. and J.B.*" Then she muttered, "Who do you think they were?"

"I don't suppose we will ever know," Tristan replied.

At that moment, a brash sound startled them from above. Looking up into a cloudless sky, they saw two snow-white tundra swans rocket past them, probably headed back to their home inland on Lake Mattamuskeet.

"They mate for life, you know," Tristan teased.

Now, Iris blushed.

"Don't push your luck, young man," she said as she patted his hand beside hers on the sand.

They sat until the sun began its westward trek and the tide rolled in to full furl. In silence, they returned to Tristan's boat, leaving the other till tomorrow, and navigated home guided by the lights and church steeples of Beaufort and a yellow waxing moon.

In its orb, two winged silhouettes made one last pass, crying longingly before disappearing like specters into the summer night.

Epilogue

Tristan McClure unfolded his middle-aged frame from the Honda and started up the trail followed by his son, Seth. His wife, Iris, had jokingly played the "you're younger" card to con him into driving their moody teenager to Western Carolina University for the start of freshmen orientation. After hours on the road with the malcontent, Tristan needed to pee and stretch his legs. The sign on the trail said, "PEARSON'S FALLS, .5 mile."

For the millionth time, Tristan tried a little small talk to break the silence. "Hey, it will only take fifteen minutes. How many times does a beach bum get to see his first real waterfall? Besides, this is in your blood. Your grandmother's people were from up here."

"Well, just for the record, the only reason I am 'up here' is because of a scholarship to Western. If we weren't so poor, I could have gone to the College of Charleston like I wanted to. Wish we had money like great Uncle Marcus."

"Well, it's not like I haven't heard that one before from someone else at our house," Tristan quipped.

"For God's sake, this is so lame. Please, let's go back to the car," Seth moaned.

His dad's stride lengthened in response. In moments, they stood before the cascades and spray of Pearson's Falls. Ever the sucker for nature, Tristan drew a long breath and whispered, "Magnificent."

Seth sighed and swore under his breath, but midsigh he caught a bit of movement from across the creek. Staring at him through a small break in the laurels was the face of a young girl about his age. She peered shyly through the blossoming branches and smiled. Seth returned her gesture with a big grin and then startled his father.

"Yes, magnificent. I think I might be able to make it up here."

The waters tumbled on in joyous torrents before them, and a jeweled hummingbird flew through the mist, across the creek, and deep into the heart of the forest.

www.ingramcontent.com/pod-product-compliance
Lightning Source LLC
LaVergne TN
LVHW091711070526
838199LV00050B/2348